THE CAPTA
FROZEN DREAM

Georgie Lee

First published in Great Britain 2015
by Mills & Boon, an imprint of Harlequin (UK) Limited,
Large Print edition 2015
Harlequin (UK) Limited, Eton House, 18-24 Paradise Road,
Richmond, Surrey TW9 1SR

© 2015 Georgie Reinstein

ISBN: 978-0-263-25581-2

A lifelong history buff, **Georgie Lee** hasn't given up hope that she will one day inherit a title and a manor house. Until then she fulfils her dreams of lords, ladies and a Season in London through her stories. When not writing, she can be found reading non-fiction history or watching any film with a costume and an accent.

Please visit georgie-lee.com to learn more about Georgie and her books.

Books by Georgie Lee

Mills & Boon Historical Romance

Engagement of Convenience
Rescued from Ruin
The Courtesan's Book of Secrets
A Debt Paid in Marriage
The Captain's Frozen Dream

Visit the Author Profile page at
millsandboon.co.uk.

To my little one,
whose obsession with dinosaurs
gave my heroine hers.

Chapter One

England—October 1st, 1820

'No, let go of me.' A woman's strained voice carried over the rolling hills of the West Sussex countryside.

Captain Conrad Essington kicked his horse into a canter, and as he crested the rise in the road he spied a gig beside it, the horse grazing lazily on the tall grass. Up a gentle hill, just beyond the shade of a wide ash tree, a man and woman stood together. The setting sun blazed behind them, turning them into little more than silhouettes. The woman tried to walk away, but the man grabbed her by the arm.

'Listen to me,' he demanded.

She twisted out of his grip. 'No, I won't hear it.'

'Can I be of some assistance?' Conrad slid off

the hired horse and flicked the reins over the animal's head.

The man let go of the woman and offered a dismissive wave. 'I assure you, we're fine.'

Conrad continued up the hill, not so easily dissuaded.

'And you, my lady?' The brown grass crunched beneath his boots, releasing the sharp aroma of warm, dry earth. Conrad pulled in a lungful of air. Even with the nip of autumn in the air, after a year and a half in the stinging cold of the Arctic, this was paradise. 'Are you well?'

The glare of the sun behind her blotted out all but the roundness of her hips beneath a dark-green dress and the light ringlets of blonde hair framing her face.

'No, not at all.' The familiar melody of her voice more than the waver in her words slowed Conrad's steps. It drew from somewhere deep inside him a happiness and comfort he hadn't experienced since he'd stepped aboard HMS *Gorgon* and set sail in search of the Northwest Passage.

She started cautiously down the hill towards him, entering the shade of the tree. The shadow freed her from the overpowering sun and brought her cheeks and fine nose into focus. Her brilliant blue eyes stopped Conrad and he stood in awe as she approached.

'Katie?' In the dark hours of the long winter aboard HMS *Gorgon*, when the sun had lain hidden beneath the horizon, months away from shining on him and his crew, he'd dreamed of this moment, of seeing her again. It was all he'd thought about during the long walk across the ice and snow, and in the ship coming home. It was the one thought which had guided him since disembarking in Portsmouth this morning. He'd sent his lieutenant, Henry Sefton, ahead to London with Conrad's official report so Conrad could set off in search of her. He hadn't expected to stumble upon her on the London road, or for her to be more beautiful than he remembered.

'Conrad?' Uncertainty as much as the fading daylight danced in her eyes, making them glow like the low polar sun on the ice. 'Is it really you?'

'It is.' He raised his hand to touch her cheek, then hesitated, afraid if he caressed her she might disappear like one of the many mirages he'd seen hovering above the Arctic sea. Returning to England and Katie had seemed like an impossible dream when he'd imagined it from the cold hold of a ship buried beneath darkness and ice. Even a mile back, when the tang of chalk from the Downs had at last replaced the mouldy stench of bilge water clinging to him, his weary mind still couldn't believe his trials were over.

Now, with the curve of Katie's small chin so close to his palm, her thick eyelashes fluttering with each disbelieving blink, the grip of the nightmare began at last to ease.

He was home.

Conrad brushed her face with his fingertips and the tender warmth of her skin made him shiver for the first time in more than a year from something other than cold. Despite the shadows beneath her eyes, the faint blush spreading under the smattering of freckles across the bridge of her nose could hold his gaze for hours. He shifted closer, craving the sweet taste of her lips parted with surprise. He'd been too long without her and the comfort of her embrace.

Conrad leaned down, ready to claim her mouth, but Katie didn't rise to meet him. His hand stiffened against her cheek while he waited for the adoring woman he'd left over a year and half ago to embrace him, but she didn't. In her eyes wasn't the love she'd seen him off with in Greenwich, nor was it simply disbelief. It was a lack of faith, the same blistering kind he'd seen in Aaron's eyes before he'd walked out into the snow to die. Conrad's stomach clenched as hard as it had the night he and Henry had watched the sea ice harden around *Gorgon*.

'Miss Vickers, do you know this man?' the gentleman asked, his intrusion as much a shock as the silent gorge opening between Katie and Conrad.

'I do.' Katie stepped back out of Conrad's grasp, her blush deepening with something Conrad sensed had nothing to do with the strength of the afternoon sun. 'Captain Essington, allow me to introduce Mr Prevett.'

Conrad straightened and dropped his hand. His fingers, stiff after months of near frostbite, tightened into a fist at his side. He stared at Katie, as unsure of his position now as when *Gorgon* had sailed north beyond the known regions of the map. He searched Katie's face for some silent explanation, reluctant to hear the one he expected her to provide.

'Captain Essington is my intended,' Katie clarified.

Conrad's hand eased. Whatever had shifted between them, at least this still remained.

Mr Prevett's gaze jerked back and forth between Conrad and Katie before an awkward smile broke across his thin lips. 'Captain Essington? Why, I can't believe it, all of England thought you were dead.'

'So did I, more than once.' Conrad laced his fingers behind his back as though on deck and examined the man as he would an unruly junior officer. 'Tell me, Mr Prevett, what are you doing out here, *alone* with Miss Vickers? Have you no care for her reputation?'

'Her reputation?' Mr Prevett snorted before a fierce glare from Conrad sobered him. 'We were searching for fossils. I've had a great deal of luck finding them in this vicinity.'

Mr Prevett, who could be no more than thirty, appeared too finely turned out for a man hunting only bones. 'It seemed as though you were having a more heated discussion than one about fossils.'

'We were having a disagreement regarding a certain line of research he wished me to pursue,' Katie hurriedly explained. 'I told him he should abandon it, as I have my own ideas about how best to proceed with my research.'

'Speaking of which, I must be getting home. My wife is expecting me.' Mr Prevett shuffled past Conrad, pausing beside him, but not too close. 'Congratulations on your return, Captain Essington. I look forward to reading your papers when you publish them.'

'I'll be sure to send you a copy.' Conrad replied, the demands of publishing the details of his expedition paling beneath the desire to be alone with Katie.

Mr Prevett hurried away down the rise and soon the grinding of wheels over dirt joined the fading plod of the horse as it drew the gig out of sight.

Katie didn't watch Mr Prevett leave, but remained focused on Conrad, sliding her opal ring on and off her finger, the movement jerky and fumbling.

'Did you really forget me so soon?' Conrad accused, suspicion hard in his voice.

'So soon?' Katie shoved the ring back on her finger. 'You promised me you'd only be gone for six months, for as long as the Arctic summer lasted, but it's been over a year since you were supposed to return. I thought you were dead, everyone did. How dare you come back now and accuse me of anything?'

Conrad trimmed his suspicions like a sail in a storm. A calm head would win the day, just as it had seen him and his men through the winter. 'I only want to know what was happening between the two of you.'

'What you saw was the result of your having been gone, of you chasing your ambitions and leaving the rest of us to deal with the consequences.'

Katie rushed past Conrad and down the hill, as livid as the day his uncle, the Marquis of Helton, had turned from ruining Katie's reputation to destroying her father's. For the better part of the last year, she'd borne the malicious whispers of London and the snubs of the Naturalist

Society alone. Now Conrad was here, tossing suspicions on the heap his uncle had worked so hard to build.

'Katie, wait,' Conrad called after her, his quick footsteps muffled by the soft earth.

She stopped to face him, further accusations silenced by the sight of him moving through the grass. *He isn't dead.*

Her heart leapt in her chest, but the pain of everything she'd suffered since he'd left trampled her joy. If only he'd come back before all the troubles had begun. 'I waited for you for over a year, I won't wait any longer.'

She turned her back on him and made for the road, the dust kicked up by Mr Prevett's gig choking her along with the biting injustice of Conrad's return. She'd prayed so many nights for him to come home. For her prayers to be answered after it was too late stung as much as the day she'd finally accepted he'd perished.

Though he wasn't dead.

She pressed her fingers to her temples, trying to take it all in, but it was too much, especially on the heels of the other shocks she'd suffered today. Her spirits dropped lower at the sight of her canvas satchel lying beside the road, set aside by Mr Prevett before he'd driven off. Inside was a selection of her papers and sketchbooks, the ones she'd been so eager to show to Dr Mantell. She curled her fingers in against her palms, her fingernails as sharp as Mr Prevett's betrayal. It was the second time she'd been deceived by a man she thought her ally in her fight to regain the Naturalist Society's recognition. She didn't know Mr Prevett had been swayed by London gossip enough to believe she would become his mistress. At least he hadn't tried to force himself on her like the other false friend.

She stopped in front of the sad canvas bag sagging over its leather bottom. Was there any person in England who wouldn't fail her? The strangling loneliness of her youth, when her father used to lock himself in his study to work for hours, filled her again.

As much as it galled her to admit it, her mother was right; the only person a woman could rely on was herself.

She snatched up the bag, then turned to see Conrad standing by his horse, stroking the length of the animal's tan nose. The changes which had shocked her as much as his resurrection were highlighted by flecks of grey in his sandy hair. He was still a rock of a man, but noticeably leaner, his jaw tighter and more angular, but it was his dark eyes which stunned her the most. They held none of the optimism and excitement which used to illuminate them before he'd left. It was as if the chill of his experiences still draped him, the way her sorrows hung around her in the quiet house she'd once shared with her father in Whitemans Green.

'It's getting late. We should be going.' The tender tones which had graced his voice on the hill were noticeably absent.

'There's an inn not far from here. I can walk there and spend the night, then take the coach home in the morning,' she feebly protested, knowing she had little choice but to join him. Even if she could reach the inn before midnight, she didn't have the money to pay for a room, or the coach to Whitemans Green.

'You know me better than that, Katie.' He came forward and took the satchel by its scarred wooden handles, his fingers brushing hers as he grasped it.

'You needn't be a hero, Conrad.' The time for him to save her had already passed.

'Then let me be a gentleman.' The circles beneath his eyes darkened with the fading daylight. It wasn't just exhaustion blackening them, but something like the despair of loss, a sadness she was all too familiar with. She slid one finger cautiously over the back of his hand, the desire to comfort him as he'd once comforted her overwhelming. He'd been the rock upon which she'd planned to build her life, then he'd sailed away.

She let go of the bag and a heaviness descended over her as he turned and walked back to the horse. With misgivings she followed, noting the ripple of his muscles beneath his faded uniform as he tied the satchel to the saddle bag, the force with which he pulled the leather straps tight telling.

Once the satchel was secure, he took the reins and settled one foot in the stirrup. Stiffness marred his movements as he mounted, but it didn't diminish the power of him. His sturdy frame reminded her of the beams used to support the quarry wall and the trees in the fields encircling the mines. They'd spent so many lazy afternoons in the tall grass together beneath such oaks, the fossils she'd collected scattered about the blanket to keep the edges down as his solid legs intertwined with hers. In the words of love and temptation he'd whispered in her ear, she'd forgotten the loneliness which had marred her life. The memory made her cheeks burn with delight and regret. She should have followed her instincts instead of her heart and never fallen in love.

He clicked his horse into a walk, bringing it beside her and extending his hand. Red patches of raw skin marred the palms, like old blisters which had healed. It tore at her to see such blinding evidence of what he'd endured, but she was careful to subdue the urge to comfort him. She, too, bore bruises from the last year and a half, only hers weren't as obvious as his.

'Perhaps we should walk.' In the face of so many startling events, she could hardly climb in the saddle with him and expect to maintain what little remained of her calm.

'It'll take too long and we're already losing the light.'

He was right, but it didn't lessen her unease as

she placed her hand in his and slid her foot over the toe of his boot in the stirrup. She exhaled with surprise at the strength he used to pull her into the saddle, the vigour which had first caught her notice three years ago when he'd sought out her father's expertise overwhelming her again.

She settled herself across his thighs, his chest against her shoulder as troublesome as the front curve of the saddle digging into her buttocks. She shifted, working to keep her balance, worried as much about being this close to Conrad as toppling over on to the ground. She gasped as he slid one hand around her waist to steady her, then took the reins with the other and set the horse in motion.

'What happened between you and Mr Prevett?' he asked.

She rocked uncomfortably against him as the steed ambled down the wide lane marked by brown parallel wheel tracks with dry grass growing in between. She kept her back straight, attempting to maintain some distance between them, and ignored the shift of his thigh muscles beneath her own. She didn't want to tell him, or relive any of the ugly moments of the past eighteen months, especially the night she'd nearly been compromised, but he'd seen too much for her to dismiss it easily. 'I asked him to drive me to Dr Mantell's so I could share with him my papers and drawings of Father's best fossil specimens. Mr Prevett mistook my request as an invitation for something more.'

'Why did he think you might indulge him?' His body tightened against hers, making her heart race, his solid presence as disturbing as his sudden return.

'Because while you were gone, your uncle did everything in his power to ruin me,' she retorted, her base reaction to his nearness more unnerving than his question. 'As you saw, he succeeded.'

'He hasn't succeeded for good. Whatever he's done, I'll undo it and make him pay,' Conrad said sternly. 'I promise.'

She looked down at his wide hand on her stomach, the fingertips spread over her dress. It would be so comforting to lean in to him and believe in his promise the way she used to when they'd lay together in the field above the slate mine with the dust of the rocks still fresh on her hands. Back then, it'd been so easy to trust in

Conrad's love and his promise to treasure her more than any reputation or expedition. Both had been illusions, like a white stone which from a distance looks like something spectacular, but up close is nothing more than a plain rock.

Pain tightened her chest and she closed her eyes to picture the bones arranged on the small table in her father's old study, the ones she'd dug from the Downs a week ago. They were clean now, the clinging dirt carefully chipped and brushed away. In her mind, she tried to imagine how each fitted together as she always did, but nothing came to her now. It couldn't, not with Conrad so close.

She opened her eyes just as they reached a fork in the road and Conrad urged the horse to the left.

'Where are you going?' Katie demanded. 'Whitemans Green is the other way.'

'Heims Hall is closer. We'll rest there tonight and in the morning I'll see you home.'

'I don't want to go there.' He'd already conjured up too many tormenting memories for her to face more.

'You needn't worry. Miss Linton should be

there and can serve as an appropriate chaperon,' Conrad offered, as if guessing her concern.

Katie heaved a weary sigh. It was Miss Linton as much as spending the night at Heims Hall which worried her. The spinster had only ever been grudgingly cordial to Katie; she wasn't likely to welcome her, or her tattered reputation, with open arms now. More than likely she'd pull Conrad aside and whisper in his ear every disgusting London story the marquis had created and spread, including the one where she'd traded her favours for a single published paper in an obscure journal.

Katie sagged a little against Conrad. She'd never thought he would come home, so she never thought he would ever have to hear the nasty things being said about her in London. Now he would hear them all. Whether or not he would choose to believe them, especially after what he'd seen today, she didn't know. Everyone else had been so quick to accept them, so why not him?

'I'm home now, Katie, you don't have to worry,' he whispered in the same soft voice he'd used to deliver the news he was leaving for his expedition. It didn't soothe her any more now than it had a year and a half ago.

'It would have been better if you'd come back sooner.' Before she'd lost all faith in him and their future together.

'I would have, but the ice had other plans for me.'

His hand against her stomach eased. Guilt swept over the back of her neck along with the faint caress of his breath. For everything she'd suffered, his suffering must have been tenfold. She laid her hand over his, noticing the slight tremor in his fingers. She squeezed his hand and the shaking stopped. Their future together might be over, but it didn't mean she didn't care for him or couldn't soothe him.

He didn't return the small squeeze, but slid his hand out of hers and took the reins. He was pulling away from her and she couldn't blame him. This wasn't the homecoming he'd expected. It wasn't the one she'd pictured either, though she'd given up imagining him returning months ago. Now he was here and she didn't know what to think or believe.

Chapter Two

The countryside around them appeared to Conrad like a dream. Familiar rocks and trees dotted the landscape and the rising full moon turned them a ghostly grey. A cool breeze brushed through the grass flanking the road, and the steady clop of the horse's hooves filled the night air. Wisps of Katie's hair danced about the sides of her face, sliding free of the slim pins keeping the tangle of blonde curls together at the back of her head.

An owl called from somewhere overhead and the horse broke its steady pace. With one hand, Conrad tugged the reins to stop the horse from bolting. With the other, he held on tight to Katie to keep her from falling. The soft inhale his grip provoked proved as jarring to his nerves as the owl's screech, more so when his manhood stirred at the shift of her buttocks against him. Conrad drew in a steadying breath. In the evening air hung the faint must of wet, fallen leaves mingling with the sweetness of Katie's rose soap. Without thinking, he drew her closer against him, the heat of her more welcome than any he'd ever enjoyed from the stove deep in the hold of the ship trapped in the hard-packed ice.

She sat rigid against him, refusing to relax the way she used to whenever they'd ridden out together in search of fossils and time alone. The distance between them unnerved him. He didn't know the extent of what had happened while he'd been gone, but he could imagine. Without Conrad to protect her, it would have been easy for Lord Helton to set the dogs of society upon a woman of Katie's humble background. He'd seen his uncle level several such attacks on his mother and knew the vicious lengths the marquis might employ to ostracise and punish those he didn't think worthy of bearing the Helton family name.

Conrad adjusted his feet in the stirrups. He'd promised Katie when they'd become engaged he wouldn't allow society or his uncle to harm her. He'd failed. It was another in a mounting pile of failures and mistakes threatening to crush him like an avalanche.

He ran his fingers through his hair, the shortness of it still a shock after he'd grown it so long in the Arctic. By now Henry must have reached London and handed Conrad's report to Second Secretary of the Admiralty, John Barrow. Conrad could only imagine what fury and damnation awaited his inability to find the Northwest Passage and bring *Gorgon* home. Mr Barrow had stood beside Conrad before, when Lord Helton had done all he could to prevent Conrad from receiving a command. He didn't know if Mr Barrow would stand beside him again or viciously denounce him like he had Captain Ross after Ross had failed to explore the bay Mr Barrow believed led to the Northwest Passage. The Second Secretary had been stealthy in his attacks against Ross, penning anonymous articles in widely read magazines and whispering against him to influential members of the Admiralty. No one could ever prove it was Mr Barrow who'd been behind the attempts to discredit and disgrace Captain Ross, but he'd never been fully exonerated either. If an attack was coming, Conrad wouldn't see it until it was too late.

The horse rounded a curve filled with trees and Heims Hall at last came into view. Conrad straightened in the saddle, indulging in the sight of it. It'd been a long time since he'd seen the sturdy brick walls lined with rows of familiar windows and the steeply pitched roof. Built in the sixteenth century, it was small and intimate, the home of a man, not the seat of a scion. Only Katie, so solid in front of him, kept him from sliding off his horse to kiss the ground in thanksgiving. There'd been too many times when he'd thought he'd never see such a glorious view again, but he'd fought nature and overwhelming odds to return.

Not all of his men would have the same opportunity to experience this relief at coming home.

His hold on the reins eased as the intermittent trembles which had plagued him since Greenland weakened his grip once more. Thankfully, the darkness covered the shaking. It was bad enough Katie had sensed it before. He didn't want her, or anyone, to know how deep the scars from his expedition ran, or how they continued to strangle his belief in himself and his abilities as a leader.

Conrad settled back down against the leather and guided the horse around the house to the stables behind, determined to allow the events of the past year to lie tonight. In the morning he'd get to the meat of them. He only prayed the damage wasn't as bad as instinct warned, either to himself, his career or his future with Katie.

In the shadow of the stable lamp, a groom rose from where he sat whittling, curls of wood falling over his lap. His eyes went wide at the sight of Conrad before he tossed the stick and knife aside.

'Captain Essington! Why, I don't believe it.' Mr Peet hustled forward on his long legs to catch the reins, his joy at Conrad's return as bright on his face as the light from the lantern. 'Mrs Peet will be so glad to see ya, everyone will be, well, excepting Miss Linton, she's never happy to see anybody.'

'It's good to be home. You remember Miss Vickers.'

'I do.' He doffed his cap at Katie. 'It's a pleasure to see you again, Miss Vickers.'

'And you, too, Mr Peet,' Katie replied, although her voice lacked the same enthusiasm as the groom's.

'Oh!' Katie breathed, as Conrad let go of the reins and slid his hands around her waist. It was smaller than he remembered and she seemed more fragile and vulnerable than when he'd left. She gripped his wrists tight as he shifted her off his lap and lowered her to the mounting block. As she stepped off it, she rocked as if she'd been on the deck of a ship for months, not on the back of a horse for a mile or two.

Gritting his teeth against the stiffness in his back, legs and hands, Conrad slid down on to the block. He turned to see Katie watching him, worry marring the small lines along the corners of her lips. She'd seen him wince, sensed the slowness of his movements and guessed he was weakened by the north. He turned to the saddle bag to retrieve her satchel, not wanting her or anyone's pity, not even his own.

With the small bag in his hand, he stepped off

the block, patting the horse's rump as Mr Peet led it away.

'Shall we?' Conrad motioned to the house.

The rising moonlight glinted off the large bank of windows making up one wall of the conservatory jutting from the rear of the house. Katie didn't want to go inside, especially with the light burning in the upstairs window. The flick of a curtain in Miss Linton's room announced the spinster's presence and her curiosity. Whenever Katie and her father had stayed here, she had gone to great lengths to avoid the thin, buck-toothed woman. More so after Katie and Conrad's engagement had been announced. The woman, only a year or two older than Katie's twenty-five, had always looked upon Katie with as little warmth as Lord Helton. However, they couldn't stand in the mews all night and Katie accompanied Conrad up the walk and into the conservatory.

She tried not to look at the marble table in the centre as they passed through the moonlit room, her shoulders brushing the delicate fronds of the many palms filling it. It was too difficult to see the empty top of the table and not think of her father working on the strange tiger-like fossil there in happier times. Through the opposite door, they entered the dimly lit hallway and the scent of scouring soap and wood oil overwhelmed her. Surrounded by so many familiar things, it seemed as if she could reach out and take Conrad's hand and the past year and a half would vanish. If it did, then all the optimism and faith she'd once possessed in him might return. She kept her hands at her sides, unwilling to expose herself to more disappointment and heartache. She'd spend one night here, then tomorrow she'd leave Conrad and their past behind.

The hallway opened into a tall entrance hall with a slate floor. In the moonlight coming through the window, she could see the scattering of ammonite fossils embedded in the flat stone. Then the dark imprints of curving shells caught the orange light of a candle from somewhere above them and Katie looked up to watch Miss Linton descend the stairs.

A plain house dress hung from Miss Linton's scrawny shoulders and her lacklustre brown hair was pinned in a tight bun at the nape of her neck.

Unlike the groom, there was no wide smile to lighten her long face. She fixed her eyes first on Conrad and then Katie, her scowl deepening with each step until she was at last in front of them.

'Conrad, what are you doing here?' It was exactly the sort of dismissive greeting Katie expected from the shrewish woman.

'Cousin Matilda, it's a pleasure to see you as well,' Conrad replied with a sarcastic bow.

'Of course, I'm glad you've returned safely,' she replied as if he'd been out in the fields, not presumed dead for nearly a year. 'It's certainly most unexpected.'

'Is the guest room and my room as I left them?'

'They are, but the linens haven't been changed or the fires lit. If I'd received some notice of your arrival instead of being startled at night, things might have been better prepared.'

'A man doesn't have to send word to his own house.'

Miss Linton stiffened at the reminder of her place. Frustrated in her effort to enforce some control over Heims Hall, she turned to Katie. 'Will *she* be staying here?'

'You mean Miss Vickers?' Conrad's voice was low and warning. 'Yes, she will.'

The little colour in Miss Linton's face drained out, leaving her an unappealing shade of white. 'But, Conrad—'

'We'll rely on you to serve as an appropriate chaperon.'

Miss Linton jerked back her shoulders in indignation, as if Conrad had asked her to walk down the high street of nearby Cuckfield naked. 'I don't think it's appropriate for a woman like me—'

'Thank you, Matilda.' He cut her off, turned to Katie and held out his arm. 'Shall I escort you to your room?'

Only the desire to vex Miss Linton prodded Katie to place her hand on the firm muscle beneath the wool coat. 'Thank you.'

Conrad guided them around his cousin and they climbed the stairs. His solid form beside her was a welcome comfort against Miss Linton's hostile stares burning a hole in the back of Katie's dress. If only he had come back sooner, before Lord Helton's lies had done their damage.

The staircase curved, taking them out of sight

of Miss Linton and Katie removed her hand from Conrad's arm, reluctant to encourage any intimacy between them.

Conrad didn't protest, but continued to escort her down the short hall illuminated by the light spilling out of Miss Linton's open bedroom door. It filled the narrow space with a wavering amber glow and sharpened the lines of Conrad's straight nose and strong forehead.

He stopped before the open door of a bedroom in the middle of the hallway. Thankfully, it wasn't one of the adjoining rooms at the end, the ones she and her father had occupied when they'd stayed here to study the tiger fossil. There were enough lingering memories to torment her, she didn't need more.

'In the morning, after we've both had some rest, we'll talk,' Conrad stated, as if the problems of over a year could simply be surmounted with a conversation.

She took the satchel from him, careful to keep her fingers away from his. 'There's little to discuss.'

She moved to enter the room, but Conrad shifted between her and the door. 'There's everything to discuss. Whatever happened while I was gone to make you think differently of me, I'll see it set right.'

Katie fingered the rough spot on the satchel handle where the varnish had been rubbed away during her father's many trips to visit scientific men. They'd appreciated his ability to find fossils, but not his theories on why the strange animals no longer existed. 'Conrad, I spent my childhood listening to my father make promises to my mother, one after another. He'd make sure she never regretted leaving her family for him, he'd spend time with her once he was done with this paper or cleaning that fossil. In the end he couldn't keep any of them.'

'I'm not your father.'

'But you have his passion for work, the all-consuming kind which places itself above anyone and everyone. When you first proposed, I told you I had doubts about entering your world, making myself visible to society. You were so gallant in your promise I'd never suffer and I believed you. Then you left and everything I feared, everything you assured me wouldn't happen did.'

A new light flickered behind Conrad. Miss Linton stood at the top of the stairs at the end of the hall, her disapproving scowl deepened by the candle she held.

He lowered his head, his face so close to hers, Katie could see the faint outline of his beard along his chiselled jaw. 'This isn't how it's going to end, Katie.'

Her chest caught at the nearness of him. If things were different, if he hadn't left, she might have risen up on her feet and touched her lips to his, fallen into his arms and known the bliss they'd once experienced together on the Downs, away from everyone and everything except each other, but things weren't different and the time for discussion had passed.

'Goodnight, Conrad.' Katie slipped into the room and closed the door behind her.

Conrad frowned as the lock clicked shut.

Matilda scurried up behind him, moving so quickly the candle flame danced and nearly went out before she raised her hand to protect it. 'Conrad, we must speak.'

'Whatever it is, it can wait until morning.' He

made for the stairs, rolling his stiff shoulders. He needed to eat and sleep in a real bed, not endure his cousin's company. Hopefully the groaning of the ship's timbers and the far-off thunder of breaking ice wouldn't haunt his dreams. Too much was already cracking up around him for him to face tomorrow exhausted.

'It can't wait.' Matilda dogged his heels as he descended, the light from her candle waving erratically over the plaster walls. 'You can't think to allow her to stay here.'

'I'll allow whomever I wish to reside here for any length of time.' He stopped on the landing and levelled a pointed look at his cousin. 'As I've allowed you to reside here and manage the estate in my absence.'

She pursed her lips in indignation. 'Then I cannot continue to remain here, risking my reputation to lend some thin veneer of credibility to hers.'

Conrad glared at her as he would a sailor who dared to question his orders. 'Careful, Matilda, how you speak of the woman who is to be my wife.'

'Don't think to cow me into withholding my

opinion of your connection to a woman of no standing who can bring nothing to your family.'

'She's the granddaughter of a baronet.'

'And the daughter of a disgraced woman who didn't have the foresight to think of her family, her name, her ancestry before running off with some poor country doctor. No wonder Miss Vickers behaved the way she did after you left. You have no idea what they're saying about her in London.'

'You're right, nor do I want to know,' Conrad tossed over his shoulder as he made for the entrance hall.

'But you must.' Matilda followed him. 'They say she and certain members of the Naturalist Society were more than professional acquaintances.'

Conrad paused in the centre of the room, tightening his fist at his side before releasing his fingers one by one. Matilda's revelation added to the unease already created by the scene with Katie and Mr Prevett on the road. Whatever had happened while Conrad was gone, the gravity of it was beginning to settle over him like a storm in the North Atlantic. Only tonight he had no time for it, or his cousin. The woman wasn't above exaggeration, she excelled in it. He brushed her and his suspicions aside as he made for his study. 'No doubt the stories are in existence because of my uncle.'

'There's no reason for an august man like Lord Helton to dirty his hands with a woman like Miss Vickers,' Matilda countered as she followed after him. She was the only one who'd ever venerated his uncle. Her slight connection to the marquis through Conrad gave her the single edge of superiority over her small group of friends and she cherished it. 'She isn't suitable to be a marchioness.'

Conrad stopped and whirled around to face her. 'What are you talking about? I'm not Lord Helton's heir.'

'You mean you haven't heard?' Her dull-brown eyes sparkled with the delight of knowing something Conrad didn't. 'Your cousin Preston is dead. You *are* Lord Helton's heir now.'

Conrad shoved open the study door and it banged against the plaster wall. The breeze of it disturbed the blue-and-gold flag from the ship of his first command hanging from the timbered rafters. The stench of stale air hit him as he made for the sideboard and the decanter of brandy sitting on top.

What the hell happened while I was gone? It was as if he'd sailed away from one world and returned to find another, more contemptible one had taken its place.

He flipped back the silver stopper and raised the crystal to his lips, ready to drown himself and all his shattered plans in the liquor. Nothing had gone as he'd intended, not his expedition or his homecoming.

Over the top of the glittering decanter, he caught sight of his father's portrait hanging over the mantel. Conrad lowered the decanter. This had once been his father's domain and he'd filled the shelves with his collection of beetles, the research of which had garnered him the presidency of the Naturalist Society. Later, his study of the insects had provided a refuge from the nightmares of the hell his own brother, the Marquis of Helton, had consigned him to for daring to defy him, the one which had ruined his health and broken his spirit.

Conrad followed the stare of his father's painted brown eyes across the room to where the spoils of Conrad's expeditions now adorned his father's precious bookcases—Inuit spears, beaverskin moccasins, wood totems and the fossil remains of animals both known and unknown. They were a silent catalogue of all his past successes and triumphs. Taking it in, his gut sank like it had the morning he'd watched *Gorgon* break apart and slip beneath the icy water, leaving them trapped. It was his blood trapping him now, the legacy his father and mother had spent years struggling to escape, the one ruled by the iron fist of Lord Helton.

Conrad took another long drink and silently cursed his uncle. Lord Helton cared for nothing except power and using it to make men in government and society bow and scrape before him. After Conrad's father's early death had put him beyond his brother's reach, it'd been a struggle for Conrad and his mother to escape Lord Helton's grasping control. If it hadn't been for Heims Hall and his mother's brother, Jack, they might never have known peace, or the security of a home and an income not encumbered by the Helton legacy.

Conrad smiled at the memory of his mother standing in the grand entrance hall at Helton Manor after his father's funeral, breaking Lord Helton's walking stick over her knee after he'd dared to strike Conrad with it for mourning his father. She'd pelted the man with the broken bits and a barrage of insults, stunning Lord Helton into silence for the first time in his life.

Conrad's smile faded. Afterwards, Lord Helton's methods had become more subtle and he'd resorted to lies and rumours to attack her instead of confrontation. When she'd passed, Lord Helton then turned his vengeance against Conrad, using his influence in government to make sure every ship Conrad received after becoming captain was more worm-eaten than the last. Yet Conrad had accepted each doomed command and made a stunning success of them all, securing his reputation as a first-rate officer and diluting Lord Helton's influence. After Napoleon's defeat left Conrad without a ship and on half-pay, he'd volunteered for the Discovery Service and built a name for himself as an explorer, one of Mr Barrow's favourites, a man who always succeeded.

Except this time.

Conrad took another deep drink, then wiped his mouth with the back of his hand. He should have turned *Gorgon* for home before the short Arctic summer had ended. Instead, he'd pushed north and others had paid the price for his mistake, sacrificing fingers, toes and even a life to Conrad's desire to accomplish his mission.

He gripped the decanter tight against his chest, hanging on with both hands to keep it from slipping out of his grasp. At times, he'd barely been able to hold his pen on the voyage home, the weakness nearly crippling him as he'd reread his journal and relived the horrors of his experience to write his report. In the cold north he'd thought it would ease once he reached warmer climes, but as time passed it was becoming apparent the weakness was driven not by cold but by memories, especially those of Aaron's hopeless eyes meeting his before he'd slipped out of the tent door and into oblivion.

Eyes as vacant as those of the skeleton of the tiger-like creature perched in front of the window.

Conrad rocked a little as he approached the animal, coming face-to-face with the long jaw and the two curving canine teeth protruding from the mouth. He slid his hand over the top of the skull, feeling the slight pits and crevices of the bones. It was an exquisite specimen, one he'd purchased from an Inuit trader in Greenland at the end of his first voyage to the Arctic three years ago. The same man had sold Conrad the skeleton that was even now in one of the many crates making their way to Heims Hall, the likes of which he'd never seen in any book or collection.

He ran his fingers over the tiger's long nose and down the back edge of one curved and serrated fang. He'd spent hours watching Katie and her father meticulously clean and piece this animal together. Katie would do the same with the creature in the crate, making sense of the jumble of bones in a way he could never understand. Her face would light up in excitement when she

did, just as it had when she'd attached this skull
to the vertebrae.

He flicked the pointed end of the fang with
his fingernail. A dead animal would receive a
warmer welcome than he had.

He backhanded the skull, knocking it free of
its neck and sending it flying across the room.
It thudded each time it bounced along the carpet
before the leg of a wide, leather bench brought it
to a sudden stop. He marched up to it, ignoring
the sting to his hand as he focused on the hollow
eyes watching him above the mercifully unbro-
ken fangs. He raised his foot to stomp the poor
thing into oblivion, to crush it and all memories
of the frozen wasteland which had ruined everything, but he couldn't.

He lowered his foot, staggering a bit before
he righted himself. He was a man of discovery,
not a destroyer, though this last expedition had
nearly crushed him. He braced himself against
a nearby desk, the wood beneath his fingers
smooth and cool, unlike the rough timbers of
the ship. The sounds of the house surrounded
him—the whinny of a horse in the mews, the
twitter of a night bird. They were as familiar

now as they'd been when he was ten and in their echoes he found a faint comfort. Then the creak of the floorboard beneath his boot sent a shock racing up his back. In the straining wood he heard the echoes of *Gorgon* groaning beneath the pressure of the ice, struggling to keep it at bay until at last she'd given up the fight.

Conrad moved uneasily to the chair beside the cold fireplace, set the half-empty decanter on the table and dropped into the thick cushions. The house was much quieter than the ship. During the long Arctic months, the wind had always been blowing and the men had been talking, complaining or playing cards, anything to fill the hours of boredom with something other than worry. The weariness of the past eighteen months, of the last few hours, settled over him like the fog of drink. He should go upstairs. He needed to sleep in a proper bed, but he couldn't move. He'd known true exhaustion and this wasn't it. Even if he went upstairs, there was no guarantee of rest, only hours of sleep jerked from him by nightmares of the cold.

It didn't matter. Years of exploration had taught him to catch sleep where and when he could, to do with as little of it as possible in order to make it through another day. Only this wasn't the North Pole, or the hull of a ship. It was the study where he'd first wooed Katie, the woman whose soft voice and love he'd hoped would silence the doubts and memories torturing him.

As the darkness closed in around him, the crack of icebergs slamming together drowned out the quiet of the house. Each thud made Conrad wince until at last it faded and a dreamless sleep brought much needed silence.

Katie peered into the dark study. In the hallway, she thought she'd heard a noise, but everything in here was quiet. She must have imagined it the way she sometimes imagined hearing her father return from a dig. She'd look up from sketching a specimen, thinking she'd see him come through the door, only to remember he was never coming home again.

It shocked her how keenly she noticed his absence. Even when he'd been home, he'd never truly been there. There'd never been anyone who'd been willing to place her above their own selfish pursuits, not her mother, her father or even Conrad.

Bitterness stiffened her steps as she moved beneath the timbered ceiling and past the books, animals and artefacts filling the room. At one time the tattered flag, seal skins and the stories behind each item had impressed her. Tonight, they were a crushing reminder of Conrad's true passion, like the tiger was a reminder of her father's.

She stopped in front of the skeleton bleached an eerie white by the moonlight coming through the window. It stood just as she'd last seen it, wired together as her father had arranged it, except for the skull. It was missing.

She searched the floor beneath the table, looking for it, irritated to think it'd been ruined by someone's carelessness. She and her father had spent hours hunched over the bones, studying, drawing and arranging them just as she had as a young girl when she'd sit beside him in their small house in Whitemans Green, cleaning away the hard dirt encasing her father's latest find. Working with him had been the only way to garner his attention and she'd taken in everything he'd taught her about anatomy and biology. He'd even spent precious money on drawing lessons to increase her natural skill, though those had been more for his benefit than hers so that she could sketch his collections.

Despite her father's selfish reason for tutoring her, those days with him were the only times she'd ever felt wanted and loved, until she'd met Conrad.

Pain squeezed her chest. If she'd known, less than a year later, Conrad would be aboard *Gorgon* and off to embrace his true passion, she would have been more cautious with her heart.

'Come to see the animal?' Conrad slurred from behind her.

She jerked up straight and focused through the darkness to where Conrad pushed himself up out of a chair by the fireplace, swaying as he stood.

She laid a shaking hand over her chest, as startled by his drunkenness as his unexpected presence. She'd never seen him drink to excess before. 'Conrad, I didn't know you were in here.'

'You'd have avoided the room if you'd known?'

Yes. 'No, I wanted to see the tiger.'

'Of course you did.' The edge in his voice disturbed her as much as the incomplete skeleton.

'Where's the head?'

'Over there.' He pointed to where the skull glowed white against the dark carpet.

She walked over and scooped it up, then turned it over in her hands to examine it. 'I don't think any permanent damage has been done.'

'Can't say the same about much else, now can we?'

Katie ignored the sarcasm as she reattached the skull to the neck.

'I suppose you've heard my status in the world has been quite elevated since I've been gone?' Conrad slurred as he staggered over to stand beside her.

'As the heir, will you resign your commission?' There was a little too much hope in her question.

'No,' Conrad answered without hesitation. 'It's what Helton expects me to do and I'm not about to do his bidding.'

'I see.' There was nothing in the world which would persuade him to cease exploring, not a title, or even love.

'Aren't you going to congratulate me?' Conrad prodded.

'I don't envy you enough to congratulate you.' There were few but the most sycophantic of people desirous of a place in government who envied a connection to the Marquis of Helton.

'You're right, you shouldn't. No one should.' The same desperation Katie had experienced during the past year, when the long days of spring had turned into summer and then autumn with no sign of Conrad or his ship, coloured his voice. He peered past her into the night beyond the window, the lines of his face hardening with a pain she felt deep inside her heart. 'I had to leave him.'

'Who?' Katie whispered, troubled by the mournful tone of his voice.

'Aaron.' He choked out the name as if it cut his tongue.

Katie swallowed hard. She remembered the red-headed Scotsman with a laugh as thick as his brogue. Of all the men who'd assembled on *Gorgon's* deck to meet her, the barrel-chested man with the quick smile and lively eyes had seemed the least likely to perish. 'I'm sorry.'

'So am I.' He staggered back to the side table and took up a heavy, square decanter, gripping it tightly in one hand as he raised it to his lips. The liquid inside sloshed as he struggled to hold it, then he lost his grip and the heavy crystal tumbled to the floor, its fall broken by the head of the lion skin lying prone beneath the chairs.

'Damn it.' Conrad stared at his fingers as though they'd betrayed him.

Katie rushed to him, laying a comforting hand on his arm, wanting to draw out his pain like a splinter and help ease both of their suffering. 'What happened, Conrad?'

The contrast between Katie's white hand on his dark, sea spray-stiffened coat was as startling as this second show of tenderness after so much reserve. It gave him hope, but not enough to make him speak. At one time he could have described to her the heart-wrenching moment he'd discovered his friend lying frozen in the snow and the agony of having to leave him where he lay. He could have described to her the pain and fears he'd experienced during the winter and the damage they'd wrecked on his confidence, body and soul. He could have told her of his concerns about his reputation once Mr Barrow received his report. The Katie from over a year ago would have listened and comforted, but not this one. 'You aren't the woman I left.'

She snatched back her hand. 'Did you really believe you could sail away and nothing and no one would change while you were gone? Did you think you could leave and come back to find everything the same?'

'I believed our love would be the same.'

'Love isn't enough. It wasn't enough for my parents. It isn't enough for us.' The surrender in her voice ripped through him like a gale wind.

He stepped closer, wanting to wrap her in his arms and soothe away the distress furrowing her brow, but he didn't. She was no frail society miss. He'd seen her break ground with a shovel in search of a fossil too many times to think her weak. But as he'd learned over the past year, those who thought they were the strongest were sometimes the most vulnerable. 'The Katie I knew before wouldn't have given up like that.'

'That Katie hadn't seen how ugly London and everyone could be and how willing you were to leave me to face it alone while you chased your precious dreams.'

His sympathy vanished. 'You know I wanted us to marry before I left. You were the one who insisted we wait.'

'Because I needed to see what it would be like to live in your world and I did, every day while you were gone.'

'That's not my world. It's my uncle's.'

'No, your world is in far-off lands,' she scoffed, her dismissal of his work and everything he was as stinging as her rejection.

'What did I do to you to engender such derision?' he hissed.

'You left.'

'You know I had no choice.'

'You could have resigned your commission. Instead, you chose to remain in the Discovery Service and put Mr Barrow's whims and wants above everyone else's. It's the rest of us who were left with no choice but to deal with it and all the consequences. Despite coming home, it won't be long before Mr Barrow snaps his fingers and you're gone again.'

'And what of you?' He levelled an accusing

finger at her. 'Are you ready to leave your work for me, to give up the fossils and chasing after the acceptance of all the scientific societies to place me first in your life?'

She recoiled, her answer in her silence.

'And you accuse me of being selfish.' He snatched another decanter from the table, using both hands to grip it. The silver tag hanging around the bottle's neck clanked against the crystal as Conrad raised it to his lips. By the time he lowered the thing, she was gone.

He dropped the decanter on the table with a thud, his failures hardening around him like ice on the masts of the ship. Katie wasn't the first person to doubt him enough to give up and walk out on him. How many more would desert him when news of his failures in the north became public? He ran the toe of his boot over the wet fur of the lionskin rug, matting and staining the tan pelt with the dirt from his sole. Perhaps Katie was right and he never should have left. The mud on his boots from one expedition was rarely dry before he was in Mr Barrow's office campaigning for another. He should have been more hesitant this time, more cautious, but he wasn't a man to sit idle in the country with nothing better to do than hunt and raise dogs.

He tilted his head to the mountain of trophies surrounding him, the silent catalogue of all his past successes and triumphs. None had come easily, not even the first commission which had cemented his reputation as a master explorer. It was an achievement he'd fought long and hard to secure, one he wouldn't surrender to his own doubts and fears.

He kicked the decanter, sending it spinning across the floor in a flurry of reflected moonlight and scattered drops. This was how weak and snivelling men dealt with their failures. It wasn't how Conrad would deal with his. He'd made mistakes, but there wasn't a captain alive who hadn't. Nothing had been decided in London or here at Heims Hall. Whatever criticisms Mr Barrow decided to heap on him for his mistakes, he'd meet them and overcome them, just as he had so many other obstacles. Whatever victories his uncle believed he'd won, Conrad would see to it they were short lived, and if Katie thought she could simply walk away from him, she was wrong. In the morning, she'd expect him to see her home, but he wasn't about to do her bidding. He hadn't fought storms and scurvy to reach her only to let his misgivings or hers defeat him now.

He took up the flint and some tinder from the holder beside the mantel, knelt down in front of the hearth and sparked a small flame. When the fire was going, he tossed in a handful of coal from the bucket, rising to watch the fire grow taller as it consumed the fuel.

He would only have a day or two before he had to return to London and face, good or bad, whatever Mr Barrow had in mind for him. He'd use the brief time with Katie to draw out the love he'd felt in her soothing touch. Despite her hasty departure, her reaching out to him revealed something of the woman he'd left all those months ago. Their love had been strained by his absence, but it wasn't gone. It was only hidden like grass beneath the snow waiting for the spring warmth to draw it out.

With any luck, the cart carrying the things he'd purchased in Greenland would arrive in the morning, before he ran out of excuses and delays to keep Katie here. On it, packed tight in sawdust and woodchips, was the one thing he knew would make her stay.

He was betting their future together on it.

Chapter Three

Katie marched across the kitchen garden to where Conrad stood by the cart, unloading crates, his jacket draped over the side. He'd avoided her all morning, leaving her to Miss Linton's scowl at breakfast before secluding himself in his study to speak with the estate and mine managers. The part of her which still cringed at the nasty accusations she'd levelled at him last night was glad he'd stayed away. She wasn't proud of what she'd said, but it was the truth and better he know it now than be led on by her silence into believing in something which no longer existed.

'You've avoided me long enough. I insist on going back with this cart once it's unloaded,' she demanded, startled when he straightened.

The strings of his shirt were undone and open, revealing the light chest hair underneath. The memory of his bare muscles beneath her palms, the soft sun caressing his shoulders as she held tight to him in the tall grass on the Downs nearly rattled her out of her purpose. They'd never gone far enough to completely compromise her, but they'd indulged in a few pleasures, the memory of which made the skin of her thighs tingle.

'You can't. It's going back to Portsmouth.' He slid the last crate off the wood and carefully laid it on top of the stack beside the wheel.

'Then call the chaise.'

'Matilda has use of it this morning.' Conrad leaned against the cart and propped his elbows on the rough wood to face Katie, not as the angry, drunken man from last night, but as the self-assured one who'd won her heart two years ago.

'Then saddle a horse. I'll ride home,' she insisted, eager to get away from him and his state of near undress.

'Come, Katie, you don't know how to ride.' He playfully tapped the end of her nose, his touch as unnerving as his jibe.

'I know what you're trying to do, Conrad, and it won't work.'

He picked up the crowbar lying beside the cart. 'What am I trying to do?'

'Keep me here.'

He slid the bar between the crate and its lid and pushed down. The nails broke free in a screech of metal against wood. 'You're right.'

'Why?'

'Because, I have something for you.' He shoved the lid aside and dug through the straw until he found what he was searching for and raised it up into the light.

Katie gaped at the sight of the elongated skull, dark from its long rest in the earth, and all desire to hurry home vanished. 'Where did you get this?'

'I purchased it from an Inuit in Greenland before we boarded the ship for home. I had a great deal of free time on the voyage and cleaned the bones, the way you taught me.'

Their eyes met and the memory of their time alone together in the evenings, sitting side by side at the table in the conservatory while she positioned his hand over the bones, passed between them. His cheek would rest against hers while she'd reach over his wide shoulder to guide the small metal pick between his fingers in the patient removal of dirt from bone. She didn't think he'd remembered the lessons, not with all the kisses and caresses which had distracted them.

She ran one fingertip over the smooth curve of her opal ring, regretting the loss of those days. They'd been some of the happiest of her life, but there was little time to ponder them or their passing as Conrad held out the skull to her. She took the heavy thing, her excitement heightened by the sweep of his fingers across hers.

'What do you think?' he asked.

She held it up to examine the row of long, dagger-like teeth lining the jaw, struggling as much to comprehend the animal as to avoid Conrad's piercing gaze. 'It's marvellous. Like nothing I've ever seen in any of the books or private collections. It's certainly not an *ichthyosaur.*'

'*Ichthyosaur?*'

'It's what the lizard with the flippers Miss Anning found is called now. Mr Konig named it in his paper to the Royal Society last year. They rejected mine.' She lowered the skull, bitterness marring her excitement.

'Then they were fools.' Conrad's solidarity was only a slight comfort. 'What will your father think when he sees it?'

'He won't see it.' Katie set the skull down on the flat bed of the cart with a thud, irritated by how little the man knew and how much she was left to explain. 'He's dead.'

Katie felt more than saw Conrad stiffen with shock. She was too focused on the skull and holding back the tears blurring her eyes. She didn't want him to see her pain, or to appear so weak and fragile around him. She wanted to be as resilient as she'd always been, but she was failing.

Without a word, he wrapped his arms around her and pulled her into his chest. He was hot from working and the heat penetrated the thin shirt to warm her tearstained cheeks. There'd been no one to hold her like this the day her father had died, or during all the lonely ones afterwards. 'What happened?'

She didn't want to answer, but she was too tired and worn down by carrying the pain alone to stay silent. 'A patient had come to see him and he'd turned her away. I was angry, we needed the money and I told him if he didn't earn some, I'd sell his fossils. He stormed out of the house, saying he'd find the one which would save us, something a private collector would pay a fortune to possess. A miner found him a few hours later at the bottom of a ladder, his neck broken.'

Katie squeezed her eyes shut, unable to block out the memory of her father's limp body as the miners had carried him into the house. The foreman had swept the dining table free of her father's fossils, making the bones clatter over the floor like pieces of broken china. Another man had crushed one beneath his work boot as he'd jostled with the other men to lay out her father's body. Then they'd filed out, uttering their apologies and leaving her with nothing but the tragedy, bills and bones. 'The only things he left me were his debts, and after what your uncle did to me there were few in England who'd purchase my finds. If it hadn't been for my American collectors, I wouldn't have had any buyers and I would have starved.'

'I'm so sorry, Katie.' His voice vibrated through

his chest, the way it had on the Downs when she'd cried against him as she'd revealed for the first time the anguish of her mother leaving. In between sobs, she'd described the loneliness of sitting in the window at Whitemans Green waiting for her to return, and the letter which had arrived three months later with news of her death. Then, just as now, Conrad had tenderly rocked her, making her feel safe and loved in a way neither her father, nor the mother who hadn't cherished her enough to stay, had ever done. 'You should have told me sooner.'

She pushed out of his embrace, her heart nearly shattering at the absence of his warmth, but she steeled herself against it and her weakness. Despite the comfort he offered, she didn't want to depend on anyone, especially someone who might disappear over the horizon as easily as her mother had. 'I didn't tell you for the same reason you didn't explain to me minute by minute the hardships and suffering you experienced while you were gone.'

'I'm not asking for the details, only the broad strokes.'

'And now you have them. So you may return to

London and Mr Barrow and publish your journals and enjoy everyone in the Admiralty and the Naturalist Society falling at your feet.'

'Careful, Katie, your anger near drips with jealousy.'

Katie stared down at the mess of bones in the crate, shamed out of her resentment. He was only trying to be kind. 'You're right, I am. No matter what I write or draw, my success will never match yours simply because of my sex. Only my connection to you and my father's work has ever made anyone take note of me before.' Even then they'd pinned her success on her feminine wiles, not her talent, listening to the vicious lies of Lord Helton and all those willing to repeat them.

'Then this could be your chance to change that. If this animal is as unusual as you believe, then stay with me and study it, draw it and write a paper the Naturalist Society won't be able to ignore.'

'Last night you said you wanted me to give it all up,' she challenged, confused by his change of heart and the wavering of hers.

His enthusiasm dimmed as he picked at a splinter on the edge of the cart. 'I think we both said a number of things last night we regret.'

Yes, she regretted saying a great deal, despite most of it being true.

'Even if I did stay and study it, I doubt anything I do, even on something as unusual as this, could sway the Naturalist Society members to support me. The last night we were at the society, they tore my father's reputation to shreds, accusing him of plagiarism. It was the reason we finally left London.'

He flicked away the splinter. 'Why would they do such a thing?'

'Because of your uncle.' She stomped her foot against the soft soil. 'He wasn't content to ruin me, but my father, too.'

Conrad banged his fist against the cart. 'Then now's your chance to ensure he doesn't win.'

'You make it sound so easy, but it isn't.' She ran her hand over the curve of the creature's skull, thinking through each of the books she'd read in the Naturalist Society library and how no animal in any of them resembled this one. 'You don't know what it was like to stand there and watch them tear him, and me, apart, to have everyone whispering about you.'

'No, but I know what it's like to fight awful odds, to keep going even when you, and all those around you, want to give up.' He shifted closer, his face set with determination. 'If you think I'm going to let you surrender to my uncle, to crawl away and hide from all the difficulties, you're very mistaken.'

'It's not your decision to make.' For the past six months she'd hidden from the world, facing no one except through letters and doing all she could to avoid criticism and judgement. She didn't want to enter it again and confront the hostile men who'd dismissed her research simply because she was a woman.

'It's my creature, and if you don't think you're up to the task of studying it, I'll hire another,' Conrad threatened.

'You can't.' Panic burned through her at possibly losing such a specimen and how much like her father she felt at this moment. She'd cursed him so many times for being too involved with his research to see her, her mother, his shrinking medical practice and the mounting bills. Even after her mother had left, the fossils and his research had determined nearly every decision he'd ever made. Katie was about to allow them to do the same for her.

'Don't be afraid to show the men of the society what you're capable of,' Conrad urged. 'This creature could be the making of you.'

He was right. With this animal, she could prove it was her brains and not her favours which had gained her past notice. If she succeeded, it would mean work as an illustrator, money from publishing books and pamphlets, and the security she'd craved since the day she'd taken over the finances in her mother's absence and seen the harsh truth of her and her father's situation.

Katie fingered one of the creature's sharp teeth. Staying was risky. Conrad was tenacious in his determination to achieve whatever it was he set his mind to and now it was focused on her. However, she had only to hold out until Mr Barrow's next order came through and pulled his focus, and presence, away from her. As much as she didn't want to be here with him, leaving Conrad meant leaving the bones and she couldn't do it.

'All right, I'll stay and examine the creature.' A smile of victory spread over Conrad's lips, as annoying as it was tempting, but she wasn't about to let him believe he'd won. She was staying for her benefit, not his. 'But it will be like it was when my father worked for you. You'll pay me just as you paid him.'

Conrad scooped up the skull and laid it back in the crate. 'I won't.'

'Then I won't stay.' She crossed her arms over her chest, as much to emphasise her seriousness as to calm her fears over losing access to the creature. 'This is to be a business deal like any other and when it's done that'll be the end of it.' *And us.*

'All right,' he conceded, picking up the lid to the crate and setting it down over the top, covering the bones. 'Draw up a list of things you need from Whitemans Green and I'll send someone to fetch them and close up your house. When you're finished with your research you may keep the fossil, and the paper, and your drawings.'

'If I'm to keep everything, what do you hope to get out of this arrangement?'

'You.' He brushed her lightly under the chin,

the same self-satisfied smile he'd worn the first time he'd stolen a kiss from her in the study drawing up the corners of his wide mouth. 'I'll have Mr Peet bring the crate to the conservatory. I expect your work to be very interesting and revealing.'

Before she could tell him what to do with his expectations he slipped into the stable, his muffled instructions to Mr Peet carrying over the shift and whinny of the horses.

Katie slammed the top of the crate with her palm, dislodging the lid. It fell into the dirt, revealing the creature's menacing smile. Her weakness and Conrad's glib determination frustrated her. She shouldn't remain here and torture herself with what couldn't be or give Conrad false hope for reconciliation, but she couldn't give up this specimen either.

Motion near the house caught her attention and she looked up to meet Miss Linton's pinched scowl. Worry slid through Katie like it had the day she'd narrowly missed being hit by a rock falling from the side of a slate mine. She and Conrad had always been careful when Katie had been here before, only intimate with one another late at night or far from the house. She wondered how much Miss Linton had seen of her and Conrad's embrace. It'd been innocent enough, but Miss Linton wasn't likely to view it in such a way and it wouldn't be long before the spinster was adding yet another nasty rumour to those already circulating. Once again Katie would be judged for something she didn't do instead of on the merit of her work.

Katie picked up the crate lid and set it back over the animal. Tracing the words burned into the wood, she wondered if there was something more for her in life than fossils and research. Her father had never given her the chance to discover it and necessity had forced her to keep on with his work.

Katie made for the house, determined not to endure the spinster's disapproving scowl or entertain her own doubts a moment longer. This was her calling, as much as it'd been her father's, and she would use it to make her way and prove everyone like Miss Linton wrong. They might scoff at her in England, but in America there were many she corresponded with, their eagerness to acquire the specimens she unearthed matched by their enthusiasm to exchange ideas, illustrations and knowledge with her. They cared nothing for her gender or the rumours circulating in London and their admiration was such that Mr Lesueur had invited her to join him as an illustrator on his next expedition West. She hadn't turned down his generous offer, but she hadn't accepted it either. There'd been a time when she wouldn't have dreamed of leaving England; now it was more tempting than ever. With the money from Conrad, she could afford passage, if she wanted it.

She paused outside the conservatory door, uncertain if she should leave, or if there was anything left in England to keep her here. She'd soon find out. Where Lord Helton and his vicious stories had lowered her, the bones could raise her up. If this animal was as rare as she believed, any paper she published about it would be the making of her. It had to be, she possessed little else to believe in.

Chapter Four

The late-afternoon sun fell through the high glass walls of the conservatory, warming it and making candles unnecessary. Katie had been hard at work piecing the creature together since yesterday, staying up late into the night, then rising early that morning to continue. Conrad had left her in solitude, but she'd caught his influence in the meals delivered to her and the supply of paper and pencils laid out by the footman. She'd tried not to allow all these small gestures to affect her, but it was difficult when tasting the cold chicken and warm bread not to think of him. She'd missed these little kindnesses when he'd sailed away, and would again when her work was complete and they parted once more.

Katie reached out and adjusted the creature's

vertebrae so she could better see the details as she drew it, determined to remain focused on her work and not think about Conrad. The dark bones stood in sharp contrast to the white-marble table top and the creamy parchment on which she struggled to render the creature as beautiful and elegant as it was in life. She'd arranged the bones more from instinct than from the memory of any species she'd seen in the books of the Naturalist Society library. She'd visited the impressive collection many times with her father, the two of them spending hours perusing the massive works of geology and biology. The Naturalist Society stood alone in its admittance of women to its hallowed halls and collections, both of which were the envy of even the Royal Society. Sadly, she would need access to the tomes again, especially once she began writing her paper. Conrad could sponsor her, and he would if she requested it, but she was reluctant to ask.

Katie picked up a knife and sharpened her pencil. The idea of facing the members who'd attacked her and her father was as disturbing as the steady sound of Conrad's boots crushing the leaves in the yard as he approached. She didn't want to rely on him any more than necessary, or return to London.

She set the knife down and returned to her sketch, filling in the dark areas around the creature's eyes when a new sensation swept over her. It wasn't the stiffness in her back and neck, but a charged awareness as Conrad's shadow filled the door.

'You've made good progress,' he remarked as he came to stand at the opposite end of the table, his tone as open and welcoming as when he used to interrupt her and her father's work.

She gripped the sides of the sketchbook to steady herself against his presence and the hundreds of memories it brought back. He no longer wore his uniform, but tan breeches tucked into high boots and paired with a crisp white shirt beneath a worn riding coat. The sweat from his day riding to oversee his lands wetted his forehead beneath his light hair, making a few small strands stick to his skin. It was the way he used to look whenever she and her father had been here before and for a moment, she could almost feel his strong hand in hers as he led her over the Downs.

Sadly, those times were gone.

'It wasn't difficult,' she croaked before regaining control of herself and her voice. 'The skeleton is much like a bird's, but at the same time different. The pits along the nose remind me of those on a crocodile's snout.'

'A reptile couldn't survive in the cold of the north. Little does.'

'That's why I don't think it's a reptile.' She picked up a flat, arch-like bone, struggling to keep the spicy scent of man, leather and sandalwood gracing Conrad's skin from befuddling her as she handed it to him. 'Look at this furcula. It's curved like a peregrine falcon's, but not as tight.'

'You think this is some kind of bird?' He set the bone back down where she'd arranged it between the ribs.

'It's possible.'

'Birds don't have teeth,' he politely challenged, tapping the table top with his fingertips as he made his way to her side, creeping up on her like the tabby cat behind the house did when stalking a mouse.

'They don't have forearms instead of wings either.' Her mouth went dry as she slid around to the opposite side, moving slowly so as not to appear as if she was running away, though she wanted to, swift and fast out of the door and away from the draw of his presence. 'But look at the feet and the position of the legs in the hips.'

Mercifully, his focus dropped to the creature. 'They certainly appear bird-like. Perhaps it's a species which no longer exists.'

'I could make a strong case for such an argument if I could compare this beast to one of the larger species of birds.'

'Such as an ostrich?'

'Exactly.' Katie met his eyes and her heart skipped a beat. He wasn't laughing at her, but encouraging her, like he always used to. It was the first time since he'd sailed away that she'd enjoyed such support. She'd nearly forgotten what it was like.

'Come with me.' He reached across the table and took her hand, drawing her around it to the door leading to the hallway.

She barely had time to set the sketchbook and pencil down as he led her into the narrow, wood-panelled passage, his grip as startling as his speed. 'Where are we going?'

'I've thought of something else which might help you.' He pulled her along the shadowed hallway towards his study.

She hurried to keep up with his long strides, holding tight to his hand, giddy and terrified at the same time. This was how it'd been before, when they would come home from searching for fossils, then seclude themselves in his study to pour over books and identify what they'd discovered.

Inside the study, he released her hand and made for a bookshelf. 'There's a bird in Australia, similar in shape and size to the ostrich. I made a sketch of it when I was there.'

Conrad knelt down before the bottom shelf and plucked out a book. His back arched gracefully beneath his coat as he bent over one of his old journals, the back of his neck just visible above his collar beneath his neatly trimmed hair. He rose and handed her the open journal, revealing a poorly drawn bird similar to an ostrich. 'If you can find a better illustration of this animal and its bones, and include it in your paper, it could bolster your case for the creature being some type of bird.'

He moved to stand behind her and look over her shoulder at the drawing. The heat of his cheek was so close to hers it nearly made her drop the book. It was too much like the last time they'd been in here two years ago, when he'd showed her the maps of the Arctic and the route he intended to take. The map she'd drawn from his description was still tucked in her old sketchbook, the timeline faithfully followed by her while he was gone, then worried and fretted over when he hadn't returned, until so much time had passed, she couldn't bear to look at it any more.

Yet he was here, close and as enthusiastic as ever about one of her ideas. The faint spark of hope she'd experienced when he'd climbed the hill yesterday rose up again, sending a more powerful thrill through her than any unknown creature could ever create. 'What if an animal like the one you purchased still exists and lives secluded in the north?'

'I don't believe they do.' He waved her over

to the globe near the wall. He spun it around to show North America.

'I've been this far and two others have been here.' He laid his finger near the top. 'There's nothing there but ice. Captain Ross saw evidence of caribou, but only up until this point. None of the Inuit I've spoken with have ever mentioned an animal like the one in the conservatory.'

'I'll need more proof than hearsay.'

Conrad stared at the globe as though it were a nautical chart on which he was plotting his course. In the look, she glimpsed something of the optimistic man who'd escorted her over *Gorgon's* deck, describing in detail his plans for the coming adventure, not the despairing and acerbic man who'd faced her in here the other night.

'Etienne Brule explored Canada for years. If something like the creature still roamed the north, he, or the natives he lived with, would have noted it. The Naturalist Society library contains an impressive collection of his works. If we left for London in the morning, we could be there by the afternoon.'

Her eagerness to prove the creature didn't still live, and was in some way related to birds, paled under the reality of stepping back through the Naturalist Society's grand front entrance. 'I'm not sure I'm ready to return so soon.'

'Yes, you are.' He wrapped his solid fingers around hers. 'I know it.'

She squeezed his hand and a faint whisper of the elation she'd once experienced with him on the Downs passed between them. All she needed to do was follow him, just like before, and she wanted to. It was a prospect as alarming as descending into a very deep mine to dig for fossils, but strangely enough, with him, she wasn't afraid of the danger. 'Yes, we'll leave in the morning.'

'Good girl.' He slid one arm around her waist, resting it on the small of her back as he drew her closer. She slipped the journal out from between them, allowing it to dangle from her hand as she relaxed against him, tilting her face up to his. The desire burning in his brown eyes proved as mesmerising now as the first time they'd kissed. She wanted to believe in him and their love and everything he promised, just as she had during all the lonely nights when she'd cried herself to sleep with grief. Only he wasn't dead, he was here, alive, warm and so achingly close.

He leaned in closer until the faint ring of gold in the centre of his eyes became clear. The journal dropped to the floor with a thud at Katie's feet as all resistance to him faded with the subtle pressure of his fingers against her back. She laid her hand on his shoulder, forgetting everything except the shift of his hips against hers and the flex of his muscles beneath her palm.

A soft knock on the wall near the door echoed through the room. Both of them turned to see Mr Turner, the mine foreman, standing there, hat in his hand, his eyes focused on the floor as though it were embedded with gold coins.

Conrad let go of Katie and she stepped back, her heart racing as much from the near kiss as being discovered by someone in such a compromising position.

'Yes, Mr Turner?' Conrad asked, no hint of embarrassment colouring his words.

Of course he didn't need to worry, he was a man. Little could touch him while the slightest whisper might further damage her already tarnished reputation, and no amount of support from Conrad or the scientific community could salvage it. Katie picked up the journal, her confidence and faith in Conrad wavering. It'd been wrong to be intimate in a place where anyone could stumble upon them. Mr Turner might be a simple foreman, but Katie knew how little time it took for stories from the common man to find their way into the drawing rooms of polite society.

'Captain Essington, we found something in the mine,' the thick-necked foreman explained. 'Miss Linton wasn't interested in seeing such things while you were away. Now you've returned, I must know if we should dig it out and bring it to you or leave it where it is.'

Katie clutched the journal to her chest, trilling her fingers as though the foreman had brought the artefact for her to feel. After her father's death, the Whitemans Green foreman had barred her from the pit, afraid she might meet with an accident, too. It'd left her with only the Downs to scour for fossils, but, while she'd collected some interesting pieces, none could match those entombed in the slate.

Conrad cocked a smile at her as a thrill crackled between them. 'Shall we go and see it?'

'We shall.'

Conrad guided the gig over the bumpy road leading from Heims Hall to the mine. He slid a sideways glance at Katie who sat beside him in the high seat. The deep green of her sturdy walking dress highlighted the apples of her cheeks, which glowed pink with the cool air. Her aqua eyes shone bright with the same excitement which had graced her beautiful face before they'd been interrupted in his study.

He flicked the reins over the horse's back, making the beast increase its pace. It heartened him to think he could draw from her as much emotion as the bones, though he envied the old creatures for the current smile decorating her full lips. It was only the second time he'd enjoyed the simple pleasure of seeing her happy since coming home.

They came around a sharp bend in the road and the gig tilted to one side as they made the turn. Katie leaned hard against Conrad's arm to keep from tumbling out until the vehicle rocked back upright.

'The bone has been buried for ages, we needn't risk our lives rushing to see it,' Katie chided with a half-laugh.

The wheel struck a small rut and her hand shot out to grasp his thigh.

'I wouldn't call it a risk.' He flung her a teasing smile. She pulled her hand away and grasped the edge of the leather seat. 'And if we don't hurry, we'll lose the daylight.'

The October sun was already low along the horizon, stretching out the shadows of trees to cover the road and fields. In the steady pulse of the horse's hooves and the sharp scent of dry earth and grass, Conrad felt something of his old self, the one who still believed he could and would accomplish anything he set his mind to. It was as big a comfort as Katie's unconscious decision to grasp him for support and their near kiss. It meant everything he'd been through hadn't buried the best parts of him. It offered a glimmer of hope for his future and Katie's.

Her willingness to come to London with him was another. He couldn't dally here in the country much longer and hope to keep Mr Barrow's support, assuming he still possessed it. If Mr Barrow set his mind on Conrad's ruin, as he had with Captain Ross, then all Conrad's influence with the Naturalist Society would vanish and with it Katie's hopes. Conrad shifted his feet on the boards, tugging one rein to guide the horse down the right path. His decisions had broken and maimed enough men already, he hated to think they might do more damage to Katie.

The horse began to slow and Conrad snapped the reins, urging the animal on faster, feeling like a fraud for entertaining his fears while he insisted Katie fight hers. Nothing with Mr Barrow had happened yet and he refused to let his worries undermine him or her. Whatever waited for him in London, he would face it as he did all his challenges and with Katie by his side.

They crested the hill and the narrow buildings of the mine came into view. Conrad tugged on the reins and slowed the horse as it trotted over the long drive leading to the open hole in the earth. The men were leaving for the day, making their way down the short hill towards the now-quiet chimneys where the cartfuls of slate were crushed and burned to create the lime needed for construction in London.

Mr Turner and a few of his men waited beside a tall ladder leading down into the pit. They removed their hats as Conrad pulled the gig to a stop in front of them. He jumped out, but before he could help Katie down, she was already on her feet and coming to join him in front of the men. One miner raised a curious eyebrow at this blatant display of female independence, but he was deferential enough to Conrad's position as lord of the manor and his employer to remain silent.

'Where is it?' Conrad asked the foreman.

'Just down there.' He pointed to another ladder perched along the mine wall, not too far from the main ladder. 'The ramp for the mules is on the other side. We can go down that way.'

Across the wide pit the ramp sloped into the grey earth. It wasn't far as the crow flies, but reaching it meant walking the wide circumference of the mine.

'We're already losing the light and walking will take time. The ladder will do just as well as the ramp,' Katie insisted, making for the wood.

The man looked to Conrad, waiting to see if there would be a disagreement but Conrad merely shrugged, then moved to step between her and the ladder.

'Let me go first.' Before she could protest, he gripped the top pole and swung himself around to catch the rung, sliding more than climbing to the bottom. He hopped off, looking up past the layers of jagged rocks to usher Katie to follow.

While Mr Turner held the top, Conrad stayed beneath Katie as she descended, ready to catch her should she fall. She managed the ladder with the agility of an experienced rigging monkey, except no man on his crew moved with such tempting grace. Her hips shifted from side to side as she took each rung and her cotton dress swung in time to her steps. As the fabric swayed, it revealed a teasing length of black stocking and a shock of white thigh just above it.

Conrad admired the hint of flesh and the memories it conjured of another evening like this one, a week before he'd left for the Arctic, when the two of them had come here after dark, lanterns in hand, to search through the rocks. He flexed his fingers, remembering the curve of her calf beneath his palm as he'd reached up to slide his hand beneath her skirts and caress the derrière hidden beneath her dress. She'd stopped in her descent and he'd waited for her to kick him away. Instead, she'd met his bold gesture with an inviting smile, dropping down from the ladder into his arms with a kiss as searing as her flesh against his.

The length of him burned with the memory of her pressed beneath him against the wall of the mine as he'd caressed her exposed thigh resting against his hips. They'd teased each other to near desperation, eager in their desire to cling to one another and forget his coming departure. He'd been careful with her, tender but restrained, satisfying her as he denied himself, not wanting to leave her with child when the dangers of his mission lingered so close. Though he'd been cavalier back then about dying, he'd known the risks, but with her breath heavy in his ear, her body trembling against his, he'd believed there'd be many more nights to indulge in the full pleasure of her when he returned.

Conrad stepped back, attempting to shield himself from the tempting hint of her legs and the heat it sent ripping through him as she manoeuvred the last few rungs. She wouldn't greet his touch with such enthusiasm today, no matter how much he needed the comfort of her embrace.

Humiliation as much as desire burned through him. He shouldn't need or want her, especially if she didn't want him, but it wasn't simply lust driving his pursuit, but the craving for peace. The night before last, when she'd clasped his hand on the back of the horse, it had stilled the trembles which had plagued him since his rescue. In the study today, with her breasts pressed against his chest, all the glories of his past exploits and all the hurtful words of that night had faded away. There'd only been her and the glimmer of love which had carried him through so many dark, Arctic nights.

Katie hopped off the last rung with a wide, exhilarated smile Conrad could feel in his core. The brisk breeze caught a strand of her hair and whipped it across her face. Conrad reached out and tucked it behind the curve of her small ear, though he wanted to wrap the gold curl around his finger, bury his face in the softness of it and make them both forget the past and the present.

Katie's dark lashes fluttered as she watched him draw his hand away. She bit her bottom lip, the anticipation in her expression urging Conrad forward, but he held back. He didn't want to push her too far and break the fragile bond they were slowly repairing.

'Hurry, I want to see the fossil before it gets too dark.' Katie quickly moved off over the loose piles of slate and around the large outcroppings of rock dotting the mine floor.

Conrad followed, stopping to join her at the base of the second ladder. Katie peered up at the length of dark bone so distinct against the grey slate and the metal stake driven in next to it to mark its place. A nearby overhang increased the shadows in this portion of the quarry, shading the mine wall and the bone.

'What do you think it is?' he asked. It was difficult from where they were standing to tell.

'I don't believe it's an *ichthyosaur*. It looks too long and thick. I must get a closer look.'

'I'll have the men dig it out for you tomorrow,' Mr Turner offered as he came to stand with them.

'No, we make for London tomorrow. I must see it tonight,' Katie insisted.

'Then I'll fetch a lamp.' Mr Turner hurried off to secure the light.

Katie crept closer to the ladder, tilting her head back and forth to try to get a better look at the bone. The curls at the back of her neck caressed her shoulders before one of them caught in the small lace of her neckline. Conrad reached up to free it and Katie jerked around to face him, then took one small step away.

'Dr Mantell found a large bone he thinks is the leg of some unknown creature,' Katie explained. 'Mr Cuvier says it's a kind of hippopotamus from before the deluge, but Dr Mantell isn't convinced. He and I discussed the matter. He's afraid to publish his paper on it for fear the societies will laugh and reject him. It's difficult to be taken seriously if one doesn't come from a titled or wealthy family.'

Katie toed a small piece of slate with her boot.

'Then all the more reason to align yourself with a man who possesses both.' It wasn't a subtle reminder of his standing and small wealth, but a powerful one. Though he'd always cherished Katie's eagerness to love him despite his money and family connections, he wasn't above using both to try and persuade her to be with him now.

Katie peered around Conrad with a frown, obviously not as enamoured with his argument. 'What's taking Mr Tucker so long?'

The sun was falling fast and the shadows deepening by the minute.

'He'll be back soon.'

'I can't wait any longer.' She marched to the ladder, sliding a little on a piece of lose slate before she regained her balance.

Conrad hurried up behind her. 'What are you doing?'

'If I managed the ladder into the mine, surly I can manage this one. Steady it for me.'

Before he could take hold of it, Katie began to climb.

Conrad grabbed the poles tight and the higher Katie climbed, the more the wood wobbled under her weight. As she ascended, the top of the poles nestled against the walls rattled, breaking off shards of slate. Conrad turned his head as the pebbles she'd knocked loose pelted his shoulders and scattered over the mine floor. By the time he looked back up, Katie was at the top, hands on the last rung as she strained to see the bone.

'Don't go any higher,' Conrad warned as she stretched up to try and touch the fossil.

'I can almost reach it.'

Holding on to the side of the mine for balance, she stepped up on to the second-to-the-last rung. She gripped the spike to steady herself and with her other hand, picked at the soft slate entombing the fossil, trying to free more of the bone. 'It looks like a femur, but bigger than any I've ever seen before.'

'Come down, we'll examine it further in the morning, before we leave,' Conrad insisted, struggling to keep the shaking ladder steady, willing his fingers not to go weak when he needed them to stay strong, but his grip was already beginning to tire.

'No, I can almost reach it.' She rose up a little higher to trace the top of the fossil and the slate beneath the ladder shifted, jerking the wood to the left. Katie's half-boots slipped and her body dropped, stopped only by her hold on the spike.

She let out a scream as a hail of rocks and dirt rained down on Conrad.

He fought to clear his stinging eyes of debris as he positioned himself beneath her. She hung ten feet above the mine floor, her feet flailing in an effort to regain her footing on the ladder.

'It's right below you,' Conrad yelled.

'I can't find it.'

Her grip on the spike gave out and in a flurry of skirts and screams she dropped towards the ground.

Conrad rushed forward, catching her in his arms. The weight of her knocked him backwards. As they fell, he clasped her to him, determined to protect her from the sharp rocks jabbing his ribs, back and sides as he thudded against the hard ground. His shoulders screamed from the exertion, but he didn't let go, clutching her to him until they rocked to a halt against the hard floor.

She trembled in his arms, curled in a tight ball, her head tucked beneath his chin, her eyes screwed shut.

From somewhere behind Conrad came the grinding of boots over rock as Mr Turner and his men hurried to reach them.

'Katie, are you all right?' Conrad whispered, easing his hold on her enough to smooth her hair off her forehead. She didn't look up, but pressed closer into the arch of his body, her hands clasped together in front of her chest. 'Katie, look at me. Are you all right?'

He stroked her cheek with the back of his finger until her eyes fluttered open.

'Yes.' She opened her trembling hand to reveal a bright red mark across her palm from where she'd gripped the spike. 'I'm fine.'

'Sir, we'll help you up.' Mr Turner and his men reached out to take Conrad's arms, but he shook them off. Despite his hips and shoulders protesting with pain, he hauled himself to his feet with Katie still cradled in his arms. As he carried her to the ramp at the far end of the mine, the memory of slogging through an ice field, every muscle aching as it did now from his exertion, near strangled him. His hands began to lose their grip and he forced them to keep a tight hold on her as he pushed through the ache in his arms and back. He carried her to the gig, ignoring the men who stood along the mine ridge watching as he put her down on the bench. When she was settled, he joined her, his hands protesting as he took up the reins and snapped the horse into motion.

With each turn of the gig's wheels, Conrad's relief at Katie having survived slowly gave way to anger. His gut tightened with the memory of her dropping through the air with nothing beneath her but cutting stone, Conrad and luck. If he hadn't been there, if he'd left for London and Mr Turner had taken her to see the bone, who knew what might have happened. If she was this careless in his presence, he could well imagine the risks she took when he wasn't around.

He shifted the reins in his hand and a sharp pain shot through his shoulder. He wanted to yell at her as he used to his sailors when they'd failed to dry out their socks and put themselves in danger of frostbite. He bit back his rebuke, keenly aware of her beside him, shoulders hunched, hair falling forward to cover her face as she rubbed her sore hand. If he yelled at her it would do nothing but make her retreat from him. Instead, he stared straight ahead, guiding the horse with less enthusiasm than he'd employed when driving them to the mine.

When Heims Hall at last came into view, he experienced a small measure of the relief which had marked his homecoming last night. When everything around him was changing, Heims Hall remained the same and the desire to hole up inside its walls proved almost as tempting as the call of exploration. The urge disgusted him as much as Katie's carelessness. He wasn't a man to hide from the world or to allow those around him to needlessly risk their lives. He hadn't allowed his men to do it in the Arctic and he wouldn't allow Katie to do it here.

Katie winced when Conrad closed the study door behind him with such methodical care; he could have slammed it for all it did to conceal his fury. He marched to the table with the liquor, seized the decanter still shiny with spirit and splashed some into a glass.

'What were you thinking, climbing to the top?' Conrad pushed the glass in her still sore hand, making the liquid slide up the side and nearly tumble over to stain her dress. 'You almost got yourself killed.'

'Don't chastise me as though I was your wife.' She gripped the glass and took a hearty drink, coughing as the alcohol burned down her throat. The warmth of it began to still the shaking which had gripped her since the fall, though not even the bright fire in the grate could drive back the chill completely.

'If I can't speak to you as your affianced, then let me speak as someone who cares for you.' His voice softened like the wind after a storm. 'What you did tonight was foolish, reckless and unnecessary.'

'I know.' The truth in his words stung nearly as much as her aching palm from where she'd clutched the spike. She stared past him to the tiger. She'd always said she didn't want to be like either of her parents, yet tonight she'd come perilously close to dying like her father.

'Then why did you do it?'

She snatched up the decanter and splashed more liquid into the glass. She raised it to her lips and tossed back the entire measure. Her eyes watered as the drink singed her tongue, dulling the ache in her palm, but not her heart. 'Why do you keep leaving for expeditions when you know you might die?'

Conrad straightened the silver label on the decanter. 'It's different for me.'

She slammed the empty glass down on the table. 'Why, because you're a man? You think you can disappear and leave behind everyone else to deal with all the problems of life while you're gone? I don't accept that.'

'I don't expect you to.'

'Of course you do. Just like my father did, just like my mother did when she walked away.' She stormed across the room to the wide leather bench and dropped down on one end. 'No one ever thinks of me before they go, not my father, my mother or you. I've never mattered to anyone.'

She pressed the heel of her hand against her forehead, struggling to stifle the sob choking her. She had nothing, was nothing, just as she'd always been. There was no reason to stay here, or in England. At least in America there was someone who wanted her, if only for what she could render with her pen.

At the sound of Conrad's muffled bootsteps she braced herself, expecting another rebuke or more arguments against her opinion. She was stunned when he knelt on one knee before her and withdrew her hand from her forehead, smoothing open her tight fingers to reveal the red mark marring her palm. He ran his thumb across it, heightening the heat already flowing through her from the strong drink.

'Do you know why I'm here and not in London?'

Katie shook her head, not understanding what difference it made.

'Because the only thing I could think about the moment the ship docked was seeing you and holding you in my arms. Nothing else mattered, not Mr Barrow, the Admiralty, nothing, only you.'

He raised her hand to his mouth and she could barely breathe as he pressed his warm lips to the exposed flesh.

She tried to tug her hand away, but he held it firm. Even with Conrad studying her as though she was his entire world, she couldn't believe him. No one ever put her first. 'But you left.'

'Every time I thought I might die in the north, every time I wanted to give up and let the cold overwhelm me, I thought of you.' He laid his hand along the side of her face, his voice like velvet across her bare cheeks. 'You were my reason for continuing on, for not giving up, for making sure I came home.'

The loneliness she'd suffered for the past year and a half began to pale under this revelation. For the first time ever someone was putting her above anything else. It wasn't possible.

'I fought so hard to reach you.' He rose up on his knees and slid one arm around her waist, drawing her firmly against him. The strength of his embrace sent a thrill racing through her like a spark along a dry length of hay. She pressed her palm against his chest, trying to create some distance between them, but his heart beating under her hand almost soothed her into surrender. 'Don't pull away from me now.'

Her arm went weak as a passion illuminated his rich brown eyes, a passion far greater than that she'd seen in them when he'd told her he'd find the Northwest Passage. She curled her fingers around his lapel as all desire to run from him, from England—everything began to fade. The happiness she'd known with him hadn't ended the day he'd sailed away. Instead, it had died slowly over weeks, and months, as every day made it more unlikely she'd ever see him again. Yet here he was alive, his eyes silently pleading for her to cross the distance between them. She couldn't deny him, or herself. 'I won't.'

She wrapped her hands around his neck, the need for solace driving her deeper into his arms. A warning like the one the miners sent up whenever a hill was about to collapse sounded from somewhere in the back of her mind, but she ignored it. His grip was too solid, the press of his lips too tender, but strong enough to ease the pain and loneliness which had burdened her for years.

He crushed her to him, his mouth meeting hers with the demanding fervour of a man too long denied. Katie surrendered to the want in his kiss, arching against his body, giving herself up to the heady pleasure swirling between them. She parted her lips to accept his seeking tongue, returning each silken caress with one of her own. She wasn't sure she could ever love anyone, even Conrad, again but his sincerity captured her as strongly now as it had the first time they'd kissed in this room.

Reaching between them, she undid the buttons of his coat, eager to be closer to him, to lose herself in his strength and heat. First one came free, then another, until at last the heavy wool gaped open to reveal the shirt beneath. Running her hands along the length of his stomach and up over his chest, she pushed the jacket from his shoulders and down on to the floor. His shirt was crisp and white beneath his waistcoat, the sleeves billowing out along his arms, the material unable to hide the taut muscles beneath.

He broke from her to lay a trail of feather kisses along the length of her neck, tracing the long arch of it to the hollow as he pressed her back into the leather, shifting his body to cover hers. She took hold of the buttons of his waistcoat and slid them slowly through the holes. He rose up on straight arms to watch her work, his breath teasing her nose. When she reached the last button he shook out of the garment, allowing it to fall to the floor before settling back down over her. With the outer garments gone, he embraced her, not as the consumed explorer, but as the man she'd first fallen in love with, the one who'd confidently overcome all her reservations to secure her acceptance of his proposal.

He slid his arms beneath her and she felt the gentle tug and pull as he undid one button after another along the back of her dress. She didn't object. For one wonderful night she wanted his touch to soothe away all her uncertainties and to feel as carefree and easy as she had during the days when they'd walked across the Downs together, the past, the future, none of it touching them. Only the present had mattered, just as it did tonight.

Sitting up on his knees, he tugged the gown down over her body and she arched her hips to allow it to slide free. She wasn't ashamed to face him in her stays and chemise, but was as eager as him to trace the flesh which made up their beings.

He took her hands and drew her up on to her knees to face him. She pulled off his shirt and cast it aside, then ran her hands over his hard chest and the taut stomach beneath. Catching her wrists, he slid them around his waist, then leaned forward to kiss first the top of one breast and then the other. She sighed, clutching his waist and revelling in the gentle pressure of his lips on her bare skin. Over the crackle of the fire, she caught the subtle swish of her stay laces sliding through the holes before the fitted garment gaped free and the chemise billowed out around her body.

He moved out of her embrace and stood beside the bench to undo the buttons on his breeches and push them down over his hips. The power of his desire for her was evident when he straightened, but there was little time to admire it as he took her chemise by the sides and pulled it over her head. He dropped it to the floor and they faced each other, the firelight dancing over their bare bodies. It wasn't the first time they'd been naked together, but they'd held back before. Tonight, Katie wanted to rush forward and lose herself in the male power of him.

He knelt down between her legs on the *chaise*, then laced his fingers in hers and with a gentle tug, pulled her forward. She didn't resist, but straddled his thighs. Trembles ravaged her as he slid further beneath her and the heat of his manhood pressed against her, eager for entrance. He'd been vulnerable with the admission of his need to reach her, now she wanted to lay herself bare to him, to allow his body to fill the loneliness in hers and warm her against the cold memories crowding her past.

Then he backed away.

'Conrad?'

He brushed her face with his hand. 'I want to, you don't know how much, but I can't. I can't risk you or a child any more now than I could before.'

Her body ached with disappointment, but she understood. Her mother had fallen pregnant with her in a moment of weakness with her father. She couldn't do the same thing and was grateful to Conrad for bringing her back from the brink and placing his concern for her above the demands of his flesh. 'You're right.'

She reached for him, drawing him down to her. His powerful body covered hers, pressing her into the supple leather as his hand slid along the curve of her waist. She gasped as he found her centre and his fingers began to tease her need. While he caressed her, he lowered himself to take one nipple into his mouth, swirling it with his tongue in time with his maddening touch, nearly distracting her from grasping his manhood.

He groaned as she tightened her hand around him, his fingers maintaining their steady pace as she struggled to hold hers. She'd been a fool for not marrying him before he'd left and sacrificing the delights of the marriage bed to her fears and worries. Under the steady rhythm of his caress, the past faded until only his skin against hers remained. He was here now, his mouth hard against hers, their breath and heartbeats nearly one until she cried out her release as she brought him to his.

Wrapping his arms around her, he settled them both down against the leather. The air of the study nipped at the perspiration covering their skin. Katie laid one leg over Conrad's, settling into the crook of his arm as she used to whenever they'd dallied in the high grass. Something of those innocent days lingered in the stillness between them, stealing their voices. Katie didn't mind the silence, fearing words would break the tranquillity created by their exploration of each other.

Conrad laid a gentle kiss on her forehead, in no more hurry to break the peace between them than she was. He settled his chin on the top of her hair, holding her close. She rested against him and, closing her eyes, listened to his breathing and the shift of the coals in the grate. Soon, his chest rose and fell with the steady rhythm of sleep, but her restless mind kept her awake.

She lazily traced the curves of his chest, sliding her hand over his damp skin. The opal on her finger glittered in the firelight and the sight of it made her freeze.

Her mother had given her the ring the day before she'd walked out of her and her father's lives for ever.

Katie rolled over and curled on her side, separating herself from Conrad, who groaned and mumbled before settling back to sleep. She twisted the ring on her finger, her bliss gone. After this intimacy, Conrad would expect their engagement to continue and for them to marry, but she couldn't. The moment Mr Barrow snapped his fingers, Conrad would be gone again, leaving her to wait and worry and wonder if he'd ever return. Losing him had been like losing her childhood and innocence for a second time and she refused to endure such suffering again.

Katie pushed herself up and reached for her chemise, drawing the rough cotton over her cold skin. She wrapped her arms about her to warm herself, but continued to shiver. She'd seen the sacrifices her mother had made for her father and how not one of them had been returned. She wouldn't make the same mistake or, like her mother, be made so lonely by wedlock that fleeing from her husband and child to die of fever in some London rookery was preferable to staying.

When, if, Katie did marry, it would be a real union of two committed people, and her children would know the one thing she'd never been given by either of her parents—true love.

She avoided looking at Conrad as she slipped back into her clothes, shame biting at her for what she was about to do. It wasn't right to leave this way, but she couldn't stay, or hope to stand strong against all his arguments for their future, not after she'd been so weak with him tonight.

She clutched her half-boots and crept to the door, nearly to it when Conrad called out.

'Where is he? Where's he gone?'

Shaken, she turned to see him lying on his back, the calm which had eased the lines of his face gone. His eyelids twitched and a line of perspiration spread out beneath his hair as he fought against the dream tormenting him.

'Find him,' he cried, his fingers digging into the leather as his head tossed back and forth. 'He can't be out there alone. He won't survive.'

'Conrad?' Katie hurried back to the bench and sat down beside him. She pressed her hand to his bare chest, his cold and clammy skin unnerving. 'Wake up.'

He didn't rouse, but continued to suffer in the grips of his nightmare.

'Henry, we have to find him. We have to get everyone back,' he cried out with cutting agony.

'Wake up, Conrad.' She shook him, trying to free him, but he wouldn't rouse.

'I can't find him!'

At a loss for what to do, Katie leaned in close

to his ear, inhaling his heady scent as she whispered to him, 'You're safe now, everyone's safe, you're home.'

She stroked his cheek as she continued to speak the soothing words until, at last, the rapid rise and fall of his chest calmed and he ceased his thrashing. His hands eased at his sides though he continued to mumble, his words growing fainter and less distinct as he settled back into sleep. She remained beside him, caressing him until she was sure the dreams were gone. Then, she withdrew her hand, slid on her half-boots and rose.

Stopping at the study door to cast him one last look, guilt twisted her stomach as much as regret. She shouldn't sneak away, but it would be a mistake to stay. He'd defied expectations and returned this time. He might not be so lucky next time. She wasn't going to open her heart to him only to have it crushed, to spend more time waiting for yet another person she loved to leave and never return.

Conrad jerked awake, struggling through the haze of dreams and reality to focus on the room and remember he was no longer trapped by the ice. He reached for Katie, desperate for the solace of her, but she wasn't there. Last night, he hadn't been able to free himself from the nightmare, but through the clinging mist of snow and cold, he'd heard her voice. It had pushed back the blinding white engulfing him until only the bliss of darkness remained. He peered through the faint dawn light searching for her, but the room was empty except for his discarded clothes on the carpet which were no longer tangled with hers.

She's gone. Panic shot through him before he settled himself. She'd been up before sunrise the day before to study the creature. She was probably in the conservatory, hard at work.

Conrad tugged on his clothes, stepped into his boots, then made his way down the dim hall, eager to sit with her and watch her draw. Despite the pleasures of their play, the most recent nightmare had left a tightness inside him only she could ease.

He pushed open the conservatory door, surprised to find it empty except for the still fronds of the palms. From the top of the table, the creature grimaced at him, as quiet in its rest as the house. The dread which had awakened him began to creep through him again but he shoved it back.

She must be in her room. He was about to go upstairs when something caught his eye. Katie's sketchbook no longer sat on the table and the books from Conrad's study were neatly stacked beside the bones. Her satchel which had rested under the table the day before was also missing. He didn't have to visit her bedroom to know she was gone.

She'd given up on him, just like Aaron.

He rested his hands on his knees as the image of Aaron's hopeless eyes meeting his from across the tent rushed back to him along with the pain of crushing failure. He'd promised to get them home, but Aaron hadn't believed in him, choosing to die in the ice instead, just like Katie had chosen to walk away instead of trusting him with her future.

Anger swept in to kill the pain and Conrad straightened. He slammed his fist down hard on the table, making the bones jump.

After everything he'd done to come home to

her, after everything he'd told her, she'd slipped away like some pilfering crewman who'd been at the rum.

He whirled on his heel and stormed through the room towards the back door, knocking fronds out of his way as he passed. His men had been more loyal to him than Katie, even when he'd driven them like sledge dogs to carry what little remained of their supplies. At night, they'd collapse exhausted in the canvas tents. In the morning, they'd look at him with their bearded and chapped faces, their eyes and lips red from sunburn and thirst as he urged them to live and struggle for one more day. When the food was nearly gone and the wind was pushing them back from every inch they'd fought to claim, he'd fed them on dreams and a future they must live to see. He once thought that future included Katie. It didn't.

Rage battered him as he stepped out into the grey of daybreak. If he'd known she'd turn on him like a mutinous crewman, he would have left her on the hillside with Mr Prevett.

Conrad jerked to a halt, his shame deepening. Maybe the rumours Matilda alluded to were correct. He'd believed what Katie had told him about Mr Prevett, but what if she was lying, just as her kisses had lied to him last night? Even if she wasn't, one indisputable fact was true: Katie didn't love him, she never really had and he'd been too blinded by his own desperate desire to reach her to see it.

He marched into the stable as bitter memories rushed in to blot out the cherished ones he'd carried with him in the snow. The way she'd resisted his proposal, creating excuses for why they shouldn't marry and forcing him to argue each one away. Then, when he'd finally secured her promise, her reluctance to set a date. Even when she'd known he was leaving, she hadn't cherished him enough to enjoy with him a few glorious nights as husband and wife. He'd done everything in his power to prove himself a man worthy of her love and trust, one who'd see her through the most difficult of trials. In the end, she'd thrown it all back in his face.

He opened and closed his hand, shaking it out in an effort to dispel the trembling. At least he hadn't told her everything, degrading himself further by revealing what the Arctic and his mistakes had done to him. No one could know.

Mr Peet stepped out of a stall, startled to a halt by the sight of Conrad. 'Sir?'

'Saddle the horse. I make for London.'

'Now?' Mr Peet leaned his pitchfork against the wall.

'Now.' He'd placed his career in enough jeopardy to reach her, and he'd been rewarded with nothing. It was time to go to report to Mr Barrow and forget her.

As Mr Peet shuffled off to fetch the saddle, Conrad worried about what waited for him in London. He'd once thought to face it with Katie, but he'd been mistaken. He drew in a ragged breath, focusing on the sharp scent of hay and horses to help shake off his concern. He wouldn't second-guess his decision to leave any more now than he had when he'd led his men off across the ice in search of a whaling station. Nor would he ever again try to create love where it didn't exist. He'd already made a fool of himself chasing after Katie. He wouldn't do it again.

Chapter Five

Six weeks later

'It's with great honour I present to you the new president of the Naturalist Society, Captain Essington,' Mr Stockton, the Naturalist Society Secretary, announced to the gathered crowd.

Conrad bowed, every muscle in his back stiff as Mr Stockton placed the heavy president's medal around his neck. As he straightened, the large audience filling the library broke into thunderous applause. The sound proved as unnerving as any Conrad had faced in the north.

He forced himself to smile as he stepped down off the stage to greet the numerous people lining up to congratulate him. While he shook their hands, the heavy gold chain holding the medal bit into his neck and he adjusted it, despite wanting to pull it off and throw it to the ground. He'd tried to bury the failures he'd experienced in West Sussex and the Arctic deep inside him along with the shame of Aaron's death when he'd ridden away from Heims Hall, but the adoration of all of London kept reviving it. Like Mr Barrow, they'd been too amazed by his return to concern themselves with his failures, and too eager to toss accolades at him he didn't deserve.

'So, you'll accept the presidential medal, but turn down the King's,' Mr Barrow mumbled as he approached Conrad.

There was no reason to repeat why he didn't deserve anyone's praise. The Second Secretary would only shrug it off as he had before. Conrad wished he could be so cavalier about his failings, but the gapped-toothed smiles and maimed hands of his men didn't allow it.

'My father once held this post, it's only fitting I should, too.' It was the only honour he'd been willing to accept since returning because it continued his father's legacy, the one Lord Helton had tried so hard to crush.

'It would be more fitting to finish your book and get it to the printers.' Mr Barrow frowned, drawing down further his long face lined with his experiences and framed by the greying brown hair spreading out from his temples.

'I'm hard at it, sir.' It was a lie. In the past six weeks, Conrad had done all he could to avoid reviewing the journal and writing the book Mr Barrow craved. While Conrad had wasted time at Heims Hall, the Second Secretary had rushed Conrad's report to the printers without Conrad's approval, assuring Conrad's fame, and the demand for a more detailed account. If it was up to Conrad, both the report and his journal would have been allowed to sink into nothingness like *Gorgon*.

'Work faster then. All England is dying to read the full story.' His order given, Mr Barrow strode away, eager to court the more esteemed members of the society.

Conrad shifted the metal around his neck again, eager to be anywhere but standing here like a trained market-bazaar monkey, but he'd accepted the duties of the office and he must face them, good and bad.

'Mr Rukin is here. I'd like you to introduce me to him,' Matilda insisted, motioning with excitement to a tall gentleman of some forty years with thick salt-and-pepper hair standing near the bookshelves. 'I understand he's a widower in search of a new wife.'

'Another time.' Conrad sighed, eager to return home instead of playing matchmaker, even if it meant staring down at the journal and all his failures. Though he didn't need the original reminder, the horrors remained as fresh now as the day they'd happened.

'You never help me with gentlemen, you only drive them off, like you and Uncle Jack did with Mr Eversham,' Matilda spat, still clinging to the perceived slight after all these years.

'If the sheriff had been more interested in you than your small inheritance, and not kept three mistresses, one of whom was with child, we wouldn't have chased him away.' Matilda had always been a poor judge of character, throwing her lot in with anyone who showed her the least bit of attention, especially if they held a modicum of influence. His aunt, on her deathbed, had asked Conrad to look out for Matilda and he'd done his best to keep his promise. Yet Matilda always wanted him to do what no one but she could—make her more palatable to others, especially men.

'Better the wife of a cheating man than a spinster.' Matilda pouted.

'Fine, I'll make the introduction.' He moved to approach Mr Rukin and mollify his cousin when Mr Stockton stopped him.

'Captain Essington, where is Miss Vickers?' The short, balding gentleman glanced around the room, then focused back on Conrad. 'We haven't seen anything of your fiancée since your return.'

'She's decided to remain in the country for the time being.' In the excitement surrounding his resurrection, there'd been no good time to announce the end of his engagement and he'd found a fake fiancée useful for keeping enamoured women and eager gossips at bay.

'Yes, well, it's probably better she elected to remain in the country,' Mr Stockton remarked with a knowing raise of one bushy eyebrow.

Conrad didn't demand the secretary explain himself, he didn't need to. He'd never asked anyone to relate the exact rumours surrounding Katie and no one, not even Matilda, had been brave enough to offer him details. However, he'd caught the hint of them in comments and sideways glances from members like Mr Stockton. Conrad didn't give a fig for their twittering; it was his uncle's interest which kept him silent about the rift between him and Katie. Once his uncle returned from the Continent and Conrad at last made his break with Katie public, the man would gloat over his success. It was the single victory his uncle would ever enjoy over him, the one Katie had handed to him when she'd walked out of Heims Hall in the middle of the night.

Conrad shifted the medal away from his neck again when a sight at the back of the room shocked him still.

'Are you all right, Captain Essington?' Mr Stockton asked. 'You look as though you've seen a ghost.'

'I think I have.' Conrad strode off towards the woman, keeping the blonde curls in sight as best he could through the ever-shifting throng of people.

'Excuse me.' He pushed his way through the crowd, his rising anger quickening his steps. He would not have this, not here, not today when he was already struggling to maintain his calm and not bolt from the room. 'What are you doing here?'

He caught the woman by the arm and swung her around, letting go as a pair of startled green eyes met his.

'Oh, Captain Essington,' the woman exclaimed, her indignation melting into admiration.

Conrad locked his arms at his sides. 'I'm sorry, miss, I thought you were someone else.' *I thought you were Katie.*

'There's nothing to be sorry about.' The woman tilted her head and batted her long eyelashes at him. 'I'm quite an admirer of yours.'

You shouldn't be, no one should.

'Thank you.' He forced the words through a tight jaw. 'If you'll excuse me.'

He wound his way through the crowd to the front of the library in a daze, too stunned by the force of his reaction to acknowledge the many congratulations tossed at him as he passed. If a woman with the same shade of blonde hair as Katie's could rattle him into forgetting himself, and in public no less, what weakness might the real Katie elicit from him?

Stopping to speak with Mr Rukin, he shoved the worry and so many others deep inside him. There was no reason to concern himself with it, he wasn't likely to see Katie again.

Conrad balled his hands into fists and rested his knuckles on the cool desktop, steadying himself against the shock threatening to undo him. It'd been three days since the Naturalist Society ceremony and the encounter with the woman he'd mistaken for Katie. Both had brought up a bevy of grief and concerns which had kept Conrad pacing the floors for the last few nights, leaving him in no mood to face the very woman who'd haunted his dreams as much as the Arctic. 'What are you doing here?'

'I came to congratulate you.' Katie twisted the opal ring on her finger as she stood across the desk from him, her face a mask of contrition he almost mistook as genuine. 'I read about your election to president of the Naturalist Society, and the publication of your expedition report.'

'I'm sure you haven't come here simply to

congratulate me,' he said in a measured voice, determined to maintain more control than he'd exhibited at the Naturalist Society.

'No, I need your help.' She shifted on her feet, her discomfort offering him little joy. 'I didn't know who else to approach.'

'Why? Is Mr Prevett no longer eager to assist you?'

She winced and inwardly so did Conrad. 'It wasn't that I didn't care for you, Conrad, only I couldn't stay. I couldn't make the same mistakes my mother did.'

Conrad narrowed his eyes at her. 'So I'm now nothing more to you than a mistake?'

'No, you were so much more.' She spread out her hands, pleading with him to understand, but he refused.

'Go back to Whitemans Green. I can be of no assistance to you.' Conrad sat down at his desk and took up his pen, determined to return to the despised journal and give Mr Barrow his damned book. He dipped the nib in the ink and began to copy out a passage about the fierceness with which winter had arrived. Weakness crept into his hand as he formed each word and only with the greatest pressure did he keep the nib steady. He waited for Katie to leave, expected it, silently demanded it, but she stubbornly remained.

'I can't go back,' she said, her voice sombre enough to make Conrad's pen pause over the parchment. 'I sold Father's fossil collection and gave up the house. There was no other way to settle his debt or keep from creating new ones.'

Conrad looked up from his work, shocked again by the exhaustion whitening her cheeks. It seemed she'd slept as poorly as he had since leaving the country. The idea of it should have offered him some sense of vindication, but it didn't. He flipped closed the journal, wishing he were as hard as some of the captains he'd served under during his first years in the Navy. He shouldn't care about her, or her plight, but he couldn't help it, any more than he could turn his back on any man who'd ever been under his command and fallen on hard times. 'Where are you living now?'

'With my widowed aunt in Cheapside.'

'And your American collectors?'

'We still correspond, but with the distance, their patronage isn't enough to sustain me.'

'What about your mother's family?'

'I wrote to them, but they ignored my letter, like every other one I've ever sent them.' A sadness he recognised choked her words. He knew such isolation, it surrounded him now. 'Even if they did deign to respond, they aren't going to consort with a woman whose reputation has been savaged by the Marquis of Helton.'

'If you'd believed in me the way I once believed in you, I would have made it right,' he reminded her with an edge of disgust he couldn't suppress.

'Then do so now and help me.' She faced him with a bravery he grudgingly admired. It revealed something of the old Katie, the one who hadn't let her sex, her father or anything stop her from pursuing her dreams, a woman who in so many ways reminded him of himself. 'I've been studying the creature from the drawings I did at Heims Hall, but they, and the few books I've secured, aren't enough to finish my research. I need to see the bones and gain access to the Naturalist Society library. If I can publish my paper, showcase what I know and what I can draw, prove to the men I'm as talented as they are, then maybe I can gain work as an illustrator, or find some esteemed gentleman to hire me to catalogue his collection.'

Conrad didn't answer right away. The image of her at the table in the conservatory, her slender back curved while her blonde hair fell forward, her light breathing matched by the faint scratch of her pencil against the paper, rose up to tease him. It was crushed by the anguish he'd experienced when he'd awakened to find she'd run out on him. 'I can't help you.'

'You must. You owe me.'

'I owe you?' He tossed down the pen and jumped to his feet. 'I offered to help you, to assist you in your work, to make you my partner in life and give you the security of my name. You rejected it all, then threw everything you meant to me and my efforts to come home to you in my face. Now you have the temerity to demand favours from me?'

'It was my aunt's idea,' she stuttered, her bravery wilting beneath his outburst.

'Then you're both very mistaken about my re-

gard for you, or any desire I have to assist you.'
Conrad jammed the pen in its stand, working to
regain his calm, afraid if he didn't Katie might
see the weakness inside him, the one threatening to chew out his insides. He rounded the desk
and marched into the entrance hall. 'Mr Moore,
please see Miss Vickers out.'

The butler pulled open the door and the dim
light of the gathering November clouds crept in
beneath the warmth of the candles.

Katie walked slowly into the hall, stopping in
front of Conrad. 'You're right, I shouldn't have
come. I won't trouble you again.'

She fled into the crush of people passing on
the street.

Mr Moore swung closed the door and Conrad
flinched as the brass lock clicked shut, the fi-
nality of it as striking as when the tent flap had
closed behind Aaron.

He returned to his study and stood over the
desk, forcing himself to look past the water-
stained journal to the framed nautical chart on
the wall. He'd failed his men by pushing north
past the date they should have sailed south and

getting them trapped in the ice. He might have found a way home, but he never should have risked trapping them in the first place, just as he shouldn't have made promises to Katie he couldn't keep. He'd once vowed to keep her safe from his uncle, and anyone else who might look down on the daughter of a country doctor for daring to marry the nephew of a marquis. It was the promise he'd made to gain her acceptance of his proposal, the one he hadn't been able to keep.

The image of Katie's blue eyes pleading for his help before he'd dismissed her haunted him. Whatever had happened in the past six weeks, it had increased the despair which had marked her at Heims Hall. He'd never seen her so desperate or gaunt. He knew what deprivation did to a man and his soul, the lengths it might drive him to, including the extinction of his very being in an effort to free himself from misery. Aaron had chosen death over another day marching through snow and starvation in search of a ship or whaling station Conrad couldn't guarantee existed. If Katie was desperate enough to come to him, what might she do?

* * *

Katie wandered down the street, the weariness which had dogged her since coming to London making each step more laborious. Approaching Conrad had been her last hope and now it was gone. Without the Naturalist Society and access to the bones, there was no chance of completing her paper, gaining employment or doing anything more than falling deeper into the poverty threatening to overwhelm her. Aunt Florence was kind enough to allow Katie to stay with her, but her aunt's means were limited. Her aunt augmented her meagre inheritance from her husband by taking in sewing, but even in this Katie couldn't assist her. Her mother, having grown up with servants and dressmakers, had possessed few domestic arts to pass on to Katie. Even if she'd known how to wield a needle, she would have had to have roused herself from her gloom long enough to sit patiently with a child and teach.

The knowledge of fossils and her ability to draw were the only skills Katie possessed, but with no connections and a tattered reputation, she wasn't likely to find work. One option was fast becoming the only path open to her.

She glanced down the street to where it ended at the river. The tall masts of ships were visible in the gaps between the buildings lining the muddy banks. Each day she studied the schedule of ships leaving for America, memorising their dates of departures, fares and expected travelling times. If she wished to reach America before Mr Lesueur set off, she must book passage within the next two weeks or even this opportunity would be gone.

Katie watched the tall mast of a ship slide behind a building, the round crow's nest at the top the only thing visible over the lead roof. There was just enough money left from the sale of her father's things to pay for the journey, but she wasn't prepared to leave yet. If she reached America, and Mr Lesueur had already set off, she'd be destitute on a foreign shore, though she wasn't sure being poor in America would be any worse than her current situation. With Conrad refusing to help, there wasn't much left for her in England and little reason to delay the voyage.

With heavy steps Katie started off towards

Cheapside. People bumped and pushed her as they passed, irritated by her slow pace, but there was no point hurrying. The research was the one thing which had kept her going during the past six weeks, the thing she'd turn to each night after spending the day packing up her father's collection and seeing it off. As the collection departed, the house had grown even more lonely and empty than before. In her small bed at night, the peace she'd experienced in Conrad's embrace had mocked her and more than once she'd regretted both surrendering to him and her fears.

With her thumb, she flicked the band of the opal ring through her thin glove, Conrad's nasty words making her cringe. Never in all their time together had he treated her so callously, though she deserved his scorn. He was right, he'd opened himself to her and she'd forsaken him, running out the way her mother had done to her and her father, but she couldn't have stayed, even if it meant security. Her father had been attentive to her mother until they'd married, then he'd forgotten her, too absorbed with his work to feed her the small kindnesses on which love thrived. Katie couldn't suffer the same tragedy, or spend another year wondering if the man she loved would ever return.

'Katie, wait,' a deep voice called from behind her, the sound nearly lost in the din of horses and carts jamming the street.

She turned to catch Conrad weaving his way through the crowd, apologising to the ladies and gentlemen he passed until the fast fall of his boots on the pavement grew louder than the cries of the hawkers. He stopped in front of her and a dangerous feeling curled inside her at the sight of him. He wore his hair longer than before and swept back from his strong forehead. A new coat of fine tan wool covered his torso and a crisp white cravat sat tucked beneath his cleft chin. He was fuller through the cheeks, having regained a good measure of the weight he'd lost on his expedition. The change in his appearance was enough to keep her fixed to the pavement though she wanted to run from him, her problems and all the troubles dogging her.

'Allow me to escort you home.' His offer was as bewildering as her strong reaction to him.

'No, you were right, you owe me nothing. It's best if we part ways.' She moved to leave, but he caught her by the arm, pulling her back from the kerb.

'I do owe you. It was my uncle who did the damage to your reputation and it's up to me to put it right.' He let go of her, but the pressure of his hand on her arm remained. 'I'm sorry if I was harsh. The last six weeks have not been easy for me.'

Katie wanted to ask why, but she bit back the question. Whatever it was which clouded his eyes with sadness was none of her concern, though she wanted to chase it away, as she had his nightmare at Heims Hall. Despite their differences, she didn't want him to suffer.

'I've thought over your proposal and believe I can be of some help to you.' He waved down a passing hack, drawing her to the edge of the kerb as the driver manoeuvred the vehicle to a stop in front of them.

She wasn't sure she wanted his help, or if she should accept it. It'd been a mistake allowing her aunt to convince her to see him. All it had done was dredge up the awkwardness of their parting and all the damage it had done to both of them. 'You don't have to help me.'

'I do.'

'Why?'

'I have my reasons.' They no doubt had more to do with thwarting his uncle than assisting her. 'Now come along.'

He placed his hand on her back and urged her into the hackney. She didn't resist, but stepped inside the musty vehicle. If his change of heart was merely a chance to strike at the marquis for the many transgressions he'd made against Conrad and his family, it didn't matter. He was offering her his help and she needed it.

He settled in beside her in the cramped hack, his arm pressing up against hers, the lack of space between them as unsettling as his unexpected change of mind.

'Where are we going?' she asked, trying to shift away, but there was nowhere to go.

'The Naturalist Society.'

'So soon?'

'The present is always the best time.'

'I don't have my notes or my things.'

He threw her an encouraging smile. 'You don't need them, I know you don't.'

Katie gripped the strap above the window,

more to steady her nerves than her body. The man who sat beside her now wasn't the one who'd looked on her with such hate and anger in his house a short while ago. This was the Conrad she'd first fallen in love with, the one who could take command of any situation and make her feel safe and protected. It was confusing to find him beside her again. 'You're right, I don't.'

She could recall nearly every word of what she'd written, each hypothesis she'd laid out and the evidence she needed to prove it. With the resources of the Naturalist Society, she could prove her theory, assuming Conrad succeeded in escorting her inside. 'Are you sure they'll allow me in as your guest?'

'I'm the most prominent member they possess. They aren't likely to deny me anything.' Conrad stared at the dirty floor of the hack, a darkness to match the one she'd seen in his study dampening his smile. 'It's one of the only advantages of fame.'

She wanted to reach out and offer him the reassuring touch he'd once have extended to her, but she kept her free hand firmly in her lap. She'd read his pamphlet. Her aunt had purchased it along with a host of other explorers' writings. Aunt Florence was enraptured by travel though she'd never ventured further than London. It'd sickened Katie to see Conrad's trials in such bald-faced terms. It had also deepened her distress at how she'd chosen to leave him in the country. With his acclaim increasing, she'd convinced herself leaving hadn't hurt him. After the vitriol he'd struck her with in his house, she knew she'd been wrong. She'd wounded him badly, though obviously not enough to make him completely forsake her.

She brushed a wayward curl from her hot cheek, her guilt at what she'd done increasing. He was helping her, as he'd always did, and she wasn't worthy of his kindness. She looked out of the window at the passing façades in St James's Street. She'd see to it this was the last time she needed to rely on him.

Katie's grip on Conrad's arm tightened as he escorted her through the wide double doors of the grand house on St James's Street. The last time she'd trod these dark, rosewood-panelled hallways had been the night she and her father had hurried out, indignation burning in her chest over the way they'd been treated. Her father had walked beside her back to Aunt Florence's a broken man, as withdrawn from her as he'd been the morning he'd handed her the parting note from her mother.

Conrad was oblivious to the stares and whispers following them as they strode past the open sitting rooms. Men looked up from their newspapers or turned from their discussions to watch them. Katie inched closer to Conrad, wishing she was as heedless of the other members as him. Their scrutiny continued to roll off of him as he led her to the large library at the back of the building. The house had once been owned by the Duke of Carling, before he'd donated it to the Naturalist Society, and the old ballroom with its high ceiling and wide floor was now the library. Tall bookshelves covered the walls and round tables filled the empty space in the centre, each one dotted with men doing research. The small stage at the end where the musicians once sat still remained. Once a month, the tables were removed and various gentlemen took to the platform to present their ideas. It was there

Katie and her father had been humiliated, with members rising to accuse them of plagiarism, men protected by minor titles and secretly egged on by Lord Helton.

It wasn't the stage which made her halt on the threshold, but the cold eyes of Mr Rukin from across the room. She met his contempt with her own, determined not to allow the disgusting man to cow her.

'What's wrong?' Conrad asked, looking back and forth between her and the barrage of harsh stares thrown at her by the men scattered at the tables.

'I don't have very fond memories of the last time I was here.' Or of the evening afterwards when she'd gone alone to Mr Rukin's to ask for his help. She'd thought him her and her father's ally in their efforts to gain recognition. She'd been terribly wrong.

'Don't let it stop you,' Conrad urged as he laid his hand over hers and drew her into the room.

She ignored Mr Rukin's sneer as Conrad led her past him to a table in the far corner.

She set her reticule down, then turned to take in the high bookshelf against the wall. It was stocked with books on birds from all over the world with large folios of Mr Audubon's drawings besides those of more obscure ornithologists. Katie's heart skipped as much from the sight of them as from Conrad's presence beside her. It was the first time in the past week when the exhaustion of packing up her things, travelling to London and counting again her meagre savings in order to calculate how long they might last didn't weigh her down.

She examined the spines, then quickly began to draw out books and stack them on the table, keenly aware of Mr Rukin and the others watching.

'There's no need to rush,' Conrad offered, as she stacked two more books on the table, then turned to select more.

'There is, as you're about to discover.' The footsteps of a gentleman approaching echoed behind them. It was someone coming to demand she leave. It had happened before when she'd accompanied her father to other libraries, a harsh reminder of how Katie's ruined reputation had marred them both.

'May I have a word with you, Captain Essington?' Mr Rukin's voice slithered over her, dragging up the desperation she'd experienced in his home.

'Yes, Mr Rukin?' Conrad demanded, turning with her to face the man.

Mr Rukin stared past Conrad to Katie, as arrogant as he was duplicitous. It made her skin crawl to remember his cold fingers digging into her upper arms and his slimy mouth pressed against hers. 'I object to a woman such as Miss Vickers being allowed in here.'

'What problems do you have?' Conrad demanded in the manner of a man used to commanding people, not obeying them. 'I have the same right as any other member to sponsor a guest who wishes to use the library.'

Katie shifted closer to Conrad and pinned Mr Rukin with a hard, condemning glare, daring him to admit his reason and his guilt.

'I— Well—' he stuttered, as much a coward today as he'd been during her last night in London.

'Our society has always welcomed anyone interested in the natural sciences, including those of the fairer sex, we've prided ourselves on it.

If any member takes issue with our policy, then they may arrange to speak privately with me about it.' Conrad raised his voice, looking around the room in challenge to the other men watching. They ducked behind their books, unwilling to contradict Conrad, or support Mr Rukin. It was a faint comfort to Katie to see him so isolated.

With lips pursed in disapproval, Mr Rukin stalked away, leaving the room and his research behind.

'I see now some of what you must have had to contend with while I was gone.' Conrad flicked a glance at Katie's hands and her hard grip on the opal ring.

She opened her fingers, pulled out a chair and sat down, disgusted by Conrad's sympathy. If he'd cared enough about her to stay in England instead of sailing off, none of the problems facing her would even exist. 'That's the least of what I was forced to endure.'

Conrad sat down in the chair beside hers and leaned in close, his breath caressing her exposed wrist above her sleeve, the tall stack of books hiding them both from view. 'Did something happen between you and Mr Rukin?'

His question carried as much suspicion as it did care and she searched his face, wondering how many of the rumours he believed. By now he should have heard them all, how her meagre success wasn't because of hard work, but midnight visits to many gentlemen's houses. At this moment, Mr Rukin was probably in the salon repeating them to anyone who'd listen and inventing some involving Conrad as well. Conrad's reputation could withstand the assault, hers couldn't. She shouldn't have come to him for help. Even with his support, it wouldn't make any difference.

'Nothing I wish to discuss, or disprove,' Katie answered at last, unwilling to delve into the details of the humiliation she'd experienced both here and at Mr Rukin's.

She slowly opened a large book on birds of Australia and pulled it close. Tracing the beautifully rendered watercolour of an egret in flight, she wondered if, had she been allowed to find it, there might have been a different path for her. If there was, it was lost to the past and only this way forward remained.

She selected a pencil and a piece of paper from

those laid out on the table for the convenience of the members, eager to shake off her despair. Conrad continued to study her, his scrutiny as troubling as the other gentlemen's disapproving looks. She didn't want him to pry, but to let her work. Too much depended on her success for her to think it was futile, or to fail.

Conrad leaned away from Katie, disturbed by her refusal to confide in him as much as Mr Rukin's presence. Whatever had passed between her and the thick-waisted member with the long legs, she didn't trust Conrad enough to tell him, or she was too ashamed.

He shoved himself up out of the chair and made for another bookshelf a few feet away, noticing the bob of men's heads as they looked up from their tomes, then ducked back down to resume their research. What did they know that Conrad didn't? He couldn't rely on Katie to tell him, although he couldn't blame her. He wasn't about to reveal to her the truth of his failures in the Arctic. Such confidences required trust, which she'd destroyed when she'd run from Heims Hall.

Conrad pulled a work on caribou off the shelf

and flipped it open. If he couldn't give Mr Barrow the book he wanted on his experiences, he'd appease him with some scientific drivel. It would give him something to do while Katie worked.

He read the first paragraph, but couldn't take in the words.

What was he doing supporting Katie when she hadn't possessed the decency to wake him before she'd fled his house? With a city full of women enamoured with him and his exploits, he might find any manner of consolation and companionship. Unlike all those women, Katie had never wanted him for the glory he could bestow upon her, or his connection to the Marquis of Helton. She'd loved him for himself and the exchange of ideas they'd enjoyed during long afternoons at Heims Hall. Sadly, the quiet days with her hadn't been enough for him.

He looked down at his right hand and the faint red marks which had all but faded from his palms. As much as he was loath to admit it, his desire to chase the Northwest Passage had been as responsible for his uncle's success in ending their engagement as her stealthy departure. If the grandeur he'd received from his adventures had been as beautiful as Katie's body beneath his, or brought him as much peace, then the sacrifice of her love might have been worth it. It wasn't. He wondered if risking his reputation to protect hers was worth it either.

Conrad snapped the book shut and shoved it back in between its mates, grimacing as the leather spine cracked. From out of the corner of his eyes he caught Katie watching him. He turned to her, the curve of her arm against the table and her slender fingers gripping the long wood of the pen moving him as much as the concern filling her blue eyes. Regret replaced his anger and he turned back to the shelves. They'd both made mistakes and it was time for him to atone for some of his, though it would be difficult to overcome people's prejudice against Katie, especially when he held his own.

It was a relief at the end of the afternoon when Conrad closed his last book. He'd made no more progress with an article about Arctic animals than he had composing the details of his expedition. The recollection of his time in the north had distracted him along with Katie's steady breathing beside him and the whisper of her faded muslin gown against her legs whenever she shifted in the chair. He didn't want her to keep affecting him, even in such subtle ways, but she did.

'Do you have what you need?' he asked as a footman shuffled behind them to light the lamp hanging from the wall, ready to end this strange day.

Katie arched against the stiffness in her back. It drew tight the faded bodice over her full breasts and sent a flood of heat tearing through Conrad. 'I believe so. Mr Brule's writings were extensive and I saw nothing in any of his drawings to suggest the creature. However, the illustrations of the emus were not as detailed as I would have liked. I need a specimen I can draw from life. Perhaps the British Museum has one. I'll visit there tomorrow on my own. They aren't so particular about who they allow in.'

She offered him a small smile he couldn't help but return. It was good to see her joking about her situation, it gave him hope she still possessed the fortitude to carry on, unlike Aaron, who'd simply given up.

He stood his book on end on the table between them and rested his hands on the top, as though placing it between them to protect himself from his weakness and her. 'Whatever else you need to complete your paper, you must gather it quickly. The last Naturalist Society meeting until spring is next week. I'll make the necessary arrangements for your presentation.'

Panic widened her eyes. 'No, I can't.'

'You must. If you don't successfully argue your thesis in front of them, then any future work will be ignored.'

She fingered the papers in front of her, folding and unfolding the corner of the top one. 'You're right, but I still don't want to do it.'

'Sometimes we must do what we must, even when we don't want to.' He sighed.

She stood and banged the stack of papers against the table. 'It's hardly a lesson you need to teach me.'

'It isn't a lesson, but a reminder.' He laid a calming hand on her arm and the tension of it eased, though it created a more unsettling one down low in his abdomen. 'Like the ones I had to give myself many times, in harsher places than London.'

'Of course.' Understanding whispered between them like the faint hiss of a sparking wick from a nearby lamp. She tucked the papers into the crook of her arm, but continued to fiddle with the dog-eared page. 'I'll need to see the creature again, to do a larger drawing, one I can use during the presentation.'

Conrad paused. He'd thought to send her on her way until next week, but as in West Sussex, the creature still linked them. He should have left the bones in the country, but instead he'd brought them with him, thinking to offer them to Mr Buckland or some other eminent biologist to study. He hadn't ordered them unpacked, but left them in their crate in a dark corner of the kitchen. 'I'll have the bones set out in the morning room. You and your aunt are free to come at any time to study them.'

'You won't be there?' Her disappointment was startling. She'd been all too eager to leave him at Heims Hall.

'I have a number of pressing duties demanding my time.'

'Preparing for another expedition?' It was as much a question as an accusation.

Conrad settled his irritation to answer in an even voice. What he did from now on was no longer her concern, just as she believed the truth behind Mr Rukin's hostility wasn't his. 'No. I think Mr Barrow finds my fame more useful for promoting the Discovery Service than a new expedition.'

'I shouldn't worry. I'm sure in time he'll send you out again.'

She guessed he was disappointed at not being given a new command, but she was wrong, though he wasn't about to admit it to her or anyone else. It was a disgrace to even think it. He wasn't a man to give into fear, or to shirk duty, no matter how much the thought of setting out again, of having another crew's lives in his hands, unsettled him.

'It's getting late,' Conrad observed. 'It's time I saw you home.'

A light drizzle fell over the dirty pavements of Cheapside as the hack stopped in front of a simple brick lodging house. The gloom from outside seemed to creep up the stairs with them and cover the cracked plaster and faded wallpaper as Katie guided Conrad up to the first floor and a lone door just off the landing. She kept her gaze focused on the stained runner covering the floorboards, her embarrassment at her new circumstances evident in the faint pink creeping over her neck just beneath the pinned-up curls.

Conrad said nothing, though he wanted very much to take Katie home and set her up in a clean room with enough food to remove the thinness from her cheeks, and a comfortable bed to soften the circles beneath her eyes.

He crossed his hands in front of himself. It was no longer his place to interfere. She'd chosen this life over the one he'd offered. There was no one to blame but herself if it didn't suit.

The door cracked open and two hazel eyes above a thin nose and a thinner chin peered out at them.

'Oh, Katie, thank heavens you're back, I was worried about you.' The door swung open and the thin woman rushed out to wrap Katie in a relieved embrace. Over Katie's shoulder, the woman noticed Conrad and gently shifted her niece aside, taking him in with appreciation. 'And is this the famous Captain Essington?'

'It is,' Katie concurred with notably less enthusiasm. 'Captain Essington, allow me to introduce my aunt, Mrs Anderson.'

'I wish you'd told me you were bringing such an esteemed guest, I'd have been better prepared,' Mrs Anderson exclaimed as she attempted to tuck a flyaway strand of greying blonde hair into a pin at her temple.

'It's a pleasure to meet you.' Conrad bowed.

'I've read all your pamphlets,' Mrs Anderson gushed, clapping her hands together in front of her flat chest like a captivated society miss. Katie wasn't as enamoured with her aunt's compliments, shooting her relation a chastising look the older women ignored. 'Your accounts are quite thrilling. Every time I complain about my life being hard, I think about what you and your men suffered and realise my troubles aren't so very bad.'

Conrad struggled to smile at her as he did the adoring green girls who interrupted his quiet time at the lending library to swoon over him. The suffering of his men and Aaron's death were too high a price to pay for a few uplifting tracts. 'Thank you, it means a great deal to me to know my writings have influenced you.'

'Please, won't you come in?' Mrs Anderson waved to a pretty little armchair by the soot stained fireplace. Beside it was a small, round table with a fine set of china on top. It appeared Mrs Anderson had enjoyed more prosperity as a wife than as a widow.

'No, I must be going. Good evening, Miss Vickers.' He slid his fingers beneath Katie's hand and raised it to his lips, the gesture surprising her as much as him. He wasn't sure when he might see her again and he wanted to draw out this parting moment. As many nights as the dreams of the ice awoke him, so did his dreams of her, her soft body and rich voice drawing him into an oblivion he craved.

He withdrew his hand and straightened, calling to mind the anger and desolation of the morning he'd awakened alone to give him the impetus to leave.

Katie closed the door and leaned her forehead against the cool, pitted wood.

'I told you he'd help you,' Aunt Florence gloated as she sat at the table and poured herself some thin tea.

'I don't know why, there can't be any benefit in it for him.' Unless it was solely to vex his uncle. Given the things he'd told her his uncle had done to his parents, she couldn't blame him for wanting to spite the man. She very much wished she could.

'He did it because he still feels for you and you gave him a reason to fight for you again.' She waved Katie over to the table, setting a cup of tea at her place.

'You've read too many novels if you believe that's true,' Katie scoffed as she sat down, rubbing the back of her hand, the impression of Conrad's kiss as strong as the small callous on her finger from where she'd gripped the pen all day.

Her aunt laid a small plate with a stale slice of cake in front of Katie. 'I wouldn't be so sure, my dear. In fact, I would say you can now give up all this business of going off to America.'

Katie pushed the cake away, too distracted by

everything that had happened today to eat. 'I can't.'

Aunt Florence nearly dropped her tea cup. 'But you can't think to leave now.'

'He agreed to help me, that's all. Nothing else is settled, not my career as a naturalist, acceptance by the society, and certainly not any future with Conrad.' There wasn't one. At Heims Hall, she'd nearly risked becoming like her mother and getting herself with child, seeing herself forced into marriage to keep from bestowing the title of bastard on an infant. If it hadn't been for Conrad's restraint, who knew what tragedy might have befallen her. 'London might be enamoured with him, but it doesn't mean Mr Barrow won't fling him to some other obscure corner of the world as soon as a ship is available. He'll be gone and I'll be forgotten, again.'

Aunt Florence gave a disapproving snort. 'He may leave, but he won't forget you. He didn't last time.'

No, he hadn't. The image of him kneeling before her at Heims Hall and telling her how he'd dreamed of her in the cold came rushing back, stirring up the guilt she'd helped settle with her research. It'd been cowardly to run out on him, abandoning him just as her mother had abandoned her, instead of staying and explaining, facing him like a mature woman. Now was her chance to make some amends for her mistake, though she had no idea how. While she needed everything from Conrad, he needed nothing from her. There was no reason she could see for why he'd changed his mind, nor was there any way to make him forget the hateful way Mr Rukin had looked at her, or to stop him from hearing all the rumours whirling around her. She'd caught the suspicion in his eyes today, the look as painful as when he'd tossed her from his house this morning.

'Don't make the same mistake your parents made,' her aunt warned as she finished her tea.

'You mean becoming too obsessed with my work to see anything or anyone around me, like my father did?'

'Things not going well between your parents wasn't all my brother's fault,' Aunt Florence chided. 'After all, he wasn't the only one consumed with a passion for the past and dead things. Your mother had her obsession just like he did.'

Katie picked up her tea and took a sip, wrinkling her nose at the bland, sugarless brew before setting it down. 'What do you mean?'

'I mean, well, she had her faults, too.' Aunt Florence coloured, then rose. She took up the wooden tray next to the table and began stacking empty plates on top of it, the china rattling as she worked with a speed that made Katie suspicious. 'But I don't like to speak ill of the dead.'

She didn't press her aunt for more. It wasn't the first time Aunt Florence had made a cryptic comment about Katie's mother, only to retreat from it with smiles and pleasantries when Katie asked for more details. Even if her aunt one day decided to explain, it wouldn't help. There was nothing Katie could do to change the past, and there were other, more ominous ghosts she needed to stare down in the coming week.

Chapter Six

'Miss Vickers is back in London and you're helping her. Those are odds I wouldn't have wagered on six weeks ago, or even yesterday.' Henry slipped the white clay pipe between his teeth, then plucked a reed from the holder and leaned forward to light it in the fire.

'We both would've lost that bet,' Conrad muttered from beside him as he watched his friend and lieutenant straighten and light the pipe. As the smoke curled around his face, it slid over the black glove covering his left hand, the one which failed to hide the absence of the smallest finger and the shortness of the three beside it.

Conrad jerked to his feet, the sight of his maimed friend unsettling him as much as the salty taste of Katie's skin still lingering on his lips.

'So, what did she do to get you to change your mind?' Henry smiled wryly as he shook out the reed, then tossed it in the grate.

'I assure you, it was nothing so pleasurable.' Conrad fingered the globe beside his chair, rocking it back and forth and making the metal holding it squeak. A few weeks ago he'd have upbraided his friend for such a ribald remark against Katie; tonight he wasn't sure if he should defend her or curse her. When he'd awakened today he hadn't expected to find himself once again embroiled in her life, or wondering if everything he'd heard about her since returning to London was true.

'Then why?' Henry crossed his ankle over his knee, his left hand hidden in his lap.

Conrad rose and wandered to the window. After leaving Katie, he'd sought solace here at the Navy Club, eager for the company and cheer of his friend and fellow officers, but calm continued to elude him. He picked up a dagger-like letter opener lying on the escritoire next to the window and flicked the dull tip with his thumb. 'I feel responsible for her.'

'Seems to me she relinquished your responsibility for her when she ran away.'

His friend was right, Conrad knew it and yet he couldn't accept it any more than he'd accepted that he and his men were doomed once *Gorgon* slipped beneath the water. 'You know I don't give up on anyone so easily.'

'And there are twenty men here in London who thank you for it.'

Conrad set the dagger down. 'It should have been twenty-one.'

Henry took a long drag of his pipe before releasing the smoke in rings over his head. 'It was his choice, Conrad, not yours.'

'But I could have done something or at least realised what he was leaving the tent to do.'

'No one could have guessed it.'

Beyond the window, the rain fell steadily, pouring off the eaves of the building to strike the pavement below. Dripping water sounded different here without the snow to muffle the drops. He was sick of cold and wet and damp, he wanted summer and warmth as badly now as last winter. 'Mr Barrow omitted Aaron's death when he published my report.'

'Will you include it in your book?'

'I will, if I ever finish it.'

'You aren't going to give all England what they crave? Tales of glory on the ice.' Henry threw out his arms in mocking exuberance, revealing again his maimed hand.

'It wasn't glory.'

'No, it was hell.' Henry took another drag of his pipe, the smoke momentarily obscuring his face.

'And I'm tired of reliving it, especially for all the fops and green girls in society.' Conrad dropped back into his chair by the fire and spun the globe. He could easily be one of those men, his mind at ease and never troubled by duty to his crew and the Discovery Service. Uncle Jack had left him the means to spend his evenings in such vapid pursuits, but Conrad wasn't lazy enough to fritter away his life the way his cousin Preston had done. It was the biggest trait his mother had instilled in him, the desire to do something of merit instead of sitting idle. Nor did he intend to spend his days poring over the past and writing it out for all of London to admire. Let them risk their lives in search of knowledge instead of reading about it from the cosy safety of their homes.

'Mr Barrow won't be pleased when you fail to deliver his desired book,' Henry reminded him.

'So he told me the other day, but I'm not his trained monkey.'

'Yes, you are, we both are, or we wouldn't be here.' Henry didn't wear the mantle of their fame, or the weight of their experiences in the north, any easier than Conrad did. All the fawning of the other officers, ladies and even the Naturalist Society members made fresh for them both the suffering they longed to forget. 'Now that you've cursed Mr Barrow, what will you do about Miss Vickers?'

Conrad propped his elbows on his knees and rubbed his temples, weary of her, exploration, everything. 'I'll help her as she's asked and afterwards we'll go our separate ways.'

'Like hell you will. You never give up on people, not even Boatswain James when he got in the rum and tried to mutiny. I'd have left him out in the snow to die, but not you.'

Conrad tossed his friend a smile. 'Good thing for you and the other men I don't give up.'

Henry held up his pipe in salute. 'Good thing.'

'Captain Essington.' A footman approached, white-faced as if he'd seen a ghost. 'The Marquis of Helton requests your presence in the south parlour.'

Conrad jerked up straight in his chair. 'Why was he admitted? He's not a member.'

'He's the Marquis of Helton,' the footman answered, as if it was all the excuse the man needed to barge into a private club and demand a meeting with one of its members.

Conrad could send back his refusal. His uncle, no matter what his pedigree, had no more right to enter the Navy Club than Conrad did to enter White's and demand an audience with the Duke of Marlborough. However, if his uncle deigned to come here so soon after returning from the Continent, and in the rain no less, in search of Conrad, it must be for an interesting reason. For the first time in his life, Conrad was curious to hear what his uncle had to say.

Conrad settled back into his chair. 'Tell Lord Helton he may join me here if he wishes to speak.'

The footman blanched at having to relay such a

message, but like a well-trained sailor he obeyed, moving off to deliver the news.

Henry rose and made for the door. 'If you'll excuse me, I have no desire to encounter Lord Helton.'

Conrad laced his hands in his lap and stared into the dancing fire. 'To be honest, neither do I.'

He didn't have to wait long for the Marquis of Helton to appear at the sitting-room door.

Conrad didn't stand or bow; the man didn't deserve his respect. Instead, he watched his uncle stride into the room with a regal arrogance Conrad despised. Yet for all his airs, there was no mistaking how much he'd changed since Conrad had last seen him riding in Hyde Park two years ago. Lord Helton's grand stature was marred by a new thinness about his chest and a marked hollowness around his mouth which increased the narrow jut of his chin. Dark circles hung beneath his eyes, but he stood as erect as ever, staring down at Conrad with as much malice as he had when Conrad was a boy.

Conrad almost felt sorry for him, thinking grief the reason for the change in his appearance. He hadn't thought the man human enough to feel so deeply the loss of his only child.

'I see you've returned from the Arctic and are once again the famous explorer.' Helton sneered the word *explorer* as he always did, as if everything without a title, a grand house or an esteemed legacy was beneath him. It killed what little sympathy Conrad harboured for the man.

'What do you want?'

'A touch of civility, as befitting a future marquis.'

'If the company is not to your liking, you may return to the gilded hallways of White's.'

'Not until we've talked.' Helton lowered himself into the chair across from Conrad's, perching on the edge as though the cracked leather would ruin his Jermyn Street breeches. He rested his hand on the gold handle of his walking stick, the metal point digging into the rug between his feet. 'I've come to discuss your future since providence has seen fit to take my son and make you my heir.'

Conrad didn't bother to offer his condolences. His cousin had never been good for anything other than molesting maids and torturing cats. 'I assume you're no happier about it than I am.'

'You've assumed correctly.' A wicked cough seized his uncle. He drew from his coat a white handkerchief and pressed it to his mouth as he fought to regain his breath. Through the older man's thin fingers, Conrad noticed the small spots of blood staining the fine linen. So it wasn't grief which had changed him, but something more sinister. The sight of it made Conrad wary. A wounded polar bear was more lethal than a healthy one.

'You could marry again, produce another heir,' Conrad offered, pitying whatever young lady the marquis might set his sights on.

'I'm too old to risk leaving the title and estate to the fate of a squalling baby.' He stuffed the handkerchief back in his pocket. 'I need a man, one strong enough to assume control of the Helton assets, take his seat in the House of Lords and bring honour to the family name.'

'Honour? Is that what you call your merciless bullying? If so, then I have no interest in furthering your legacy.' Conrad crossed one ankle over his knee, facing his uncle's determination with a carelessness Lord Helton had always detested. It was the one weapon he'd possessed against the marquis as a boy and it still held the power to taunt the wicked man.

'What about your own legacy, Captain Essington?' Helton countered, the sound of Conrad's title on his uncle's tongue as eerie as the calls of whales vibrating through the hull of a ship.

'I've already secured it.' He spun the globe on the stand next to him, then jammed his thumb against the white expanse at the top, bringing it to a rattling halt. 'In spite of everything you ever tried to do to ruin it.'

'Yes, you have, but through sheer brute force, not brains. You won't be young and strong for ever.'

Conrad flexed his hand, disturbed by how close to the mark his uncle had come with his attack.

'When you're too feeble to chase after your invisible meridians, what will you do then?' Lord Helton continued, his lip curling in disgust. 'Sit in your study and regale small children with your past glories?'

'I wouldn't be the first.' Conrad shrugged, his

false glibness at odds with the truth. The long faces of the older officers who haunted the Navy Club and told any man who'd listen stories of their past exploits came to mind. However much he hated his uncle for pointing it out, it was his future, assuming the cold or a tropical disease didn't kill him first.

The image of Katie standing in his study at Heims Hall, her eyes filled with fear for what might be, cut through him, and his mortality settled against his shoulders like his epaulets. He caught a glimpse of what Katie saw and how she'd been right to doubt their future. At moments like this, Conrad doubted it, too.

'As a powerful man with the ear of other powerful people, you can see to it expeditions are better funded so men like yourself will be well provisioned,' Lord Helton continued.

There was some truth in the proposal, enough to nearly tempt Conrad and make him as disgusted with himself as he was with his uncle. 'According to Mr Barrow, I can already persuade people to fund expeditions based on my reputation, not my ability to intimidate.'

'By bowing and scraping, begging and pleading? Follow me and you won't have to demean yourself or the Helton name in such a manner.'

Conrad leaned forward and caught the faint yellow in the whites of Helton's eyes. 'I wouldn't follow your example if it meant finding the Northwest Passage.'

'Then you're a fool. With my guidance, you could become one of the most powerful men in England, able to step into my place and continue to cloak the Helton name in honour and rewards. Women of rank will hurl themselves at you and you can choose a marchioness of privilege and influence instead of some peasant who picks through the dirt like a mudlark.'

Conrad levelled a hard glare at his uncle. 'I'll thank you not to address Miss Vickers in such a way.'

'You should thank me for driving her from London. She isn't worthy to bear the Helton name.'

'You haven't driven her away. In fact, she just returned this morning.' He said nothing of their broken engagement, unwilling to give the old man the satisfaction of learning he'd won. He'd figure it out in his own time.

'You're like your father.' Helton grimaced, trilling his long fingers over the handle of his walking stick. 'Wasting your strength and effort on someone so obviously beneath you.'

Conrad jerked to his feet and stared down at his uncle, wanting to thrash him for the insult to his mother and what he'd done to Katie. 'And you're a tired old man, full of hate and bitterness. If you think to savage Miss Vickers' reputation again, I'll see to it you regret it.'

'Don't you dare threaten me.' Helton shoved himself up to meet Conrad.

'Attack Miss Vickers again and I'll tell society the truth behind my father's illness and how you're to blame for it, and his early death.'

The wrinkles around Lord Helton's eyes smoothed as his lids opened wide with his shock. 'You have no proof of it.'

'You know as well as I do society doesn't need proof, just stories, especially when they concern such a well-loved and *esteemed* man like yourself.'

'Insults, how charming.' He narrowed his eyes at Conrad. 'Don't think you can intimidate me with threats. I didn't spend my whole life building up the Helton name only to have you drag it through the dirt with your poor choice of mate.'

'Thankfully, you won't be here to see such a travesty,' Conrad mocked.

'I'm not dead yet.'

'You are to me.' Conrad turned his back on the man and left, rigid with rage. The hours he'd spent in the library at Heims Hall watching his father cough and shiver, his body and spirit broken, made Conrad want to speed Lord Helton along on his journey to hell. The only thing which kept Conrad from returning to the sitting room to do it was the promise he'd made to his mother. She'd refused to let Conrad waste his life in search of revenge, or allow the ugly hate which fed Lord Helton eat Conrad up from the inside until there was nothing left but a bitter shell. She'd wanted Conrad to overcome his uncle by succeeding, not sinking to his disgusting level, believing providence would wreak justice upon the marquis far better than either she or Conrad could. It seemed with Preston's death and the consumption eating at his lungs, she was right.

His anger easing, Conrad continued down the

hallway in search of Henry, then paused at the library door, surprised to see Lord Mardling inside perusing the shelves. He'd been a fine captain before his brother died in a coaching accident, making him the earl. Lord Mardling could be found here most nights during the Season, but rarely in the winter.

Conrad entered the library and approached the earl. He had a great deal of his uncle's work to undo where Katie was concerned and Lord Mardling might be a man to help him. 'Lord Mardling, what are you doing in London in November?'

'Captain Essington, good to see you alive and well.' Lord Mardling looked over the tops of his spectacles. 'A council meeting has brought me and the countess back to London for the week. She isn't very happy about it, afraid of what people might say and all that. I rather enjoy the chance to return and select a few more items to keep me amused when the country snow sets in.'

Conrad flexed his hand at the thought of the coming bad weather. 'Do you still have your collection of exotic skeletons here in London?'

'I'd give up the paintings or the furniture before I'd let them go. Wife wouldn't want to hear me say it, but it's true.' The older man slipped off his spectacles and wiped them with his sleeve. 'What interest do you have in the skeletons? Looking to abandon the excitement of exploration for the study of anatomy?'

'No, it isn't for me but for—' He wasn't sure how to finish the sentence. 'Miss Vickers. I'm sure you remember her and her father from the Naturalist Society. She's quite the lady scientist. She'd be in no end of raptures if she could examine a few of your more exotic specimens.'

Lord Mardling slowly set the brass frames on his nose, taking great care to hook the ends behind his ears. 'Well, I— You see, Captain Essington, the thing is, I'm not sure it would be prudent to invite the young lady to my house. My wife has strange notions about her, stories she's heard and the like.'

Conrad fought to keep the shock from showing in his expression. For a man like Lord Mardling, who took little interest in gossip, to allude to such things was akin to Lord Helton attending a botany lecture. 'Lord Mardling, do you think I'd risk my reputation by associating with a woman of loose morals?'

'You were gone a long time, Captain Essington.' Lord Mardling plucked a book from the shelf and turned it over in his hands. 'And the rumours were quite specific about her and certain members of the Naturalist Society, especially Mr Rukin.'

Conrad fingered the lion-headed button on his coat, trying to slip from the suspicion coiling through him to maintain his current course. 'I assure you, Lord Mardling, there's no truth to the rumours, only lies invented by my uncle to strike at me and Miss Vickers. You know how he is, and you've been around long enough to remember the things he said about my parents and all the other whisperings.'

Rumours of Lord Helton's part in Conrad's father's poor health had been rife for years after his father had retired to the quiet of Heims Hall. It wasn't until Conrad was grown and his mother on the verge of joining her husband when she'd told him the truth. Conrad had secretly blamed his father for years for not standing up to his brother, and when he heard the reason why, he finally understood. His father had held his ground against the marquis in order to marry Conrad's mother and he'd paid a heavy price. Once again, Conrad admired the force of will his mother had used to keep the marquis from becoming Conrad's guardian after his father had died. His life would have been very different, and painfully empty, if she'd failed.

'Yes, quite a dreadful business all those whisperings, especially when your father was so ill.' Lord Mardling tapped his thumbs against the book. 'I hear Lord Helton isn't well.'

So, it wasn't just Conrad who'd noticed the changes in Helton, though Conrad had known too many sailors who'd lingered for years once they developed the cough to predict Lord Helton's imminent demise. 'Even if he's ailing, you know his type, they're too stubborn to die. They insist on holding on to make as many people as possible miserable before they go. It'll be years before I inherit.'

'Yes, I had a grandfather like that. Still, when Lord Helton does finally let go of life, you'll be the marquis.'

Lord Mardling looked curiously down his long

nose at Conrad, as if seeing for the first time Conrad's future and how doing him a favour now might benefit him later. The realisation made Conrad uneasy. He didn't want the influence of the Helton name to be the deciding factor in any man's dealings with him. His uncle had traded on his title for too long, coating it in a greasy slick of fear and intimidation. It would take a lifetime for Conrad to free it from the mire.

'For the moment I'm simply one captain asking another for a favour. What do you say? May we visit your collection?'

Lord Mardling stopped fiddling with the book and studied Conrad, as though weighing the desire to show off his impressive collection against the possible wrath of his wife. In the end, his pride won and he slapped the book against his palm. 'Why not? Come around tomorrow at noon. Wife will be off to the glovier and won't give us any trouble. I'll be happy to show the young lady my collection.'

'Thank you, Lord Mardling. I'm grateful.' Conrad would have been more grateful if Lady Mardling was included in the visit. For all Conrad's influence with the men, he knew the challenges both he and Katie faced were with the women. Though he wondered what such a success might achieve. It would take more than a few days to undo the months of damage to her reputation, and truth be told, it might never recover completely. There were many in society who still refused to recognise the Countess of Thurlow despite the years which had elapsed since her days on the stage and her marriage to the Earl. It didn't matter. Henry was right, Conrad didn't give up on those who depended on him, not mutinous crewmen, shrewish cousins, or wayward fiancées. Conrad would see this through, just as he'd seen his men through the bitterest of winters. In the end, as it had made a difference to his men and their lives, it would make a difference to Katie and perhaps ease his guilt at having left Aaron behind.

'Lord Mardling's?' Katie gasped as Conrad's chaise made the turn from Conrad's quiet neighbourhood into the crowded streets around Hyde Park.

'He's agreed to show you his collection of skeletons, included in which is an emu you may sketch.'

'That's very generous of him.' Katie tried to cover her nervousness with manners. She hadn't expected to wade in with the sharks of society so soon upon her return to London, yet it seemed as though Conrad was determined to make her swim. If she wanted his help, then she must follow him into the water, no matter how deep.

Despite last night's rain, the day was sunny and they drove with the hood of the chaise down. Above the tops of the crowded houses on their left, the blue sky spread out over the streets with only scattered grey clouds to mar its expanse. To their right, Hyde Park stretched out in softly rolling mounds of brown grass dotted by bare-limbed trees. The red-and-orange leaves covering the ground crinkled and swirled beneath the horse's feet as the chaise made steady progress.

The cool winter air rushed over Katie, piercing the folds of the blanket covering her lap. Her gloves weren't thick enough to protect her hands from the crisp air and neither was her blue pelisse or the green dress beneath. She slipped her hand under the blanket, struggling for warmth. If things had been different between her and Conrad, she could have pulled him close to settle the chills racing through her, but things weren't different and she kept the length of the seat between them.

To distract herself from the cold and the temptation of Conrad's heat, she watched the park pass by. Couples walked huddled together against the stiff breeze, the ladies' hands covered with warm muffs Katie envied. Despite the chill, it felt good to be out in the air. In the weeks since coming to London, she'd missed the smell and sight of nature. In the darkness of Cheapside, with the stench of smoke, horses and the river always in the air, she realised again how difficult it'd been to leave Whitemans Green. It was one tempting aspect of a possible journey to America—the chance to be among nature while putting her abilities with the pen and her knowledge of the natural world to use to earn her living. If only it wasn't so far from everything she'd ever known or the idea of leaving didn't remind her so much of her mother, running from her troubles instead of dealing with them.

The chaise stopped to wait for a stream of carts

and carriages to pass so it could turn left into Grosvenor Square, when a sight near the edge of the park caught Katie's notice. There, in an open-topped landau, sat Lord Helton, his riding companion none other than Miss Linton.

'How well acquainted is your cousin with Lord Helton?' Katie asked.

'Only in passing, though I think she'd commit murder if he'd simply nod at her.'

'Then she must have killed someone because she's with him in his carriage.' Katie motioned in the direction of the fine landau with the deep-green sides and richly appointed leather seats. It was drawn by two perfectly matched black horses and a driver in livery so well turned out he could have been the envy of the most deco-rated admiral in the Royal Navy.

'Well, I'll be, I hadn't thought him to look to a poor spinster to sire a new heir in a hurry.' Con-rad let out a low whistle. 'She must be in a twit-ter to be so honoured by the man.'

Conrad could make light of it, but seeing the marquis with Miss Linton raised the hairs on the back of Katie's neck. 'I don't think it's an heir he wants, but something else.'

'Like gossip.' It wasn't a comfort for Conrad to so quickly understand her meaning.

The traffic cleared and the chaise turned down the street leading to Grosvenor Square. Katie rubbed her hands together, glad to be driving away from the marquis. Whatever Miss Linton was telling Lord Helton, her being seen with Conrad would only work to confirm Miss Linton's lies and validate whatever ugly story the marquis was inventing.

Conrad settled back in his seat and tapped a steady beat on the edge of the phaeton. 'I'm sure nothing will come of it. There isn't anything she knows worth telling him.'

'Except we were alone together at Heims Hall.'

Conrad's fingers paused in the air before resuming their rhythm. 'She saw and knows nothing.'

'I hope you're right.' She and Conrad had always been careful when she'd been at Heims Hall with her father, enjoying their pleasures away from the house. To think they'd been so careless this time and it might come back to harm her burned. It was another of the many mistakes she'd made in regards to Conrad, ones she'd make sure to never repeat, though she wasn't likely to get the chance. Her current time with Conrad was limited and once he was done helping her, he'd turn to the affection of another woman, one who was more willing than her to tolerate his long absences. It shouldn't matter to Katie, but strangely enough, it did.

'Don't look so despondent,' Conrad soothed, not guessing the true reason behind her frown. 'There's little Lord Helton can say or do to hurt us.'

'Of course there is. He has the ear of everyone in society and their respect.'

'It isn't respect, it's fear and the first chance those he's intimidated get to turn on him they will and I'll gladly help them. I know things about him he doesn't want others to know. He'll stay silent about us, or he'll regret it.'

'Either way, they'll listen to him long before they listen to us. I'm surprised Lord Mardling was so gracious as to invite me to his house since he sits with your uncle in the House of Lords.'

'Lord Mardling is one of the few men with enough money and influence of his own to disregard my uncle's threats. More than likely he's helping me simply to spite my uncle.'

'Is that wise?' She knew the damage the marquis could do with a few words and how difficult it was to recover from such a strike.

'That's for him to decide and, apparently, he has.' Conrad's mouth drew tight at the corners, the unexpected tension making Katie uneasy. 'Though in the course of our conversation, he alluded to a rumour concerning you and Mr Rukin.'

Katie gripped the side of the chaise as it hit a hole in the road. A curricle carrying two purple-clad matrons passed them driving the opposite way. Even beneath the shadow of their hats Katie could see the whites of their eyes widening with shock before they huddled together in furious conversation. 'It's a lie like all the rest.'

'Lord Mardling isn't usually a man to gossip.'

'Apparently he is or he wouldn't have mentioned such a thing.'

'Perhaps he told me to warn me.'

'About what?' she demanded, hating this cagy approach. It wasn't like him and it troubled her as much as him entertaining the vile rumour.

This one possessed more truth than any of the others, a truth she didn't want to discuss or remember, not while Conrad fixed her with such suspicion.

'That's exactly what I'd like to know.'

'Would you like me to go through each and every story and discredit them for you?'

'Yes, then I won't be taken by surprise whenever a new one surfaces.'

'Which they are sure to do now that your uncle has returned.' The chaise rolled to a stop beneath the portico of a large house and behind the tall, wide columns separating the front from the traffic of the street beyond. A footman hurried forward to open the chaise door. 'I don't believe now is the time to discuss it.'

'No, but at some point we will.'

Of course they would. As she'd learned from her mother, rumours attached to women never truly disappeared and nothing, not marriage, distance, time or even the truth could make them fade.

The unease Conrad's accusations created increased as Katie entered Lord Mardling's grand hall. Katie looked up at the plaster ceiling and the cherubs gazing down at them from their painted clouds. She and her father had passed this house many times and, despite knowing of the impressive collection of animal specimens inside, she'd never once imagined entering it. Naturalists of Lord Mardling's pedigree didn't consort with men like her father.

'Welcome, Captain Essington, and you, too, Miss Vickers.' Lord Mardling was all smiles as he came down the stairs to greet them. 'It's a treat to show off my humble collection. Though it doesn't exactly rival Mr Hunter's in variety, I'm proud of it. I should be getting a monkey soon from a friend in India. Wife hates this hobby of mine, but I hate paying her exorbitant dress allowance so I believe we're even.'

'Thank you again for having us.' Conrad smiled for the earl, but the tension from the carriage showed itself in the tightness of his stance. Katie wondered if he regretted vouching for her, especially with a man he'd one day outrank. If he did, it was too late for either of them to change course now.

Lord Mardling proudly hooked his fingers

in the pockets of his waistcoat as he turned to Katie. 'Captain Essington told me something about your theory, though not enough to give it all away. I'm curious to read your paper when you publish it.'

'May I dedicate it to you, my lord?' Katie asked, emboldened by his enthusiasm. With Lord Mardling's support, it would be difficult for others to dismiss her work.

Lord Mardling's smile stiffened at the corners. 'Let's discuss such things when the time comes, no point rushing into it. Why, there might be men more esteemed than me who deserve your praise.'

Katie's spirits dropped. She could practically hear the story of her and Mr Rukin rolling through his mind. He must want to vex Lord Helton very much to have agreed to Conrad's request. She almost wished he hadn't. She was tired of reliving the past year and having people stare and whisper at her, especially with Conrad now casting the same aspersions her way.

'Come, I keep the collection in here.' He ushered them towards the back of the house.

Whatever misgivings Katie held about being

here and with Conrad, they were forgotten the moment Lord Mardling pushed open the double doors to the large room filled with books and skeletons. A tall bank of windows at the back arched up over the top like a conservatory to let in the sun. In the bright light, Katie read the small print on the spines of the books crowding the many shelves. It wasn't all biology, but old works from the time of good King Henry, Greek writers and medieval texts. Though she couldn't read Latin, she knew enough from her father's anatomy lessons to recognise a few of the words in gilded letters on the old spines.

This is what money can purchase. It'd bought some northern factory owner her father's collection. Once Conrad became Marquis of Helton, he'd have access to such wealth while Katie would continue to struggle to earn her living. The iniquity of it stung and in the darkest parts of her mind, the idea she'd given up on Conrad and his future position as a marquis by leaving Heims Hall grated. However, she wasn't mercenary enough to marry simply for her own selfish reasons, or foolish enough to raise herself to such exalted heights and risk being shunned by the *ton*. It was difficult enough dealing with those of her own class and profession without suffering the pelting insults and cuts of the better sort.

She made her way past the impressive collection of animal bones displayed on red velvet beneath glass, focusing on them instead of all her other troubles. Aquatic animals dominated one case, while the next held reptiles, followed by small mammals and then birds. Katie looked over the skeletons in the last case, not finding one with a furcula like the creature she was studying.

It wasn't until she reached the tall case at the end and spied the creature inside that her lack of money and all her other problems were forgotten. In the tall case stood the full skeleton of the emu, its toes and the position of its legs in the hips so similar to the creature's it made her heart race.

'Will this do?' Conrad asked.

'It will.' Katie moved forward to lay a gloved hand on the glass separating her from the emu, jealous of Lord Mardling and the money which allowed him to amass such an impressive collection. Her father had done his best to mimic these great men, but he'd never possessed their means, though at times he'd spend as though he did to acquire a rare fossil. The rest he'd obtained through hours of patient digging and hard work, his pride in his collection no less than Lord Mardling's. It was his pride in what he'd achieved which had made the Naturalist Society's attack so cruel and increased Katie's pain when she was forced to sell the collection. However, if he'd ever thought of her and her future, set aside even a small amount of the money he'd paid for the more exotic items to pay bills, or employed even the smallest effort to maintain his medical practice, Katie might not have had to part with the fossils.

'Captain Essington, I have a lovely French wine in the drawing room,' Lord Mardling announced. 'Would you care to help me consume it while Miss Vickers completes her study?'

Conrad turned to Katie. 'Do you mind if I leave you?'

'Not at all.' She needed peace to work. 'I'll be fine.'

Conrad handed Katie the sketchbook and the

case of pencils, something of concern replacing the subtle condemnation he'd shown her in the carriage, as if he regretted leaving. She wished he regretted having mentioned the rumours of Mr Rukin more, then she might believe it was his care for her and not the lost chance to pester her with his suspicions which made him hesitant to leave. His willingness to believe the gossip was a sad reminder of why, when his current help was done, there was no future for them together.

'We'll be down the hall in the library. The footman can help you if you require anything,' Lord Mardling instructed as he led Conrad from the room.

Once alone, Katie dragged a chair from a nearby escritoire and set it in front of the case, determined to focus and not waste this precious opportunity fretting about Conrad or anything else. She opened the sketchbook across her knees, selected the sharpest pencil and set to work. She sketched the creature as a whole, then moved closer to complete a detailed drawing of its feet, hips, legs and chest.

More than once while she worked, the deep

roll of Conrad's voice through the quiet house teased her. The steady cadence of his words would make her smudge a detail and long for his presence, silent judgement and all. The wide room with the dead animals felt cold and her pencil moved slower over the paper without him there to joke and tease her like he used to at Heims Hall. She wanted to speak with him about what she was seeing and how similar the creature's stance was to the emu's. Such discussions would have to wait until later and the quiet of the chaise, assuming his demand for information about Mr Rukin didn't dominate the conversation.

Her pencil slipped, leaving a marring line across the thigh bone. Katie smudged it away, wishing the last year was as easily erased. She didn't want to talk about Mr Rukin, or the accusations attached to her by him and so many other men. She picked up her knife and roughly sharpened the end of the pencil, making the shavings flick off the wood and fly over her skirt to land on the floor. She hadn't earned her knowledge on her back, but by the same long hours of research as any of the men. Her work held as much merit as theirs and could stand up to the scrutiny of a hundred different societies.

She set down the knife, cleaned up the shavings and returned to drawing with a new determination. For all the creature's similarities to this bird, it was astoundingly different and she'd be the one to reveal it to the world. It would force the Naturalist Society to take note of her and give them a presentation to debate and discuss for years.

The light in the room shifted as Katie continue to sketch. Then the clock on the mantel began to chime the two o'clock hour. Numerous drawings filled her book and she was putting the final details on the emu's head when she caught the swish of footsteps behind her. She ignored them, thinking it a footman or maid since she could still hear Conrad and Lord Mardling chatting down the hall.

'And who, may I ask, are you?' a woman demanded.

Katie jumped to her feet and whirled around, sending her pencil case clattering to the floor.

The woman might not have recognised Katie, but Katie knew her at once.

'Good afternoon, Lady Mardling.' She dipped a respectful curtsy.

The shock which swept across Lady Mardling's face, then settled into a horrified sneer, was enough to make it clear Lady Mardling knew exactly who Katie was.

'What are you doing here in my husband's curio room unaccompanied?' the countess demanded, shoulders squared, ready to do battle.

Katie fought to remain calm, seeing no reason for the woman's hostility. She'd done nothing wrong except return to London after the damage Lord Helton had wrought and dared to show her face in the Mardling house. There were worse sins a woman could commit, though in society's eyes this was one of the gravest.

'Your husband has graciously allowed me to sketch this bird for my research.' Katie picked up the pencil case, then closed the sketchbook, tucking it under one arm.

Lady Mardling looked down her aquiline nose at Katie as though she were some kind of street urchin who'd crept in to steal one of the long strands of pearls wrapped around her neck. 'And what exactly did you do for my husband to make him so eager to provide access to his collection?'

Katie stiffened in shame, biting back a vicious reminder of the rumours about Lady Mardling and a certain French nobleman which had circulated last year. She would get nowhere with Lord Mardling if she insulted his wife, nor would standing up to such insults further Conrad's efforts to clear Katie's reputation. Instead, it would only prove the Countess's suspicions about Katie's character and provide yet another story for people to use against her. Once again she was forced to endure the taunts and insults of others while she remained quiet and waited for their attention to turn elsewhere.

Katie dared a quick glance over the woman's shoulder to the doorway, but it was depressingly empty. To hope Conrad might appear to extricate her from this situation was not only futile but foolish. He hadn't been there through all the other insults she'd borne; she could hardly expect him to be present for this one. She would face the woman as she had all the others, alone.

'Well?' Lady Mardling demanded, eyeing her

with all the contempt with which she might examine a stain on an expensive gown.

Katie met her imperious look, determined not to fidget, or fumble her words. Katie had been invited into this house. She wouldn't cower before its chatelaine like some criminal. 'I didn't seek out your husband and press him for an invitation. Captain Essington spoke to Lord Mardling on my behalf and is here now in the other room with your husband.'

Lady Mardling came forward, the whisper of her expensive silk gown over the carpet nearly as threatening as her disapproving glare. 'My husband may see fit to cavort with those so obviously beneath him, but I refuse to pollute my house with people of low character, no matter how they managed to gain entrance.'

The pencils rattled in their case as Katie gripped them tight, holding back the rage welling inside her. She'd never done anything to deserve such treatment except love a man above her in station whose uncle had been determined to separate them.

'Is everything all right, Miss Vickers?' Conrad strolled into the room, moving like a sure ship upon steady waters. The light from the large windows heightened his square jaw and the cleft at the end of his chin. Relief rushed through Katie and it was all she could do not to run to be by his side.

Lord Mardling followed behind him, taking quick stock of the situation and looking less gregarious than when he'd left her. Katie held her breath, wondering if the high man would turn on her and apologise to his wife for having soiled her house with a woman of Katie's reputation, or if he would stand up to her and let her know it was his right to invite whomever he wished. He did neither, but remained silent by the door, obviously hoping not to be noticed.

'Good afternoon, Lady Mardling.' Conrad paused to bow before coming to stand beside Katie, making his support for her clear. Even if he acted out of duty, instead of the deep regard he'd once harboured for her, the one she'd killed, she didn't care. He was here at last and she was thankful.

Lady Mardling offered Conrad a polite curtsy in return, her lips twisting into an unsteady smile. 'Captain Essington, what an honour it is to have you grace our house.'

It was clear Lady Mardling's admiration for Conrad had more to do with his new position as a future marquis than as an esteemed explorer. It provided a glimpse into the future Katie might have known if she hadn't broken the engagement. Regret mingled with nervousness. Perhaps she shouldn't have tossed Conrad away or allowed her fears to govern her instead of her heart.

No, it wasn't fear which had guided her, but experience and good sense. As a marchioness, Katie would be forced into these people's company and her children made to endure the rumours whirling about her, just as she'd heard time and again the stories of her mother's downfall and the mistakes she'd made with Katie's father. Katie wouldn't put a child through such torture, not for all the manors, diamonds and titles in England.

'I was enjoying a fine conversation with your husband. I'm glad to see you've extended an equally warm welcome to Miss Vickers.' Conrad smiled.

Lady Mardling's back lost some of its indignant straightness, though she wasn't entirely cowed. 'Miss Vickers informed me of my husband's invitation to view his collection.'

'Your husband is a very generous patron of science.' Conrad laced his hands behind his back. 'He's keen to get at the truth of a matter instead of relying on the speculations and theories of others, especially those who are often misinformed.'

'Of course it's always better to learn things straight from the source than it is to trust others for your opinion, though sometimes the opinions of others are correct,' she countered.

'It's a rare occurrence.'

Lady Mardling blanched, her puce gown emphasising the sudden lack of colour in her skin. Before she could think of a retort, Conrad shifted his attention to Katie, offering her his arm.

'Shall we be off?'

Katie hesitated, eager to be gone, but unable to believe he'd defended her against Lady Mardling after being so suspicious of her in the chaise. Deciding to accept his help instead of questioning it, she took hold of his arm with her free hand, hoping the slight tremble gracing her fingers went unnoticed by him and Lady Mardling. While the countess might have missed it, Conrad didn't, laying his hand over hers and giving it a steadying squeeze.

'Thank you, Lady Mardling, and you, Lord Mardling, for your hospitality today.' Conrad bowed as befitting a man descended from peers.

'My pleasure,' Lord Mardling mumbled, garnering a threatening look from his wife.

Conrad escorted Katie to the carriage as though he were already the Marquis of Helton. Katie maintained his easy pace despite wanting to bolt from the house and all the way back to the country, though there was nothing left there for her to return to. The house in Whitemans Green was gone, like her reputation.

It wasn't long before she and Conrad were in the chaise and Lord Mardling's impressive house was receding into the distance.

'Don't let Lady Mardling discourage you,' Conrad encouraged. 'She's but one woman and an ignorant one from what Lord Mardling tells me.'

'Yes, but many share her opinion, just as you seemed to on the way here.'

Conrad trilled his fingers on his thigh. 'If you'd tell me the truth, it might set both our minds at ease.'

Katie stared out of the chaise at the grand houses, catching through their windows the movement of a maid of some regal lady. Conrad had stood up to Lady Mardling, risking his good name to defend hers. Despite his doubts when they were together, in public he'd showed faith in her. She owed him an explanation.

'The night after the Naturalist Society turned on me and my father, I wanted to make it right, to help him. I went to Mr Rukin's to ask for his assistance. I knew he'd been at the meeting and he'd always been so supportive of us before. I thought he would be again. I was wrong.' She picked a sliver of wood off her skirt and flung it out of the chaise. 'We were alone in his study when he tried to force himself on me, saying if I wanted his help I'd submit. Thankfully, his housekeeper interrupted him and I got away. Father and I left London that night. In my absence, a different story spread, one your uncle encouraged and I couldn't refute because no one believed me and there was no one to challenge him.'

* * *

Conrad's heart dropped as if the unseen hole under the snow which had swallowed his best sledge dog had opened beneath him. Suddenly Mr Prevett's advance on her in West Sussex made terrible sense, as did Mr Rukin's objection to her yesterday.

'You should have told me sooner. If I'd known the truth, I never would have said the things I did, or blamed you.' *Or failed you again.* She'd come to Conrad for help and he'd treated her no better than those men, the ones whose heads he wanted to rip from their shoulders.

'There was no point in telling you sooner. There's nothing you could have done.'

'I could have broken the man's neck yesterday, or ground Mr Prevett into the ground.' Conrad banged his fist against the squab, disgusted at society, his uncle, himself. 'I'll see to it Mr Rukin is driven from the Naturalist Society, his work discredited. A man so disreputable in his personal life is surely shoddy in his research. I won't let him get away with what he's done.'

'You'll do to him what your uncle has done to me?'

'They deserve it, you don't.'

She stared out of the carriage at the passing trees, her expression as desolate as those of his men when they'd watched *Gorgon* founder. 'I shouldn't have come back to London.'

The resignation marring her features turned Conrad's blood to ice. She couldn't give up, he wouldn't allow her to surrender to her fears, or his stupid, idiotic doubts. 'Don't let them intimidate you.'

'It isn't intimidation, it's exhaustion,' she shot back. 'I'm tired of fighting the men, the women and all their petty rumours.'

He caught her hand in his and rubbed the skin above the glove with his thumb, shocked by the coldness. 'You're frustrated. It will pass, I promise.'

'It's more than that. You have no idea what it's like to face such censure again and again and again.'

'You think I didn't see what the marquis's relentless attacks on my parents did to my mother and father? My mother might've had the strength to stand up to it, but my father didn't and my uncle destroyed him. I don't want the same thing to happen to you.'

She tried to pull back her hand, but he refused to let go. 'You can't be with me every day, or challenge every person who whispers against me.'

'Maybe not, but Lady Mardling and her ilk are not the only society in London.' He shifted to be beside her on the squab, heartened when she didn't move away. 'I've been invited by Miss Etheldred Benett to attend a dinner party tomorrow night at her house. You're to attend as my guest.'

'I'm to meet Miss Benett?' Her stiff hand relaxed in his and the excitement brightening her eyes eased the worry scratching at Conrad's insides.

'And other influential men, the kind who don't look askance at a lady scientist. Miss Benett has cultivated their support, you will, too,' he assured her, trying to draw out more of the optimistic Katie.

The hope in Katie's eyes dimmed. 'As a woman she can hardly afford the taint of associating with someone of my reputation.'

'Miss Benett is hardly one for convention, or the opinions of polite society. She's assured me you're most welcome.'

Katie watched Conrad's thumb continue to make circles on the inside of her wrist, his skin warming hers as much as his body beside hers made the lap blanket unnecessary. As elated as she was at the prospect of meeting Miss Benett, with Lady Mardling's remonstrations still ringing in her ears, she was reluctant to accept the generous invitation. Though there were many who admired and accepted the lady geologist, there were more closed-minded society men who cast aspersions on her interest and made her struggle to be accepted as difficult as Katie's.

The leather glove stretched over the back of Conrad's hand as he continued to hold hers, his assurances along with the steady stroke of his thumb easing her concerns. If Miss Benett was willing to consort with Katie, in spite of the rumours, it was an opportunity she must seize. Attending would allow her to cultivate the acquaintance of many well-regarded figures and perhaps find a position as an illustrator or an assistant. It was imperative she establish herself in some meaningful employment before Conrad sailed off to his next adventure and left her alone.

She turned her hand over in his, trapping his thumb beneath hers, not wanting to let go. For all their troubles, London would be lonely without him. 'I'll accompany you.'

'Good.' He slid his arm over the back of the squabs behind her, his fingers brushing her neck as he moved. They sat so close she could tilt her head to rest it against his shoulder if she wanted, if he wanted her to. The invitation to draw together lay in the weight of his hand in hers and the steady rise and fall of his chest beneath his dark redingote, but neither of them moved, unwilling to wade into such uncertainty.

'Conrad.' A man's voice carried over the din of the street. 'Driver, stop the chaise.'

Katie and Conrad slid apart on the squabs, Katie's hand instantly cold without his as the driver pulled the horse to a stop.

They turned to watch Henry Sefton bring his mount alongside the carriage. He wore a light-blue coat with a white lining reminiscent of his naval uniform. The clean lines of his sleeves blended seamlessly into the dark black riding gloves covering his hands.

Katie tried not to react as she noticed the missing finger on his left hand, despite the deft way he hid it by removing his D'Orsay hat. 'Miss Vickers, it's a pleasure to see you again.'

'And a hearty welcome to you, Lieutenant Sefton.' She wondered how much he knew of the end of her and Conrad's engagement. It was difficult to gauge in the liveliness of his greeting, one which discouraged her from pitying his wound. If he refused to allow it to dampen his spirit, then neither would she. 'I'm glad to see you looking so fit and well after your trip north.'

'It's a pleasure to be back.' He tapped his D'Orsay down over his dark hair, his cheer fading as he turned to Conrad. 'Mr Barrow wants to see us at once.'

Katie met Conrad's eyes from across the seat and her heart dropped.

'What does he want?' Conrad asked, the excitement which used to mark any summons from Mr Barrow noticeably absence.

'Only one way to find out.' Lieutenant Sefton worked to keep his horse steady beside the chaise, as glum about the news as Conrad.

'Then I'll meet you at the Admiralty within the hour.'

Mr Sefton nodded to Katie, then rode off, giving his jumpy horse free rein to trot across the cobblestone.

A gravity as heavy as a mine cart settled over the carriage. Conrad stared out into the traffic, one hand on his chin and the other tight on his thigh.

'Do you think he's going to offer you a command?' Katie asked, rubbing the outline of her ring through her glove.

'I don't know what he has in mind for me.' Conrad's voice lacked his usual veneration for his employer, making Katie's fingers still on the ring. If he no longer held Mr Barrow in such high esteem, then perhaps there was hope for a continued friendship between her and Conrad, and a chance he might remain in England. 'I'd best see you home.'

'Perhaps I may examine the creature this evening?' Katie prodded, trying to coax back the connection they'd enjoyed a few moments ago.

For all her eagerness not to rely on him, to her shame, she did. 'Aunt Florence can accompany me as a chaperon.'

'Whatever you like,' he replied casually, as he stared out over the street to where Henry had disappeared around a corner, his expression grave. 'Mr Barrow probably wants to discuss the publication of my journal, nothing else.'

She wasn't sure who he was trying to reassure, her or himself.

Chapter Seven

Conrad and Henry strode down the halls of the Admiralty, passing magnificent paintings of the Battle of Waterloo and the more famous ships of the line covering the walls. Despite his confident steps, worry dogged Conrad. It wasn't only the meeting with Mr Barrow which pressed down on him, but Katie's revelation in the carriage. Conrad had been a heel to condemn her because of the rumours, proving himself little better than half the members of the Naturalist Society. He'd allowed his anger to prejudice him against her instead of believing in the woman he'd once loved, the one he continued to care deeply about. It was difficult to admit his feelings still coursed so strongly, but it was impossible to deny, not when her story of Mr Rukin's attack made him want to destroy the man. He'd make it his priority to ensure Mr Rukin paid for what he'd done, as soon as he concluded his business with the Second Secretary.

Up ahead, the imposing double doors to Mr Barrow's office came into view. Out of the corner of Conrad's eye, he caught the white flash of Henry's glove as he swung his arm in time to his steps. Conrad fingered a button on his coat, the reminder of Henry's scars making him just as uneasy as his misstep with Katie and his worries about the summons. Conrad dropped his hand to his side and stood up straighter. Whatever it was, he would face it, just as he'd faced and overcome every other challenge in life. He was no coward.

They paused long enough to announce themselves to the secretary who ushered them into Mr Barrow's office.

'Welcome, gentlemen. Please, be seated.' Mr Barrow rose from behind his desk and waved them into the caned chairs situated in front of it. The nautical charts and paintings of shipwrecks on the walls were lost in the clutter of spears, shields and tropical totems making the office more of a curiosity shop than a space for the Second Secretary.

As Conrad removed his cocked bicorn and settled himself against the caning, he attempted to gauge something of the reason for this meeting in the older gentleman's pale eyes. The man who'd scraped his way up from humble beginnings to become first an interpreter to the English ambassador to China and later Second Secretary of the Admiralty revealed nothing. He stared at Conrad with the same impassiveness he always displayed whether he was reading a report or handing him a new commission.

'Thank you both for coming so quickly. We have a great deal to accomplish in a short amount of time,' Mr Barrow announced.

'A short amount of time until what, sir?' The joints in Conrad's fingers began to ache.

'You leave for Melville Island, near Australia. You'll determine if Melville Island or any of the smaller ones around it can support a settlement. His Majesty is keen to secure our trading position there before the Dutch can settle theirs. Can't have them controlling trade in the area.'

'Sir, do you think it's wise for me to take command, especially so soon after the loss of *Gor-gon*?' He flinched from adding more details and at the faint weakness the question implied.

'No ice to worry about so far south.' Mr Barrow stroked the point of his chin. 'Besides, you came back, even if the ship didn't, bringing with you much-needed information.'

'It wasn't just the ship I left in the north, but Mr Dubhach,' Conrad reminded his superior, struggling to remain deferential and failing, judging by the warning look Henry threw at him.

'Yes, terrible business that, but you aren't the first captain to lose a man or two.' Mr Barrow dismissed his words with a flick of his hand. 'Most come back having buried half their crew from fever, assuming they come back at all. Look at Captain Tuckey—he barely reached the Congo before he was dead of dengue. You've only ever lost the one ship and the one man. A commendable record given the number of expeditions you've led.'

'He was an excellent first mate, perhaps the best.' Conrad chafed under Mr Barrow's callous response to the end of Aaron's life. It was knowledge Mr Barrow sought and he was willing to pay the cost of obtaining it in men's lives, caring little for the death of anyone beneath the rank of lieutenant. Common men like Aaron might be of little consequence to men like Mr Barrow, but the loss of a friend was one Conrad couldn't forget, or forgive himself for.

'Of course he was,' Barrow replied blithely as he sat forward, ready to move on with his business. 'And it'll be difficult for you to find a man to replace him, especially on such short notice, but there's to be no delay. Funding has been granted and I'm appointing you leader. You'll depart as soon as the ship is victualled and outfitted and you've chosen your crew.'

Conrad exchanged an uneasy look with Henry. Neither of them had expected to face the challenge of another expedition so soon. Conrad's grip on his hat began to weaken and he set it on the chair beside him. The weakness disgusted him as much as the discovery of Boatswain James breaking in to the stores to steal precious food had during their entrapment.

'How were you able to secure funding so fast?' It was nearly unheard of.

'Surprisingly, Lord Helton pushed it through.'

Conrad tightened his fingers into a fist over the chair's arm to cover both his anger and the trembling. This was his uncle's attempt to separate Conrad from Katie and bring Conrad to heel for not following his lead. It forced Conrad to choose between two unappealing decisions—thwart the marquis and relinquish the command or accept it and leave Katie. Lord Helton was wrong if he thought to back Conrad into a corner. Conrad wasn't about to shirk from duty or let Katie and the Discovery Service down, no matter how much the acceptance of a new command made his fingers shake. He would find a way to make sure she was secure before he left and see to it his uncle knew he wouldn't win or bully Conrad.

'I'll send word when I need you to oversee the purchase of your personal supplies,' Mr Barrow continued, oblivious to Conrad's silence or lack of enthusiasm for the new mission. 'Good day, gentlemen.'

Their futures sealed, Mr Barrow ushered them from the room.

It was a sober leaving, with none of the elation

which had greeted the appointing of their last command. Then, they'd indulged in a drunken celebration with fellow officers, facing death as though they were invincible. They weren't, as they'd discovered in the Arctic. Any drinking tonight would be to dull the realisation they were leaving again, not to celebrate it.

Once outside, beneath the tall columns marking the entrance to the Admiralty, Henry adjusted the ribbon on the cock of his bicorn, his maimed hand hidden by the hat. 'I didn't imagine we'd be sent out before late spring.'

'Neither did I.' Nor did he think he'd once again be the cause of his friend's misery. If it wasn't for Conrad's blatant defiance of Lord Helton, Henry might have been allowed more time to recover here in England. So might Conrad. 'I could select a different lieutenant and you could stay.'

Henry pulled the hat down over his forehead with a determined tug. 'I wouldn't dream of relinquishing my place any more than you would.'

'I'm not so sure.' It was the first time he'd ever

considered declining a command and it sickened him.

'So you'll stay then, angering Mr Barrow and being placed on half-pay so you can grow old and fat like Captain Standish?' Henry slipped his pipe from his pocket and fingered the wizened face engraved on the bowl.

'No.' He'd suffered a great shock in the north and it would take more than a few bottles of port or time in London for him to fully recover, but he would, he must. He opened and closed his fist, fighting to keep his fingers pressed against his palms. The mistakes he'd made in the north had shaken his confidence and he'd have little more than a month to regain it. There was nothing as deadly, not storms or disease, as a captain unable to command and he wasn't about to disappoint another crew.

'Then it looks as though we'll set sail.' The pipe clicked against Henry's teeth as he bit down on the stem. 'Miss Vickers will be as thrilled to hear of our new command as we are.'

Conrad groaned at the reminder of the other

challenge facing him before departure. 'She hasn't forgiven me for the last voyage.'

'Then you'll have a great deal to atone for between now and when we depart.' Henry went off down the stairs, leaving Conrad in the shadow of the pillars.

Conrad stood in the doorway of the sitting room, watching Katie as she bent over her sketchbook, her slender fingers curled around the pencil as it scratched against the paper. The sun had disappeared behind the dark clouds covering the city, strengthening the orange light from the candles burning around the room. Two plates of refreshments sat on the tea table, one with crumbs, the other untouched, the cheese slightly greasy from the warmth. Only the sketch taking place beneath her nimble fingers consumed Katie now, not hunger, exhaustion or anything else. It reminded Conrad of the numerous times he'd left his dinner to grow cold in his cabin while he'd stood on deck to watch a foreign coast grow larger on the horizon, or to examine a herd of creatures passing on a nearby shore.

'I see you're still here.' Conrad approached the

table and picked up one of the many sketches littering the perimeter.

Mrs Anderson slept in a deep wingback chair near the fireplace, her mouth agape as she snored softly.

'You know I have a difficult time stopping once I begin.' Katie set down her pencil and rolled her wrist against the stiffness. 'The quickness with which I must complete my paper is not helping.'

'I wish I could give you more time to prepare, but I'm afraid I can't.' Their days together had already been truncated by Mr Barrow.

Mrs Anderson snorted, then mumbled something before settling back into her nap.

'Your aunt is failing in her duties as chaperon,' Conrad teased.

'If she is, it's your fault. She isn't accustomed to rich food and richer wine.' Katie's humour eased some of the distress which had accompanied Conrad home from the Admiralty. 'How was your meeting with Mr Barrow?'

Conrad set down the sketch, careful not to block her view of the creature.

'Quite routine,' he lied, hesitant to inform her

of his new appointment, knowing she'd view it and him with the same disgust she'd shown in the country. Even if he owed her nothing beyond the help he'd already promised, he wanted to enjoy more of this Katie, the happy, peaceful one who reminded him of the better days before the tragedy of the Arctic. 'He had concerns about the progress of my book.'

'You're having difficulty finishing it?' Katie took up a small knife to sharpen the end of her pencil.

He picked up one of the curled shavings and crushed it between his fingers. 'It's not a time I wish to remember in detail, yet I find, quite often, I can't forget.'

She set down the knife and pencil and tilted her head to study Conrad. 'It must be difficult to tell so many stories of your struggles to all the people who want to know.'

'It is.' Her gentle voice was inviting, leading him into a confidence he couldn't fight. He'd been vulnerable with Katie so many times before, and though she'd run out on him, she'd never disparaged his weakness, only allowing herself to be guided by her own. 'Some nights

I don't sleep. I can still hear the crash of ice in the distance, slowly coming for us. I thought it would end when I came home, but it hasn't.' He straightened one of the creature's ribs, stone cold beneath his shaking fingers. 'I still see my men shivering in the tent, their cheeks sunken, their eyes blaming me for their misery, but Aaron's eyes haunt me the most. When he rose to leave the tent, I could see his desperation, the desire to be free. I should've chased after him. I shouldn't have let him go.'

Katie reached out and took his hand, her gentle squeeze calming the trembles. 'It's not your fault, Conrad. You did the best you could under circumstances no one could have foreseen, or expected you to survive.'

He let go of her, unworthy of her or anyone's comfort. 'It was my fault we were trapped.'

'You couldn't have guessed the weather.'

Conrad stepped up to the window and stared out into the grey London evening. Over a church spire, lightning flashed, followed by a deep roll of thunder. The shame of her having noticed his shakes was equal only to the guilt of what he'd done. He shouldn't tell her, or anyone, but it weighed too heavily on him for him to remain silent. 'The weather didn't trap us, my ego did. I should have made for home sooner, not pressed on, but there was an inlet, an open channel of water and I followed it, hoping it would lead to the Northwest Passage. The only thing it led to was ice.'

Thunder rumbled through the sky overhead and in the deep roll Conrad heard the crack of icebergs closing in around *Gorgon*. He opened and closed his hand, willing away the memories, but they wouldn't leave him.

The swish of skirts overcame the fading echo of the distant thunder and Katie was beside him, her small hand cupping the curve of his shoulder. The faint brush of her body against his drew him back to London and away from the past. 'You were following orders, doing what Mr Barrow commanded.'

'No, I was the one who made the decision to stay, to sail on even as winter was approaching. Henry wasn't the only one who lost fingers; others lost toes to the cold or teeth to scurvy. Some nearly lost their minds in the endless nights and desolation. I tried to distract them as best I could. Keeping up the routine onboard ship, teaching to read those who couldn't, encouraging games and whatever else I could to keep them from thinking of the cold, the darkness and our increasing hunger.' He turned to her, and for a moment the understanding Katie, the one he'd dreamed of during so many nights in the desolate wasteland, stood in front of him again. If only he was worthy of such sympathy. 'We were buried alive, Katie, and when the light finally returned and I thought we'd be free, the ship sank. My men looked to me to keep them safe, to act like a leader, but instead I sacrificed them for my own aggrandisement just like my uncle has been willing to sacrifice so many people for his.'

She laid her hands on either side of his face. 'No, Conrad, you're better than that, you're better than him.'

'You don't understand. I failed, myself, my men, you.' Conrad slid his hand over hers, her faith in him bittersweet because he couldn't hold on to it. In less than a month he'd sail off and she wouldn't wait for him this time. Instead, she'd curse him again for going. Until then, he wouldn't disappoint her, or leave her to suffer as he had before. He pressed his forehead against hers, screwing his eyes shut tight. 'I won't let you down again, Katie.'

It was a promise to her, his men, himself, and one he was desperate to believe in and to keep.

'I know,' Katie whispered, her breath easing the tension pooling inside him.

'Do you?' He needed her faith as much as his own.

'Yes.'

He opened his eyes to meet hers and the cold distance which had hardened them against him in West Sussex was gone. In their blue he experienced something of the salvation he'd known when he and his men had crested the last hill of ice to see the whaling ship anchored in the glittering bay. As then, he could hardly trust his troubled senses to believe what was before him.

He slid one arm around her waist and she melded against him, as tender and accepting as she'd been before he'd left. Despite the cold which had built a wall of doubt and distrust between them, some vestige of their love lingered. He was cautious of scaring it away just when it was growing bold enough to appear, but he wouldn't be denied the tranquillity of her embrace.

Conrad pressed his mouth to hers, near groaning at the sweetness of her lips beneath his. Her pulse fluttered against his fingertips as he cupped her face with his hands to draw her deeper into him. His body stiffened against her stomach, desire rising up in him to blot out his better sense. He'd dreamed of her warmth in the coldest days of winter, longed for their breaths to mingle as they did now. Here was the Katie he remembered, the brave, passionate woman from the Downs who'd captivated him with both her beauty and her intelligence. He never should have allowed her to get away from him so easily or to cave in to her doubts before he'd left, but he should have fought for her as hard as he'd fought to live.

Her fingers tightened against the skin of his neck as he took her earlobe between his teeth, her hair sweeping his cheek as he sucked the soft flesh. Brushing the skin of her neck with his lips, he traced the long arch of it to the hollow. Flicking his tongue against the warmth, her sigh gave him courage and he bent down to press a kiss against the top of her rounded breasts through the thick net of the fichu.

Then Mrs Anderson let out a snort loud enough to shake her awake. She sat up, groggy, rubbing her face before appearing to notice Katie and Conrad standing on opposite sides of the table, both attempting not to look ashamed.

'I think I fell asleep.' Mrs Anderson blinked, then rubbed her heavy eyes.

'You did.' Katie took up her pencil, trying to appear as if she'd been working all along. Her act was no more convincing than Conrad's intense study of the atlas on the stand near his desk.

Mrs Anderson pushed herself up, pressing one fist to the small of her back as she stretched. 'Then I think it's time we were going.'

Regret flickered across Katie's face, matched by the subtle ache in Conrad's heart and lower down in his body. There'd been something in this moment and he wanted to hold on to it, strengthen it the way he'd strengthened his men when they'd reached Greenland and the food and spirits waiting there.

'Thank you again, Captain Essington, for

your generous hospitality,' Mrs Anderson offered as she gathered up her and Katie's cloaks and gloves.

'Of course, you're most welcome any time. My carriage will see you both home.'

Conrad held out his hand to Katie, inviting her to touch him again, to rekindle for the most fleeting of moments what had just passed between them.

She slipped her hand in his, not with the startled wonder she'd greeted his parting kiss with at Mrs Anderson's, but something more giving and willing. The slight inhale which met the press of his lips to her skin was worth more to him than all the glories which had been heaped on him since returning to London. He hated having to part from her, letting yet another night pass without her beside him.

'Come now, Katie, we've taken up enough of Captain Essington's time and we must get home before it gets too dark,' Mrs Anderson urged, pulling on her gloves as she made for the entrance hall.

A biting breeze swept into the room as Mr

Moore opened the door, but neither Katie nor Conrad shivered.

'Until tomorrow night, Katie.'

'Until then.' She withdrew her hand, hiding the tender skin beneath her worn gloves as she followed her aunt outside to his waiting chaise.

He watched the vehicle until it disappeared down the street, the outline of it lost in the fading sunlight and the crush of traffic. Conrad didn't know what the unexpected kiss meant to either of their futures, but until his duty separated them, he'd do everything he could to redeem himself and her, to rouse her as he had his men, encourage her to persevere, to hold up under challenges and keep going until she found whatever she considered her salvation.

If only he could find his.

Chapter Eight

'Mr Rukin, a word, if you please, in my office.' Conrad stood over the man in the Naturalist Society sitting room, wanting to knock him from his chair, but refraining for the moment. Brawls in the Naturalist Society were frowned upon.

Worry drew down the corners of Mr Rukin's mouth before he recovered something of the bravery which had prodded him to approach Conrad the other day. 'Of course.'

He rose and the gentlemen he'd been speaking with exchanged looks, as curious as Mr Rukin was reluctant.

Conrad didn't wait, but turned abruptly and made for the hall, leaving Mr Rukin to hurry after him.

'Might I ask what it is you wish to speak with

me about?' Mr Rukin fingered the knot of his cravat as he accompanied Conrad to the president's office.

Conrad pushed open the door and waved the man inside. 'It's best we discuss it in private.'

Mr Rukin slid into the room and Conrad closed the door behind him.

When the geologist turned to face him, Conrad grabbed him by the coat, lifted him off his feet and slammed his back into the wall.

'What are you doing?' Mr Rukin yelped.

Conrad wanted to connect his fist with the man's face, but he didn't want to leave any marks. It would be his word against Conrad's after this interview, and Conrad wasn't about to give the man evidence against him. 'Miss Vickers was kind enough to inform me about how you tried to force yourself on her the night her father was disgraced.'

Mr Rukin's skinny fingers clawed at Conrad's hands. 'I don't know what you're talking about.'

'You know exactly what I'm referring to.' Conrad banged him against the wall again, making the man whimper in well-deserved fear. 'She came to you for help and you tried to take advantage of her. You did it because you knew I was gone and you thought I wasn't coming back. You were wrong.'

Conrad let go and Mr Rukin slid down to the carpet, dislodging an old spyglass from the table of curiosities beside him.

'How dare you attack me like this,' the man whined from the floor, cowering as Conrad stood over him. 'I did nothing. It's a lie.'

Conrad pulled the man to his feet by the collar of his coat and dragged him over to one of the chairs in front of the desk, forcing him into it. 'I'm to believe that someone who's plagiarised the early writings of John Walker, a man too long in his grave to defend his work, in order to further his own career wouldn't try to take advantage of a young lady?'

'You have no proof of either charge,' Mr Rukin tried to assert, drawing up his courage. 'You think I can't see you're only doing this because she's your intended and you believe her lies.'

'Here's your proof.' Conrad lifted a paper off the blotter and slammed it against Mr Rukin's chest, driving the breath from him. 'The society librarian was kind enough to unearth one of

Mr Walker's old treatises and I compared it to yours. They're nearly identical.'

'It was Lord Helton who told me not to support Miss Vickers,' Mr Rukin wheezed. 'He was the one who suggested she might be amenable to my advances.'

'Then you were a fool to believe him.' Conrad shoved a piece of paper and pen in front of Mr Rukin. 'Now compose your confession for the society and tell them how you lied and stole to get published and recognised.'

Seeing his life's work slipping away, Mr Rukin straightened his back. 'I will do no such thing.'

Conrad slammed his hands on the arms of the chair and leaned in close to Mr Rukin's face. The frightened man drew back, his eyes wide. 'You'll do exactly as I say or I'll call you out for insulting both my and Miss Vickers's good name. So, unless you want a lead ball in your gut, you'll write.'

Conrad grabbed the pen and shoved it in Mr Rukin's hand.

With no more protests, Mr Rukin wrote out his confession in shaky, uneven words.

'What will you do with that?' Mr Rukin timidly asked.

'Present it to the board, then see to it you're drummed out of this society and every other one in England.'

'It'll be the ruin of me,' he wailed.

'Yes, it will.'

Mr Rukin jerked to his feet. 'You Heltons are all the same. You think because of your name you can tread on anyone and get away with it.'

'Don't blame me for your weaknesses. You brought this on yourself.' Conrad advanced on Mr Rukin, barely able to hold back from striking the coward. 'Get out of my sight before I break your neck.'

Mr Rukin scurried towards the door, rattling the knob as he worked to twist it. At last it swung free and Mr Rukin darted into the hallway, stumbling against the wall before he righted himself and fled for the entrance.

Conrad stepped out of the office to watch him, refusing to chase him like some terrier after a rat, despite wanting to shake the life from him.

'Mr Rukin, what happened?' one of his friends

enquired as Mr Rukin hustled by. 'Where are you going?'

Mr Rukin didn't stop to answer, but rushed out of the front of the building and into the noise and bustle of St James's Street as fast as his spindly legs would carry him.

The friend looked to Conrad, but, meeting his warning glare, thought better of pressing him and stepped back into the sitting room.

Conrad retreated into the sanctuary of the president's office. He stared at the confession on the blotter and the splatters of ink marring the hastily scratched words. He wanted to march into the middle of the Naturalist Society library, hold it up and reveal Mr Rukin's dirty practices to the entire membership. Instead, he left the paper where it lay. This was the one time when the direct route wouldn't serve him best. He'd give the evidence to Mr Stockton and have him bring Mr Rukin up for a reprimand, then allow the board to devise Mr Rukin's final disgrace. It would hide Conrad's involvement in the matter.

Conrad picked up the fallen spyglass and turned it over in his hands, noting the many scratches marring the brass surface. In this mat-

ter, he did act too much like his uncle. He set
the spyglass on the table, pressing one finger to
the top to steady it. This subtle manipulation of
people was exactly the way Lord Helton worked,
rarely coming out from behind the protection of
those eager to win his favour by doing his bidding. It disgusted Conrad to take the same tack
but he had no choice. Conrad was doing this for
Katie and, if he was too obvious about his reason
for pursuing the matter, it'd be difficult to press
the case against Mr Rukin without tainting it.

The flower-shaped water clock in the corner
began to chime five times, calling Conrad to
his next duty. He'd silenced one critic. Katie's
appearance before the society next week would
work to silence many more. In the meantime,
she needed friends to support her in his absence
and he'd see to it she had them.

Katie smoothed her hand over the black dress
as she and Conrad followed Miss Benett's butler
up the stairs to the first floor of the lady geologist's town house. It was a much more modest
dwelling than Lord Mardling's, but the wealth of
Miss Benett's family was evident in the highly

polished furniture, well-executed paintings, servants and the smell of turtle soup filling the house. While Katie had thought nothing of entering Lord Mardling's in her simple green walking dress, appearing tonight before a woman she esteemed, with the possibility of being in the presence of so many others, nearly stopped her on the stairs. She'd read all Miss Benett's works and envied her career and ability to move among all levels of the scientific community. She never thought to find herself a guest at one of her dinner parties.

She fingered again the lace Aunt Florence had added to the bodice of her black mourning dress. It was one of only two gowns Katie owned which wasn't pocked with stains or near threadbare. There hadn't been much time to mourn her father, not with the mounting bills and the need to don her more rugged dresses to search for fossils to sell to pay her way.

'You look wonderful,' Conrad complimented her as they climbed the stairs, though it failed to ease her nerves.

Since Conrad had arrived to collect her and her aunt, who walked behind them mumbling in awe at the portraits of classical ruins hanging over the staircase, there'd been no opportunity to discuss what had passed between them last night. Even if they'd been left alone to talk, she wasn't sure what she would say. The kiss had rattled her belief that she could be with Conrad and remain aloof. His honesty about his fears had touched something deep inside her. She didn't want him to suffer, but she wasn't ready to seek a second engagement, nor was she as eager to be away from him as she'd been their first day together at the Naturalist Society.

What last night's kiss meant to their future faded beneath the concerns of the present as they entered Miss Benett's sitting room. On every surface stood colourful geodes and blinding white quartz, the insides catching the candlelight and creating small rainbows in the rock's depths. A large, curving nautilus took pride of place on top of the piano which stood silent, unlike the guests. Many of the men, who Katie recognised from the Naturalist Society stood in clutches around the room, hands waving as they debated the latest scientific article in the

Gazette, or the last paper presented at the Royal Society.

Miss Benett didn't stand with the men, but held court on a wide blue sofa in the centre of the room. Beside her sat her sister, Mrs Anne Marie Lambert, and beside her was her husband, the esteemed botanist, Aylmer Lambert. Mr Lambert had fostered both his wife's interest in botany and his sister-in-law's study of geology, helping Miss Benett to gather friends from the simple Dr Mantell to the esteemed Oxford don, Mr Buckland. To Katie's disappointment, Mr Buckland was not in attendance tonight. Dr Mantell sat on Miss Benett's other side, enjoying a small plate of tarts. So engrossed was everyone in their discussions, they failed to notice Katie and Conrad until the butler announced them.

The discussions faded as all turned to view their arrival. A few of the men narrowed their eyes disapprovingly at Katie, including Mr Stockton, who stood near the window with three other gentlemen. The rest were welcoming, smiling brightly and hailing them with congenial nods. Whether it was Conrad's influence or their own welcoming natures which provoked such greetings, Katie wasn't sure, but she intended to take advantage of their acceptance to become better acquainted with them and some day perhaps their equal.

Miss Benett rose from her seat and swept forward to greet them, her deep-crimson dress setting off her dark hair. A spinster of some forty years, she was stout around the middle, with a face free of lines yet full of experience. 'Captain Essington, it's been too long since I've seen you. I was so sorry to hear about your travails in the Arctic. You have my deepest condolences for the loss of your friend Mr Dubhach.'

'Thank you.' Katie felt more than saw Conrad flex his hand as he accepted Miss Benett's condolences. 'The loss of my ship was a tragedy, too, for there were quite a number of specimens on board which I'd collected specifically for you.'

'Liar. I know they were all meant for Miss Vickers.' She took Katie by the arm, drawing her away from Conrad and to the sofa. Conrad and her aunt followed. 'Thank you so much for coming. It's rare for me to have so many ladies in attendance. It's usually only myself and my sister, which isn't always as pleasant as one might think.'

'Nonsense, Miss Benett, you know we're always open to your ideas,' Dr Mantell offered, as Miss Benett settled back down between him and her sister after seeing Katie and Aunt Florence seated on the matching shield chairs across from them. 'I'm especially intrigued with what Captain Essington told me of your research into the creature he brought back.'

'I find it difficult to believe a large animal could live so far north since the plant life there can't possibly support much in the way of prey for a beast,' Mrs Lambert offered.

'You're quite right, my dear.' Mr Lambert patted his wife's hand, pride, not condescension, in his compliment. She rewarded his support with a tender smile and Katie's heart caught. She glanced at Conrad's hand on the chair back near her shoulder, so close to her yet unlikely to reach out and join with hers as Mr and Mrs Lambert's did. They'd kissed last night, but the intimacy had been fleeting, easily disturbed by her aunt just as their love and future had been disrupted by Conrad's expedition.

'I don't believe the creature does still exist, for that reason and many others,' Katie explained, struggling to concentrate on her work and not Conrad. His presence proved as distracting as the many luminaries wandering about the room. She never thought to be in such company, at least not outside the walls of the Naturalist Society. Now she was with them, accepted as if she'd been working with them for years, and not a newcomer among their ranks. 'I also don't believe the creature is still living in some unexplored corner of America. Mr Jefferson sent out an expedition and they recorded no evidence of such a beast.'

'Speaking of unexplored regions, Captain Essington, I know Mr Weston is eager to speak with you about the Arctic weather. Would you mind if I introduce you?' Mr Lambert enquired, rising from the sofa.

'Not at all.' Conrad's fingers pressed hard into the chair until Katie saw the knuckles turn white, but nothing else about his demeanour changed. If she hadn't known how raw the memories of his expedition were, as he'd revealed last night, she, too, might have missed the subtle change.

She reached up and covered his hand with hers, giving it a small squeeze, not caring if anyone around them saw the intimate gesture.

'Will you be all right, Miss Vickers?' Conrad asked.

'Of course.' There was no way to assure herself he was going to be well, too, not without revealing the weakness he struggled to hide.

With a respectful nod, Conrad slipped his hand out from beneath Katie's and followed Mr Lambert to where a group of gentlemen stood near a table with a small obsidian obelisk on top.

'I must say, Miss Vickers, you're looking very well,' Dr Mantell complimented her. 'Much better than the last time I saw you.'

A lean man of thirty with thick dark hair, Dr Mantell was one of the more striking gentlemen in attendance tonight, though his dark looks could not compare in Katie's mind to the sturdiness of Conrad's, especially his sandy hair and the faint, lingering tan from his time beneath the Arctic sun.

'No doubt it's due to the return of Captain Essington,' Miss Benett teased and Katie regretted having been bold enough to touch Conrad, and to stare.

'Yes. I'd feared all was lost for so long,' Katie offered through a forced smile before exchanging an uneasy look with her aunt. Katie possessed no desire to correct anyone's assumptions about her and Conrad's engagement, especially when her own were so muddled. A few days ago, in his study, she thought he'd hardened his heart against her for good. Last night, it was clear he still harboured feelings for her, though how deep they ran, she wasn't sure. He'd been hurting and she knew all too well how weak and vulnerable pain could make a person.

'Now, you must tell us in detail your entire theory as to the creature,' Miss Benett demanded.

'Of course.' Over Miss Benett's shoulder, Katie watched Conrad move to join another discussion. The confidence in his stride and the set of his shoulders beneath his dark uniform was striking, but it was the faint echo of vulnerability which lingered in the subtle lines of his face and eyes which called to her. For the first time ever, Katie didn't want to discuss fossils or science, or her troubles. She wanted to be beside him, offering him as much comfort as she drew from him. It frightened her.

'Miss Vickers?' Miss Benett prodded as she, Mrs Lambert and Dr Mantell leaned forward, eager to hear what she had to say.

Lacing her fingers together over her knees, Katie cleared her mind of everything else as she launched into a description of the teeth and furcula and her theory that the creature was more bird than reptile. 'I'm to present my paper on the creature next week at the Naturalist Society meeting.'

'You may have a hard time of it, Miss Vickers,' Dr Mantell warned, reaching for one of the small tarts on the low table in front of them. Katie's Aunt Florence had already helped herself to a plateful and was thoroughly enjoying them. 'It is difficult to change people's minds once they've formed an opinion.'

Katie nodded her agreement over their shared frustration with the established scientific community. There were brilliant gentlemen more willing to take the word of a wicked man like the Marquis of Helton simply because of his title rather than a humble man like Dr Mantell or a brilliant woman like Miss Benett. Despite the quality of Dr Mantell's work, his profession as a country doctor without wealth worked to prejudice many against him as much as Miss Benett's sex.

Another gentleman came over and urged Dr Mantell to join a discussion about Mr Buckland's ideas on geology. Even her aunt's attention was pulled away by Mr Edgar, a tall, elderly man who sat down beside her and found a very willing audience for his argument against Mr Lamarck's theory of transmutation.

'I don't envy you the challenges you've set for yourself,' Miss Benett commiserated once they were alone. 'I'll do what I can to support you, but my advice is to keep Captain Essington close. As much as it galls me to say this, a woman's best champion, as experience has taught me with Mr Lambert, is a man with a good reputation. It smooths the way to success.'

Katie shifted on the chair, uneasy at the notion of relying on Conrad, not simply because it would undermine any effort to achieve success on her own merits, but because he was fast becoming more than a champion for her research.

'Thank you, Miss Benett. You don't know how much it means to me to speak with a woman who understands the challenges I've faced.'

'Oh, I do, for there were many times in the early days of my study when I would have given my most prized crystal to have had another woman who understood.'

'Why do you think the men are so against us helping them?'

'Because they're men.' Miss Benett shrugged. 'Yet we still adore them, don't we?'

Katie looked to where Conrad stood with the men, his profile highlighted by the candles behind him. Even in the midst of his own turmoil and all that had happened between them, he still wanted to help her. After so many years of loneliness, of fending for herself and taking on the burdens of her parents, she'd been a fool to throw away such a gift. It was his caring as much as his optimism and belief in himself which had first drawn her to him and now it did the same again. Some day he'd set sail again, but at this moment he was here, giving her the strength and conviction to face all the people who'd scorned her. 'Yes, we do.'

Even though we shouldn't.

Conrad caught little of what Mr Winston said about the climate in Canada and his work studying the logs of various whaling ships plying their trade in the north. It was Katie seated across from Miss Benett who captured his attention. Tonight, among those who accepted and listened to her, she glowed. There were times when he'd catch a shadow of sadness dimming her excitement, but it disappeared quickly, replaced by an enthusiasm as bright as any he'd ever witnessed on the Downs.

Conrad tugged at the cuffs of his sleeves. Neither of them had mentioned the kiss from yesterday, but the effect of it lingered in the way Katie had viewed him, both here and in the chaise. Despite the presence of Mrs Anderson, Katie had been more generous with her smiles. They weren't the coy glances of a young girl naive about the intimacies between a man and a woman. Nor were they the heated gaze of a woman with too much knowledge of a man, the kind the rumours suggested. They were private glances which conveyed a deeper understanding between the two of them. Telling her about his fears had helped him to understand some of hers and how they could command a person enough to make them turn away from even love.

Conrad took a glass of champagne from the silver tray of a passing footman and enjoyed a deep sip. Guilt heated him like the fireplace behind him warmed his wool uniform. The moment he told her about the Melville Island expedition, it would be like pulling a belaying pin out from the centre of a coil of rope and watching it unwind. That's how fast she'd flee from him. He couldn't blame her.

He watched the bubbles rise from the bottom of the flute to cover the liquid's surface before they popped and, for the first time ever, pondered resigning his commission. As the heir to the Helton title, it would be the prudent thing to do and wouldn't raise many eyebrows. Such a convenient excuse would spare him the pain of having to invent another, more elaborate one to cover his true reason for wanting to remain ashore.

Fear.

Conrad threw back the rest of the champagne, disgusted for thinking like a coward instead of a commander. He wouldn't run away and allow his fears to defeat him any more than he permitted Katie's to defeat her. He would accept this command, as he had all the others, and prove he was the man, the captain, worthy of the praise and glory being heaped on him. Though nothing he could do in the islands would bring Aaron back.

'Captain Essington,' Mr Tines interrupted Mr Winston. 'Tell us something of your magnificent exploits in the north.'

Conrad set the champagne flute down on the mantel, afraid the tremor would make him drop the glass. The men peered at him as if he were a hero and Conrad wanted to yell at them that they were wrong. What he'd done wasn't heroic or brave, it was selfish and self-serving, the act of a desperate man determined to survive after making an incredible blunder. It was nothing to celebrate, especially not when a man still lay frozen beneath the ice. 'In truth, there isn't much to tell.'

'Then describe some of the plant life you saw there,' Mr Lambert suggested, ever the botanist.

Somewhat relieved, Conrad indulged Mr Lambert's interest, describing the red algae which dotted the ice flows in the spring. He thought such topics safe, but he was wrong. When Conrad described how the vegetation had disappeared with the summer, the tremors threatened to return.

Conrad met Katie's sapphire eyes from across the room and the trembling subsided like the stinging cold from his hands over a blazing fire. If her mere presence in a room could comfort him, he might experience a greater peace in her arms. Leaving her would be like a man shivering with malaria refusing quinine, but he couldn't resign his commission.

Katie broke from his glance and fell back into conversation with Miss Benett. Conrad tapped each finger with his thumb, smarting at the ache in his joints. She might calm him with a look, but her leaving at Heims Hall had shaken him as deeply as Aaron's departure. It would be more prudent to lose his grip on every champagne flute from here to Mayfair than risk waking up humiliated and alone in his bed after a night with her.

Katie slipped into Miss Benett's library and heaved a sigh of relief. The purple amethyst crystals displayed on the tables and shelves twinkled with the light of the coals in the grate. She dropped into a chair beside a table with a large ammonite fossil perched on it and stared at the pair of curving tusks dominating the centre of the room. Mammoth, she guessed, by the discolouration of the ivory, but she didn't hurry to inspect them. It was quiet she sought now, not the treasures. After months of isolation in Whitemans Green, so much conversation proved as taxing as it was stimulating.

'I see you've come here to seek some solace as well.' Conrad's voice echoed through the quiet as he stepped inside and shut the door behind him.

Katie straightened in the chair, her breath catching as he moved into the room. The white lining of his coat shone, stunning against the darker wool covering his chest and the light of the fire deepened the thick gold embroidery around each buttonhole. 'I've spent so much time working alone on fossils, I've forgotten what it's like to be in such animated company.'

'I understand. It was much quieter in the north than here in London. It's taken me some time to adjust after coming home.' Conrad circled the table with the amethyst crystal, admiring it before picking up one of the smaller samples. 'I have some news for you. I dealt with Mr Rukin today.'

Katie tapped her fingertips together in her lap. 'It sounds rather ominous.'

'It is for him.' Conrad explained about the plagiarism and his method of handling it.

'To think, a man acting as he did dared to look down on me,' Katie fumed, rising to pace in front of the chair, as disheartened by Conrad's news as she was encouraged. 'The hypocrite. Though I suppose society is full of such people.'

'Sadly, it is.' He turned the crystal over in his hand and dark sparkles flickered in the purple. 'Some day, I'll be forced to deal with them on a more permanent basis, perhaps sooner than I'd like. As the future Marquis of Helton, society will expect me to resign my commissions and prepare to take my place in the House of Lords.'

The faintest hope ignited in her heart, but the reminder of his future position quickly snuffed it out. 'A great many things will be expected of you—becoming a politician is surely not one of them.'

He set the amethyst down with a thud, then made for the tusks. 'What if I could do more for expeditions as a member of Parliament than the captain of a ship?'

'Which is exactly what your uncle wants.'

He stopped on the other side of the ivory, his eyes fierce. 'What he wants doesn't matter, it never has. It's what I can accomplish. I could see to it the ships are well funded and supplied. It could mean the difference between life and death to many future explorers.'

'Perhaps, but you wouldn't be content reading about other men's journeys instead of taking your own.' She knew he wouldn't, any more than she was able to read about other naturalists' scholarly accolades and not covet them. It was a weakness to be pitied, but a reality she couldn't dismiss for either of them.

'You're arguing as if you want me to leave again.' He ran his finger along the curve of one tusk. 'I didn't think you wanted me to go.'

'What I do, or don't, want you to do doesn't matter any more.' He had his own goals to pursue while here in London, as evidenced by his blue uniform. His goals were not hers and, as she'd painfully learned before, they superseded everything else.

His fierce eyes met hers from across the ivory. 'It does matter.'

He said it with such conviction, she almost believed him, but she wasn't convinced. Worry over his past expedition led him to speak as he did now, but when the fears faded, he'd set out again. She was sure of it. 'If that was true, then I could have persuaded you to stay before.'

'You could sway me to stay now.' He came around the tusks to where she stood. 'I don't want men to know depredation because of my mistakes. I don't want anyone to suffer for my ego or my choices.'

He raised his hand to her face and she noticed for the first time ever in his eyes not fear, but worry. She laid her hand over his, pressing it against the curve of her cheek. He was hurting with a grief she understood, as if the invincibility of youth had been stripped from him, leaving him bare, open and wounded. It was the same thing she'd experienced the morning her mother had fled, when her childhood had ended and she'd been left to see to the house, the food and the bills. It was the day all the ugliness of her parents' relationship was spread out on the grass for her and the entire village to see and she'd learned how the people who love you the most can still walk away.

'If you resign your commission, tether yourself to shore, then, when younger, less competent men are winning accolades, you'll resent them and their glories. Eventually you'll resent me, too, just as my mother resented my father for everything she'd sacrificed for him.'

'I've never blamed anyone for my mistakes. I won't start now.' He traced her cheekbone with his thumb, his touch tender and seeking. 'We don't have to forge ahead alone, Katie, neither of us. We could find a new way forward, together, perhaps in directions we've failed to consider before.'

The words to tell him of Mr Lesueur's expedition danced on the tip of her tongue. They could both leave England and all the people fawning over Conrad and scowling at her, set off as a team to explore unknown lands. They might discover if some of the animals she'd excavated still lived in the wilds of America. She opened her mouth to speak, then closed it again, hesitant to place them on such a path, when there was so much left for her to do here. She wasn't ready to leave England, not when the chance to prove wrong all the men who'd scorned and doubted her was only a few days away. Conrad would be there beside her when she did it, believing in her just as he always had. If only her rank in society and his didn't stand between them, then she could hold on to him and his care for good.

She slid both hands along the sides of his face, the faint stubble of his beard pricking her palms. Tenderness flickered through his eyes like sunlight in a crystal, drawing her to him as powerfully as the fossils drew her back to the Downs. In the weight of his hand on her cheek and the sultry scent of wine on his breath, it was as if they were alone in the countryside again, all the promises of their future as one waiting to be seized. Time had damaged them, hardened their hearts as it did the bones she dug from the earth, but like the bones they were still here, waiting to be made whole again. Maybe, like the animals, the love she and Conrad had broken could be pieced back together.

She traced the firm line of his brow with the tips of her fingers, then buried her hands in his hair. She drew his face down to hers, meeting his lips with a sigh of relief as deep as the temptation. Whatever course their lives took, tonight she didn't care. He was here and hers and even if it was only for a brief time, she wasn't alone.

Conrad savoured the pressure of Katie's tender lips against his. She hadn't laughed at him for considering resigning his commission, or chastised him for being weak or afraid. Instead, she'd listened, then argued against it, understanding why he couldn't leave the Discovery Service and everything he'd spent his life building and achieving. She knew the kind of man he was and in her embrace he sensed, at last, her acceptance of it and him.

Her sighs enticed him to bolder conquests and running his hand up her side, he cupped one breast through the stiff bombazine. With two fingers, he reached over the top of the bodice and drew back the thin lace lining it to reveal more of the creamy skin beneath. He bent down to press a kiss to the supple flesh and her fingers tightened against the back of his neck.

'Conrad, we shouldn't,' she gasped weakly as her hand slid beneath the wool of his jacket. 'The others might find us.'

'Let them. I don't care.' Nothing mattered except her and the calm settling in beneath the excitement urging him on. In her arms was the peace he'd sought since returning to London, the peace he'd found with her at Heims Hall and believed he'd lost when she'd run away.

Katie didn't care either, not about the geologists in the sitting room, the Naturalist Society, the past or her uncertain future. Nothing existed except Conrad pressing her against the wall, his mouth on the tops of her breast as she undid the buttons on his uniform. She wanted the cursed jacket off his shoulders, hating the way the brass

buttons winked at her in the firelight and reminded her of everything which had come between them over the past year and a half. She
didn't want memories or thoughts or anything
but his hard chest against hers and their bodies
together as one.

He straightened to claim her mouth, his hand
drawing up the hem of her skirt. She raised her
leg to rest on his hip as he slid his hand beneath her thigh, following the curve of it to her
buttocks. As his fingers caressed her flesh, the
heavy wool of his jacket at last gaped open to
reveal the white waistcoat beneath. She tugged
the jacket off his shoulders and down over his
arms until the weight of it pulled it to the floor.
Then she set to the buttons above his manhood,
losing her grip on the curved ivory as his exploring hands found the heat of her centre. Grasping
his shoulder to steady herself, she rose up on the
balls of her feet, eager to end this play and be
filled by him, but at the same time not wanting
this stolen moment with him to end.

'Conrad, I… We…' She panted as he met the
rhythm of his caress with the steady sweep of
his tongue against her arched neck.

'Patience, Katie. Patience,' he whispered in her ear.

With each long, slow stroke of his fingers, her patience grew closer to its end. Unable to work the buttons on his breeches free, she slid her hand inside the wool to take hold of his erect member. He groaned as she clasped him, the steady pace of his caress faltering as she stroked the length of him, failing to maintain the quickness of her pace as her release began to crest. Closer and closer it came, threatening to shatter her when the deep metal gong of the dinner bell reverberated through the room.

Katie and Conrad froze, their hard breaths filling the quiet as they listened.

'Dinner is served,' a butler announced from somewhere in hallway too close to the room.

The outside world they'd been so eager to forget intruded with the steady muffle of voices and footsteps filling the hall. She glanced to the door, seeing the key upright in the lock, the door free to open to anyone who might try it.

'We must join them or we'll be missed,' Katie gasped, barely able to hear the words over her pounding heart, her entire body aching for the fulfilment promised by Conrad's touch.

Conrad banged his forehead against the panelling above Katie's shoulder, his frustration mimicking hers.

'We could enjoy a quick dessert first,' he suggested, teasing her neck with one feathery kiss.

'No, we can't. Miss Benett and her guests might be open-minded, but I don't think they're that open-minded.'

The heady intoxication of his kisses cleared as Conrad withdrew from her and she lowered her leg. They reluctantly separated, rushing to straighten each other's clothes the way they used to after an hour or two of pleasure in the meadow. When they were ready, Conrad took her hand and they hurried through the house and down the stairs, stepping up to the end of the line as the guests began filing into the dining room. Aunt Florence stood a few couples before them, still listening to Mr Edgar talk about his theory, neither of them showing any signs of fatigue of each other's company.

If her aunt or anyone else had missed Katie and Conrad, they didn't reveal it as they took their places at the long table. Conrad escorted Katie to her seat between Mr Winston and Mr Stockton before making for his chair on the other side of the table. She didn't want Conrad so far away, but beside her where she might slide her foot against his calf and use his confidence to bolster her own. His presence would keep all eyes fixed on him instead of her and the flush of pleasure she felt sure still coloured her cheeks.

As dinner began, Katie tried to engage Mr Stockton in conversation, but he gave his attention to the man on his other side, leaving her to Mr Winston's company.

'I've been studying the northern-weather patterns for a number of years by reviewing the logs of whaling ships to determine when the ice floes form and then break up. Winter has been coming earlier over the past four years. I believe such information could be of great help to men like Captain Essington and others searching the rugged climes,' Mr Winston explained before launching into a detailed description of his findings.

Katie listened with only half an ear, too focused on Conrad across from her. He discussed the fauna of Australia with the men on either side of him, his conversation as steady as if he'd just come from the sitting room and not from indulging with her in Miss Benett's study. Katie hoped she appeared as unruffled, though more than once she thought she saw Miss Benett suppressing a knowing smile as she observed her.

'Tell me something of your work, Miss Vickers,' Mr Weston prompted when he was through.

Mr Winston listened intently as Katie explained her work and she prayed his enthusiasm offered some indication of the reception she might receive at her presentation next week. It also provided a glimpse into what it must be like to be Conrad and have the whole world in envy of what you do. He'd never had to seek approval; it'd always come easily to him. Though, as she'd seen over the past two nights, it wasn't anyone else's faith in him he needed so much as his own. The Arctic had pummelled it out of him and he was struggling to regain the sure footing on which he'd built his life, just as Katie had struggled to find her own after he'd left and her father had died.

Catching his smile from across the table, she

offered him a teasing wink which caused him to raise one surprised eyebrow. Perhaps he was right and they could seek out their futures together, reclaim both their past relationship and their faith in themselves before men like Mr Barrow and Lord Helton intervened again.

'The Egyptian Hall has a fabulous specimen of an ostrich,' Mr Winston suggested, drawing Katie's attention back to him. 'You must view it.'

'Did someone mention the Egyptian Hall?' Miss Benett demanded from her place at the head of the table. 'I'm going there tomorrow to attend Mr Sedgwick's lecture on the rock strata in Devon. Let's all make a day of it. Miss Vickers must view the fossils and animals on display there if she wants to make her research more complete.'

Many raised their glasses in agreement while those who couldn't join the excursion muttered their disappointment. Mr Stockton didn't share his fellow diners' enthusiasm and took a deep drink of Madeira to avoid participating in the hearty enthusiasm for the outing.

Katie joined in the excited chatter, hoping everyone mistook the faint glow of her skin as anticipation for tomorrow. Even if they didn't, Katie didn't care. Nothing, not even Conrad's fiery glances from across the table, could dampen the thrill of this evening. She was among people of science who accepted her, her body still warm from Conrad's touch. They'd made no promises to one another and she wasn't ready to fall again into the thorny tangle of losing her heart completely to him, but something deeper than help and assistance was growing again between them. It was like the early days at Heims Hall when the optimistic adventurer had overcome the reservations of the daughter of a country doctor during long afternoons on the Downs. It was possible he could surmount them again and, in doing so, teach her to leave them in the West Sussex ground, along with all the old heartaches of her mother and father's lives. Perhaps the threat of having to go to America to make her way could finally be put aside, even if she wasn't ready to discard Mr Lesueur's letters just yet.

Chapter Nine

Despite the biting chill in the air outside, inside the Egyptian Hall it was hot and mufflers and scarves were quickly abandoned by the mass of curious visitors making their way through the crowded galleries. Many were here seeking a respite from the dreariness of the weather and their ranks were swelled by the number of men in attendance for Mr Sedgwick's lecture.

A steady hum of conversation punctuated by hearty laughter and gasps of amazement filled the stifling air as Katie, Conrad and Miss Benett moved along the glass cases. The cases were packed floor to ceiling with birds, insects, animals and other assorted specimens from England and the far reaches of the world.

Katie leaned in to examine a tray full of

beetles pinned to a piece of black velvet, as light and happy as one of the green girls being escorted by her beau along the perimeter of the room.

'Your presentation before the Naturalist Society is scheduled for Tuesday,' Conrad announced, leaning in beside her to examine a particularly large green beetle from Egypt.

Her lightness dropped around her like a dislodged window curtain. 'That's only three days from now.'

'I wish I could give you more time, but I can't.' His eyes shifted from hers to the collection of animals in the middle of the room. She knew this week marked the last meeting of the Naturalist Society until spring, but she couldn't help feeling there was something more to the rush. Conrad's summons to Mr Barrow's office came to mind and she wondered if he'd been assigned to another mission, giving him some reason to believe he wouldn't be here when the society reconvened in April.

'Maybe I should wait until the first meeting in the spring,' she suggested, trying to draw out the truth from him, but he was stubborn in his desire not to reveal it. Perhaps she was seeking something which didn't exist. Maybe Mr Barrow had only wanted to discuss Conrad's book. It was difficult to believe Conrad would keep something as important as another expedition from her, and at the same time, it wasn't.

'I wouldn't advise it. Most of the titled members of the Naturalist Society have gone to their country houses for the winter. They're the ones who were most likely swayed by Lord Helton to attack you before. Without them there, you'll have a more receptive audience.'

'Yes, you're right.' It would be easier to gain the acceptance of those who were closer to her in rank and more likely to be sympathetic to her need for recognition and employment.

Miss Benett approached with her sister and Mr Lambert. 'Come, Miss Vickers, you must see the stuffed ostrich near the elephant.'

Miss Benett accompanied Katie and Conrad to the main gallery, all the while sharing her anticipation for the forthcoming lecture. Mr and Mrs Lambert walked on Miss Benett's other side, their heads tilted together, deep in conversation. Frequently, they would break from their talk to engage Miss Benett with a question or draw her into the discussion.

Katie had once wondered at Mr Lambert's enthusiastic support of Miss Benett. There were some malicious people who'd attributed it to a relationship between the spinster and her brother-in-law. Seeing him now with Mrs Lambert on his arm, the two of them exchanging sweet glances, Katie understood it wasn't love for Miss Benett which drove Mr Lambert, but love for his wife. He encouraged her and her sister because it made Mrs Lambert happy.

Jealousy pricked at her as she watched them, wishing she knew something of familial love. Her father had encouraged her work with the fossils, but it was always for his benefit, not hers. That she'd enjoyed the work had been a lucky coincidence. It would have been wonderful to have had siblings and parents to engage in lively speculation with as Miss Benett enjoyed with Mrs Lambert now, but it hadn't been. There were no more children after Katie. Then, after her mother's death, with Katie taking care of everything so her father could work, there'd been no reason for him to remarry and give her siblings, or the benefit of a woman to guide her. Her parents had designed her entire life to leave her in solitude and fate had continued their efforts.

She slid a glance at Conrad and tightened her fingers on his arm. Her heart fluttered when he met her teasing look with one of his own. Maybe her fate and his were about to change.

'You've been here before, Miss Vickers?' Miss Benett asked, drawing her attention away from Conrad.

'Once, last spring, when Lieutenant Colonel Birch held his sale for Miss Anning.' She and her father had spent an entire day admiring the impressive collection of fossils the lieutenant colonel had placed up for auction to benefit poor Miss Anning. It wasn't just the sheer number of bones and curiosities for sale which had amazed Katie, but Lieutenant Colonel Birch's willingness to support an unknown country woman with a gift for finding fossils. Katie had viewed his support with a small amount of jealousy, wishing she could garner the attention of esteemed men. Never did she think she would be back here a year later, walking with Miss Benett and Conrad.

It was a stark contrast from the lonely life she'd lived in Whitemans Green. She didn't want to return to such a solitary existence and she wouldn't. She would face the Naturalist Society and win them over as she'd won over Miss Benett and her friends. With Conrad beside her, it didn't seem like such an impossible feat. He'd already brought about such a transformation in her situation, it was difficult to believe it wouldn't change more and for the better.

'You're absolutely glowing,' Conrad remarked. 'Is it the visit here, or something else?'

'Yes, on both accounts.' She gazed up at him through her lashes, relishing the heat it brought to his eyes.

'I'm glad to hear it.'

They entered the main gallery which was filled with people waiting to go into the larger room where Mr Sedgwick would speak. 'Though the exquisite specimens on display might play a small part in my excitement.'

'I thought perhaps they would, though whatever brings such light into your face makes me happy.'

Katie revelled in the compliment. There'd

never been anyone who'd been concerned with her happiness the way Conrad was and she realised again the mistake she'd made by leaving him in West Sussex. It wasn't too late to undo it, if she wanted to.

They stepped up to the railing separating the crowd from the exhibit of large animals arranged in the centre of the room. It was more a jumble than a scientific grouping, with an elephant from Africa posed beside an American wolf. Even a polar bear stood among them, its white fur eye-catching amidst the grey of the rhinoceros and the ostrich.

'You saw many of those in the Arctic?' Katie questioned, motioning to the bear.

'Not as many as I would've liked once we ran out of food.' Conrad tore his gaze from the bear, fixing a smile on his lips though it wasn't as lively as before. It hurt Katie to see him struggling to crush down the awful memories the way she used to whenever she'd awake late at night in a feverish chill, calling for a mother who would never come.

'Will you be joining us for the lecture, Miss Vickers?' Miss Benett interrupted.

'No. I have far too much sketching to do here.'

'Then you must accompany me, Captain Essington,' Miss Benett pressed as a crowd of sombrely dressed men began to make their way to the lecture hall. 'We can't have you distracting Miss Vickers. A great deal relies upon her ability to sway the men of the Naturalist Society. If she succeeds, it will give many lady scientists hope for their own acceptance. Perhaps the Royal Society will even consider opening its doors to us, too.'

'There's always hope,' Conrad agreed, though none of them believed it would happen. The members there were too rigid in their beliefs to be swayed by a man of even Conrad's fame.

Miss Benett led Conrad off to the lecture, leaving Katie alone in the exhibit hall to ponder her words. In gaining Miss Benett's confidence and friendship, she'd elevated her own quest to be accepted into something more. It added a pressure and importance to her work she wasn't sure she wanted. It would be difficult enough to put aside the awful memories of last year in order to make her presentation without thinking so much else hinged on her efforts.

She found a place on the bench just outside the iron railing with an excellent view of the ostrich. The way the animal stood would help her wire together the creature's skeleton and perhaps some day she'd see it on display here, her name linked with the fascinating animal for ever. Before her imagination could get the better of her, she set to drawing, chiding herself for such a ridiculous thought. There were so many obstacles still to overcome, so many people to persuade. It was too soon to dream of a glory as big as the Egyptian Hall.

No one bothered her while she worked, except one old man who shuffled up to sit beside her on the bench before settling down to wait until his grandchildren beckoned him to join them in another part of the museum.

She was so engrossed in her sketching, she failed to notice the room filling again as the lecture ended and the audience returned to the main hall.

'Are you done or do you need more time?' Conrad asked, coming to sit beside her.

She wiggled her stiff fingers, the tips black from the lead. 'I shouldn't be much longer.'

'Then I'll leave you to it.' Conrad left her to join Mr Winston by one of the fake metal palm trees surrounding the animals.

Katie struggled to return to her work and not watch Conrad, or the way the white breeches of his uniform stretched across his thighs, leading up to where his coat cut away to reveal the front of his hips, hinting at what she'd missed last night. She gripped the pencil tight, pressing it so hard against the paper that the tip broke and she was forced to retrieve another, duller one. By then Conrad had turned, the dark of his coat facing her, emphasising his shoulders and the narrowness of his waist. It wasn't as delightful a view as his front, but easier to resist as she set to finishing her drawing of the ostrich's feet.

The bench shook as someone dropped down on the other end.

'I see you weren't content to ruin just your father's reputation, but mine, too.'

Katie jerked up to meet Mr Rukin's taunting jeer, his lips curling in disgust as they had when she'd rejected his advances.

'You deserve what Conrad did to you.' Katie

flipped closed the sketchbook and rose, forcing him to his feet.

'What favours did you promise Mr Winston and Mr Lambert to make them humour your pathetic attempts at science?' He made no mention of the women, considering them, like Katie, beneath him. 'They barely give me or my papers any consideration.'

Katie narrowed her eyes at the nasty man, amazed to think she'd once considered him her colleague and friend. 'What reason would they have to acknowledge someone who plagiarises in order to succeed?'

He stepped closer, the toe of his boot tapping hers. 'Don't give yourself airs about your research. I know the only reason you're here is because you're bedding Captain Essington and the entire scientific community knows it, too.'

'How dare you,' Katie seethed. 'I work as hard as any man for what I have.'

'On your back.'

Out of nowhere, Conrad appeared and clapped a hand on Mr Rukin's shoulder and spun him around. A sickening crack filled the air as Conrad's fist rammed into Mr Rukin's face, knocking him to the floor.

'You broke my nose,' Mr Rukin wailed, blanching at the blood covering his fingers and staining the white cuffs of his shirt.

Conrad grabbed him by the cravat and hauled him to his feet, drawing him up eye to eye with him, oblivious to the blood dripping on his hand. 'Speak to her like that again, in public or private, and I'll break more than your nose.'

He shoved Mr Rukin away and the man stumbled, coming to a hard stop against the bench.

Conrad took Katie by the arm and pulled her towards the entrance. She struggled to keep hold of her pencils and sketches and to ignore the crowd of surprised onlookers. It wasn't just the couples and grandparents who watched them with a mixture of disapproval and horror, but Miss Benett and all the scientific men milling around after the lecture. Some nodded their silent approval at Conrad's behaviour. Others weren't so supportive, scowling at them or huddling to whisper as they passed.

Even in the shadow of Conrad's chaise, Katie couldn't shake the sting of the disapproving looks. She could practically hear the story whisking through society, especially among the learned men she was trying so hard to impress. The chaise set off, rocking in time to the horse's gait, the motion more irritating than soothing. No matter how hard she tried to avoid scandal and gossip, there seemed no way to escape it.

'You didn't need to hit him,' Katie chastised, the tension between her and Conrad riveting the air more than the rub of leather straps against the wooden sides.

'I was defending your honour.'

'Most won't see it that way.'

'What does it matter? Most believe we're still engaged and view it as a fiancé protecting his intended.'

'But we aren't engaged and some day the truth will come out. Then what will people think? They'll call me your whore and say Mr Rukin was right and everything we've struggled to build will be ruined.'

Conrad rested his elbow on the edge of the carriage and pressed his fingers to his temples, viewing her with sickening disappointment. 'Even when I help you, you blame me for your troubles. No matter what I do, you'll never see me as anything more than the man who failed you by leaving.'

'No, that's not it at all, only you don't understand what I've suffered, what I continue to suffer day after day. No one's ever looked down on you or scorned you for things you never did.'

He sat forward, his anger simmering just beneath his control. 'Yes, my life has been one pleasurable experience after another, especially during the last year and a half.'

She twisted her hands in frustration, unsure of how to make him understand. 'But everyone still looks on you as a hero.'

'You're right. How could I know what it is to endure harsh looks and whispers when I was fighting for mine and my men's lives?' Conrad cried.

Katie moved into the corner, clutching her sketch pad to her chest. 'Your suffering is over and some day time will lessen the pain of it while mine continues. It always will because I'm a woman.'

'My suffering isn't over.' Conrad slipped a handkerchief from his coat and rubbed at the maroon drops on the top of his hand. 'It's with me each and every day, just like yours. Only I don't blame you for all my miseries.'

Katie turned to the window, watching the small snowflakes catch on the glass, then melt in fat drops to run down the pane. He was to blame for making her believe in their future together at Heims Hall only to take it away by leaving. He was responsible for leaving her vulnerable to his uncle's attacks and not being there to defend her. He was the one who'd chosen to strike Mr Rukin today. No matter how glad she was to see the man suffer, it was a fleeting happiness since this story would further soil her name.

The chaise rocked to a halt in front of her aunt's lodging house. Katie reached for the door, ready to bolt from the carriage, eager to be alone, but Conrad shifted forward to turn the handle and step down on to the pavement. He held out his hand, waiting in stiff silence for her to take it. There was no warmth in his grip as he helped her out into the biting and fetid wind of Cheapside.

He stared straight ahead as they climbed the stairs to her aunt's door, acknowledging nothing and no one else, not even her. His indifference cut as deeply as Mr Rukin's insinuations. She thought of the letter in her satchel and the remaining money from the sale of her father's things hidden beneath the floorboards. America still loomed, but just as she hadn't given up on herself when faced with Mr Rukin's criticism and insults in the Egyptian Hall, she wasn't ready to abandon everything. If Conrad had taught her nothing else, it was to stand tall and fight for herself and there was one battle left to be waged, assuming Conrad intended to still sponsor her before the Naturalist Society.

They stopped at her door and Conrad finally faced her, his jaw tight, his shoulders stiff. 'I have business to attend to in the next few days. I won't be available to assist you with your research.'

She shifted the sketchbook in her hands and swallowed hard. This was the same type of response she used to hear whenever she'd approached her father's associates for help during the first days of the Marquis of Helton's whispering campaign. Now Conrad was distancing himself from her, too, and she feared, unlike the day she'd first approached him in his study, there would be nothing to make him change his mind about helping.

'And the presentation to the Naturalist Society?' She held her breath, waiting for his answer. There was little reason to continue her research, or stay in England, if she couldn't present it.

'I'll fulfil my promise to sponsor you.'

'And afterwards?' It shouldn't matter if Conrad refused to involve himself with her again. It was better to let him go now than to spend another day on the docks searching for any sign of his ship. Yet the idea of being separated from him scared her more than the thought of standing before the harsh glares of the members. It shouldn't, but it did.

He moved to leave, then stopped, scratching at a red stain on his shirt cuff with his fingernail. 'Last night, when you argued that I shouldn't resign my commission, I thought it was because you understood me and who I am. I see now I was mistaken. You weren't arguing for why I should continue on, but for why you believed I'd go again.'

'But you will, won't you?' Even if he winced at her question, it was the truth and they both knew it.

He tugged his cuff straight, then dropped his arms, but didn't answer. His silence was as much a confirmation as if he'd spoken.

There was no vindication for Katie in being right, only a hollowness which sat heavy on her chest. 'It's not simply about your leaving.'

'Of course it is.'

'It's more than that. Can't you understand?' She reached for his arm, but he shifted away from her.

'I do. I know what your mother did, I remember how you cried out the truth of it in my arms in West Sussex.' He did understand. It should have elated her, but the hardness darkening his eyes offered little sympathy, or reason to be glad. 'We aren't our pasts, Katie.'

'Don't pretend your past doesn't consume you as much as mine.' She wouldn't accept all responsibility for the strain between them now.

He was just as culpable for letting his legacy govern him.

'Yes, we both have our demons to wrestle. It's a fight I thought we could wage together. Apparently, I was wrong. After Tuesday, you may follow whatever path you choose. I won't burden you with my presence any longer.'

He made off down the stairs, disappearing out of the door faster than the heat from a poorly vented fireplace.

Small flakes of snow which had swept in when the door was open dropped to mix with the puddle of mud and grime staining the old floorboards. He was gone, as if he'd set sail again, and she nearly chased after him to call him back. Instead, she remained on the landing, determined not to move. No matter what his kisses had suggested the other night, what tantalising promise his caresses had held, the events of today had proven there was no future for them.

Katie slipped the key out of her reticule and into the lock of the door, letting herself into the plain room. The coals in the fireplace were low, her aunt having gone out to collect her sewing work for the week. This wasn't the first time she'd come home to lonely and cold rooms either here or in the country. She should be glad for the solitude, the chance to work undisturbed, but she wasn't.

Katie set her sketchbooks on the small tea table and lit one of the tallow candles, not wanting to stoke the fire and use any more of her aunt's precious and expensive coal. Leaving her pelisse on to keep warm, she fetched the satchel from where it sat in the corner of the room. From inside the faded canvas, she withdrew her books and papers and spread them out on the table beside her sketchbook, determined not to waste a moment of the next three days of research. Tuesday was her last chance to redeem herself and create the life she'd craved since leaving Whitemans Green, the only life still left to her.

While she read, she struggled to focus on her work and not Conrad or the things they'd said to one another in the chaise. She didn't have time to worry about it, or to do anything except prepare, but no matter how much she concentrated, Conrad's words echoed through the quiet room. *I don't spend every day blaming you for all my miseries.*

Katie closed the book and sat back. He'd accused her of being selfish in her pain and he was right. She'd lost her reputation while he was gone, but for her there was always America and the chance to start again. Unlike her good name, his friend could never be resurrected.

Shame settled over her as she looked at the papers and books in front of her. Every single one of them was a testament to Conrad's care and generosity. She picked up a paper close to her, studying the co-ordinates Conrad had provided from his log to support her claim no animal could survive so far north. Next to each was a sampling of the daily temperatures, a stark reminder of the harsh conditions he'd faced. The small numbers were shaky and uneven, as if he'd struggled through the tremors in his hand to make them, just as he'd struggled through the ice to reach home, and her.

She set down the paper and picked up the drawing of the creature she'd made the other night. The back of the skull was incomplete because Conrad had interrupted her to reveal his secret shame and pain. The faraway look which had come into Conrad's eyes then, and again today when he'd faced the polar bear, haunted her. He'd suffered things she couldn't imagine, things which still tormented him, and when he'd confided in her she'd been unable to put aside her own troubles to truly comfort him. Instead, she'd ignored his grief to wallow in her own, just like her mother used to do.

Two tears fell from her cheeks to smudge the lines of the creature's teeth. For all her efforts to avoid becoming like her parents, everything she did seemed to mimic them and bring about more unhappiness. It was as if there was no way to escape it or the damage it wreaked on her and Conrad. Yet even when she'd insulted him and everything he'd suffered in the north, he was still determined to stand beside her and keep his promise.

She didn't deserve it.

She set aside the creature and wiped away the dampness on her cheeks, not wanting to surrender to the hopelessness gnawing at her. She'd made so many mistakes with Conrad, not in accepting him, but in pushing him away, and they couldn't be undone. When he was gone, she would be alone again to make her way as best she could, as she always had. Her work would keep her going, though tonight it seemed a very hollow and sad companion.

She shouldn't have let Conrad walk away.

She set aside the sketches and returned to his page of temperatures, trying to keep the regret at bay. Even if she chased after him, there was nothing she could say. Any apology she might make would be too weak, words not enough to close the wounds between them. There needed to be something more, but there was nothing of value or influence she held which she could offer him. It was another glaring reminder of how selfish she'd been after all his generosity.

She was about to set the paper with the temperatures aside when a snippet of her conversation with Mr Winston came back to her.

'Winter has been coming earlier over the past four years.'

She read down the list of temperatures, seeing the cruel way they descended before rising again in the spring, though never as high as they'd been the year before.

Winter came early.

She tapped the table with her fingers, wishing

she'd paid more attention to what Mr Winston had said, but with Conrad smiling at her from across the table, it had been difficult. Staring at the falling degrees, she cleared her mind and forced herself to focus.

'I believe such information could be of great help to men like Captain Essington.'

Katie sat up straight. Conrad blamed himself for the loss of *Gorgon*, but maybe he was wrong, and maybe Mr Winston could prove it. If so, then it was the single way she could apologise and thank him, the only one which held any meaning.

'No matter what I do she keeps pushing me away, blaming me for her troubles. Then, when I provide solutions, she blames me even more.' Conrad paced in front of Henry, nearly wearing a hole in the Navy Club sitting-room rug. Her accusation in the carriage, her swift dismissal of his suffering, singed his insides like a freezing wind. He didn't deserve her scorn, any more than his father had deserved Lord Helton's. 'I was ready to marry her once, but even then she was more willing to live in poverty surrounded by the memory of her father and all his failings than accept me and security.'

'I think it's time to realise whatever you and Miss Vickers enjoyed before you left is gone.' Henry crossed his ankle over his knee as Conrad stopped before the window. Outside, in the fading twilight, the bright lanterns of the carriages glowed with the flecks of falling snow.

'I have.' He'd have nothing more to do with her after Tuesday and never again subject himself to her constant doubts about his faithfulness.

'Then cut her loose now. Don't bother with the Naturalist Society.'

'I can't. I pledged to stand beside her and I intend to see it through.' He resumed his pacing, feeling more like a caged dog here than in *Gorgon's* cramped quarters. 'I can't fail anyone else. I've already let down myself, Aaron, you.'

He motioned to Henry's gloved hand. Henry flexed his fingers, then slid them between his thigh and the chair to slip a bag of tobacco from his pocket. 'I don't blame you for what happened.'

'Aaron did.' *And so do I.* 'I saw it in his eyes before he left the tent.'

'We thought Aaron the toughest man aboard ship. He boasted as if he was, but he wasn't.' Henry pulled open the strings of the pouch. 'All his swaggering was his way of concealing his weakness.'

Like Katie's act of pushing Conrad away was meant to conceal hers. Conrad balled his hand, but his fingers failed to hold the grip and he relaxed them. 'Aaron didn't deserve to die because he put on a good show of being strong.'

'No, he didn't, but he knew the dangers of signing up, just like every man did, and he accepted them.' Henry packed the pungent tobacco into the bowl of the pipe. 'So did you.'

'Which is why I ordered everyone to get up and walk, even when they wanted to lie down and die.'

'And we all obeyed and lived, except Aaron. It was his decision to disobey, not yours.'

Conrad splayed his fingers in front of him, not bothering to conceal the tremor as he struggled to accept what Henry said. It was the truth, but still Conrad couldn't find absolution. 'What fate awaits Katie when I finally turn my back on her?'

'She isn't Aaron, Conrad.' Henry lit his pipe, as blunt with his opinion today as he'd been aboard ship in the privacy of Conrad's quarters. 'Continuing to help her won't bring him back, or make any man whole again.'

'I know.' Yet the two had become inextricably entwined in his mind. 'I once thought to find peace with her.'

Henry took a long drag of his pipe, then exhaled the smoke before he answered. 'You both need to find your own peace before you can find it with each other.'

'If she'd married me, she'd have found some security, but she wouldn't.'

'Her objections to a marriage and a life with you are reasonable.' Henry held up his hand to stop Conrad from protesting. 'I've been where she's been, I know what it is to move among men not of my class, to get my hackles up when some incompetent buffoon with a titled father is promoted while I stagnate. Yes, you suffered under your uncle's heavy hand, but you did it with a house over your head and plenty of food in the larder, luxuries not all of us enjoyed. We've had to struggle and fight even more than you have to get where we are. Society can be a nasty place and not everyone has the stomach for it.'

'I know,' Conrad admitted, his frustration easing. 'It's why my parents walked away from it.'

'And Katie has, too. Now, it's your turn to let her go.'

'I can't.' The sense Katie was becoming the second person he couldn't save overwhelmed him like a wave across the deck of a ship during a storm. He couldn't just let Katie go, like he'd let Aaron go.

'I didn't think you would.' Henry rose and approached Conrad. 'Now I find, like you, the melancholy of the Arctic hasn't quite left me. I'm sorry, Conrad, but tonight I must make for merrier company.'

Conrad levelled a cautious look at his lieutenant, not offended by his desire to seek out more temperate climes. If he could, he would, too. 'Careful you don't risk losing a different extremity by swimming in certain seas.'

The pipe smoke obscured Henry's sly grin. 'I know better than to dally where there's too much danger. I plan to visit a sweet little widow with a taste for men of adventure.'

'Then I wish you a hearty evening.'

'It will be a hearty one indeed.' With a whistle, Henry strolled away, a trail of smoke following him out of the door.

Conrad's smile faded with the scent of the tobacco. He should follow his friend's lead, enjoy himself and shake the melancholy encircling him, but it wasn't pleasure he was after tonight, but purpose. Katie had come to him to lead her through the perils of the Naturalist Society and the scientific community and he'd agreed. He wouldn't fail her.

He strode from the room in search of men sympathetic to lady scientists, ones who could support Katie on Tuesday and afterwards. Once she was secure in a position or with a patron, he would go to Melville Island and she to her research. It wasn't the future he'd planned in the ice and it didn't warm him any more than the idea of sailing in the tropics, but it was the way of things and he must deal with it. He'd fulfil his promise to her and then they'd be done.

'That was quite a scene Captain Essington treated us to at the Egyptian Hall.' Mr Winston chuckled as he handed Katie a warm cup of tea. Outside, a light snow collected in the corners of the study windows. It would cover the streets by morning, mixing with the mud and muck to make them fouler than before. 'I haven't seen such excitement there since Mr Hawkins and Mr McGowan fought over who should bid on the *proteosaurus* skull.'

'Yes, it wasn't the kind of ending I'd imagined for such a day.' Katie sighed.

'It certainly set tongues wagging.' Mr Winston took a drink, the steam fogging the spectacles perched on the end of his round nose. Like most men of science, Mr Winston's study was cluttered with books and notes. They covered every surface except the small tea table between them, the one the rumpled old maid had set the tea service on before giving Katie a disapproving scowl for arriving so late and without a chaperon. Katie ignored the woman, more concerned tonight with helping Conrad than protecting her already battered reputation.

If Mr Winston noticed, he didn't seem to mind or find her lack of a protector discomforting.

Other things occupied him just as they'd always occupied her father.

'You've certainly given Mr Stockton a new reason for harping on about why ladies are only a distraction to science,' Mr Winston informed her. 'It was all he could discuss after you and Captain Essington left. Needless to say, it didn't make Miss Benett happy to hear him prattling about it.'

Katie turned the tea cup in its saucer, wondering what damage the scene had done to her efforts to befriend the lady geologist. 'Yes, it was a most unfortunate situation.'

Mr Winston set his tea on top of a stack of books beside him, his humorous manner turning serious. 'But I suppose you didn't come here to discuss the Egyptian Hall.'

'No. I need your help.' He shifted in the chair and she could hear the polite refusal forming behind his large lips. 'Not for me, but for Captain Essington.'

At once his demeanour changed and he sat up straighter, ready to listen. 'What could a man of his reputation possibly need from me?'

'Proof it was the early coming of the Arctic

winter, and not his insistence on pushing north, which led to *Gorgon* becoming trapped.'

'You wish me to provide research to help Captain Essington?' He laid his hand on his dull and wrinkled cravat, appearing as honoured by her request as if the King himself had asked him to predict the weather. 'I've always hoped my work might assist such a renowned man, but I didn't think it would happen so soon.'

'Indeed, as soon as possible would be best.'

'Then I'll do what I can, at once.' No doubt he was seeing the rewards he might obtain by presenting Conrad, a future marquis, with such research. Katie didn't care why he helped her, as long as he did.

'Could you prepare something by Tuesday? I'd like to present it to Captain Essington before I give my lecture on the creature.' Tuesday might be the last time she would see Conrad. Afterwards, there'd be no reason for them to spend time together, or for her to approach him.

'It will be a rush to compile the necessary information so soon, but...' he held up one determined finger '...I like a challenge.'

Their meeting concluded and Katie rose and

followed Mr Winston to the door. At the threshold he paused and faced her, his brows knitted gravely together, reminding her of her father, though the silver hair above his short forehead was better kept than her father's had ever been. 'A warning to you, Miss Vickers. Mr Stockton is not alone in his opinion of the inappropriateness of women in the Naturalist Society. Nor is Mr Rukin the only man questioning Captain Essington's motivation for assisting you. Until the two of you marry, people will continue to whisper.'

'Of course,' she choked out through the tightness in her throat. When the news of their broken engagement was finally made public, it would make her critics more vicious in their condemnations. Hopefully by then she'd have the strength of the work to protect her. She wouldn't have Conrad.

'I don't mean to upset you, but as a fellow naturalist, I'm sure you appreciate a clear view of the lay of the land as much as anyone.'

'I do. Thank you.' His warning ringing in her ears, she slipped out into the fading daylight, eager to be home before darkness fell. It would be a few days before she knew if her theory about the early winter was correct and if the proof of it would make any difference to Conrad. He deserved some rest from the memories persecuting him and hopefully she would be the one to help him find it. It was the least she could do for him after all he'd done for her.

Chapter Ten

'Don't look so worried, Miss Vickers. I sense you're on the verge of a great triumph tonight, both for yourself and all lady scientists,' Miss Benett reassured Katie from her place beside her in the Naturalist Society library.

Katie twisted the opal ring on her finger. 'I hope you're right.'

She hadn't realised the intense interest in her presentation until she'd entered the library. The tables usually filling the wide space were gone, replaced by rows of uncomfortable wooden chairs. They were not enough to accommodate the crush of people filling the room any more than the street outside the Society had been wide enough to contain all their carriages. Those without a seat crammed into the centre aisle and the two along the sides.

Katie sat in the centre of the front row, her aunt on one side and Miss Benett and a long line of gentlemen on the other. Conrad wasn't one of the people sitting near her. As president, his place was beside Mr Stockton at the back of the stage, as distant from her now as during the ride here from her aunt's dwelling. Though she'd entered the room on his arm, she might as well have walked in alone for all the encouragement he'd offered her. The only thing his presence beside her had done was keep the gentlemen civil, even if some continued to pin her with nasty scowls.

Katie clutched her notes in her lap, the faded leather of her father's folio sticking to her sweaty palms as she tried to drown out her worry by silently reviewing her speech. She'd practised for hours with her aunt until the notes she'd prepared were unnecessary.

'Order, order,' Mr Stockton called out as the conversation in the room began to rise to drown out Mr Edgar who stood at the podium.

There were three speakers tonight and Katie would be the last, the unofficial conclusion to the society's year. One had already gone and now Mr Edgar presented his arguments against transmutation to an uninterested audience. She pitied the soft-spoken man, for only her aunt and a handful of others showed him the respect he deserved.

Her own nervousness made her ability to focus on Mr Edgar difficult. She'd enjoyed little sleep or food in the past three days as she'd toiled in near isolation to draw together the research she and Conrad had collected. Each night, she'd stay up late working, her eyes straining in the dim glow of the smoking tallow candle as she read her notes. Then, when she could no longer keep her eyes open, she'd catch a few hours of fitful sleep before rising with the sun to start anew.

The exertion weighed on her as much as the whispers of the few women in the audience—wives of Naturalist Society members unable to resist the spectacle of watching Katie either succeed or be crushed. She wished she could rely on their support, but many of them thought as their husbands did. Sex was no guarantee of solidarity.

Katie shifted in her chair to ease her body's tension and her eyes met Conrad's. She silently willed him to offer even one of the smiles he'd so easily graced her with just three days ago, but he refused, turning his attention back to Mr Edgar. When he'd arrived to fetch her tonight, her Aunt Florence's constant presence had prevented any conversation between them except the most mundane. There'd been no chance to discuss with him the events of three days ago, to apologise for what she'd said or to show him the note Mr Winston had sent her moments before Conrad's arrival. There'd been no details written in the older man's neat script, only the words:

You were right about the weather. I'll explain further at the meeting.

Whatever Mr Winston had discovered, it would have to wait. He hadn't been here when she'd entered. She turned in her chair to search for him again, but he wasn't among the guests or any of the people who continued to trickle in, finding places where they could along the back of the room.

All too soon Mr Edgar brought his presentation to an end and the society politely applauded. Mr Stockton rose to thank him and usher him from the stage, and a strange quiet settled over the audience. Mr Stockton's booming voice broke it as he took to the podium to make a few announcements. When he was done, he turned to Katie.

'Miss Vickers, will you please come forward.'

A silence similar to the one she'd known during all the lonely trips to the Downs to hunt for fossils moved through the room as she approached the stage. Conrad rose from his chair and came forward, offering her his hand to help her up. The memory of him reaching down from atop his horse flashed across her mind. Despite all the aspersions she'd cast on him and their time together, even here he was a gentleman, just as he'd been in West Sussex.

She offered him a small smile in thanks, but he didn't return it as he stood with her off to one side of the stage while Mr Stockton made her introduction. Conrad had risen for no other speaker tonight, or stood beside any of the other waiting men. Katie and all in attendance recognised at once the credence his actions lent to her research and her presence here. He was supporting her and silently challenging anyone who objected to her to face him. No one did and Katie wasn't sure she deserved such protection. She'd failed him so many times and still he stood beside her. It was time to make amends.

'You weren't to blame for *Gorgon* becoming trapped,' Katie whispered as Mr Stockton continued his introduction.

'What do you mean?' Conrad muttered, his eyes on the audience.

'You were wrong about continuing north leading to your trouble. You didn't linger too long. Winter came early.'

'Miss Vickers, the stage is yours.' Mr Stockton waved her forward.

Katie moved to take the podium, but Conrad clasped her elbow, stopping her.

'How do you know?'

'I asked Mr Winston. He told me.'

'Miss Vickers, now, please,' Mr Stockton demanded through a tight smile.

Conrad let go and Katie hesitated. It wasn't the presentation she wanted the most now, but to calm the confusion her comments had created in Conrad's expression. She should have waited to tell him instead of throwing it at him when there was no time to explain, but she didn't have a choice. She didn't know if they'd have any time alone together once tonight was over.

With reluctance, she stepped away from him and made for the podium.

She laid her folio on the smooth wood and looked out at the audience, meeting the eyes of all the members and their curious wives over her research. A fear like none she'd known before nearly sent her back to Conrad's side, but she forced herself to stand. She hadn't come all this way, suffered and endured so much to turn tail now. There might be few here to support her, but she believed in the validity of herself and her work. It was time to convince others of it as well. Clearing her throat, she opened the folio, set her notes before her and began.

Conrad took his seat at the back of the stage, shocked out of the reserve he'd demanded of himself since fetching Katie over three hours ago. The past few days had been difficult. He'd spent most of it in conference with Mr Barrow, reviewing the arrangements for the Melville Island expedition. At the end of each day, worn out from planning and wrestling with his ability to captain another ship so soon after *Gorgon*, he'd missed Katie's steady company and the distraction he found from his troubles by helping her with her own. What he hadn't missed was defending himself against her constant doubts and aspersions.

He studied the back of her, her face not visible from where he sat. She moved her hands in elegant timing to her words, her slender body straight and confident at the podium with only the hint of her hips visible beneath her black dress to tease him. Her figure wasn't what he should be focusing on tonight, or anything else in regards to Katie except seeing through the promise he'd made to bring her to this stage. He'd fulfilled his end of the bargain; now he could free himself from her and all her misgivings and accusations. Except it wasn't disbelief she'd struck him with before she'd stepped up to speak, but an affirmation he'd never thought to hear, especially not from her.

It wasn't your fault. The winter came early.

He tapped the arm of his chair, rubbing the spot worn down by the many other illustrious men who'd occupied this seat, including his father. Conrad pressed his fingers into the wood as he recalled the swiftness of the ice drifting in to surround *Gorgon* until the night the temperatures had dropped and frozen the sea solid.

He racked his mind, trying to remember how the cold had set in, whether he'd missed the signs of its approach or, as Katie's brief words suggested, it'd come in fast, silent and unexpected.

I asked Mr Winston. He told me.

Conrad searched the audience for the white-haired man, desperate to speak to him, but he wasn't in attendance. He spotted Henry who stood along the wall with so many other men.

I don't blame you for what happened.

Conrad shifted in his chair. Maybe Henry and Katie were right. It was as difficult to imagine as ever being warm again had seemed when he'd plodded through the frigid snow. It ached to not be able to pull Katie back from the podium and demand more answers.

Settling himself, he looked over the audience again, noticing at last the rapt attention being given to Katie's speech. The members and their guests exhibited a reserve not usually seen during a presentation. Conrad wasn't willing to believe it was a sign of acceptance any more than he was ready to believe he wasn't at fault for the loss of *Gorgon*. Curiosity and an ingrained respect for Katie's sex probably had more to do with their courtesy than her ideas. It wasn't likely to last as she unfurled the drawing of the creature.

Agitation swept through the crowd along with gasps of surprise as men turned to one another in astonishment. Conrad stilled his hand, ready to jump to his feet and call the audience to order if they began to speak out, but they didn't. Instead, they listened, curious as she described the similarities between the creature and large birds.

She was succeeding, yet strangely, it wasn't her presentation which commanded his attention. During the past three days, Conrad had kept his distance from her, but she was ever on his mind. It seemed she might have thought of him, too, and his suffering, not just her own work, spending precious time in conference with Mr Winston instead of at her books.

Conrad rubbed the end of his chin, noting how the flickering of the lamps from around the room highlighted the faint amber streaks in Katie's hair. He'd accused her of being too wrapped up in her miseries to recognise his, but maybe she wasn't. Maybe she had considered Conrad's suffering enough to obtain the one piece of information which could lift the heavy yoke of blame from his shoulders, and bring him peace.

Katie began to explain the similarity between the creature's furcula and a peregrine falcon's when a commotion near the back door caught Conrad's notice. The crowd parted, jostling to find space to make way as Lord Helton entered accompanied by Mr Prevett.

The hairs on the back of Conrad's neck rose as they had the morning aboard *Gorgon* when Boatswain James and the cooper had cornered him on the gun deck to threaten mutiny.

Lord Helton appeared more cadaverous since Conrad had last seen him, but his light, wolf-like eyes remained clear and hard as he pinned Katie with the same condescending disgust he used to throw at Conrad's mother.

Katie caught sight of the two men, stopping mid-sentence to exchange a worried look with Conrad. With an encouraging nod he set her back on course and she shuffled her notes, resuming her talk, though a noticeable waver marred her words. Whatever confidence she'd gathered to take to the stage, it was beginning to falter under Lord Helton's malevolent sneer.

He leaned over to Mr Stockton. 'What's Lord Helton doing here? He isn't a member.'

'Mr Prevett invited him. Didn't you hear he would be in attendance?'

'No, I blackballed his membership years ago. He has no right to be here, even as a guest.'

Conrad slid from the stage and made his way along the side of the room, trying not to draw attention to himself. His uncle spied him moving through the crowd and a wicked smile cracked the deep lines of his face. Conrad could almost smell the relish the man took in the destruction he was about to wreak. It was the same look Conrad had endured the day of his father's funeral when Lord Helton had demanded Conrad's mother turn Conrad over to him to raise. It wasn't love or concern which had prompted him to seek guardianship, but the craving to mould Conrad as he'd never been able to mould his brother. He'd failed then and Conrad would see to it he'd fail in whatever he intended to achieve tonight, but the crowd along the walls was thick, hampering Conrad's progress.

Seeing him detained, Lord Helton strode up the centre aisle. The people catching sight of him shuffled aside, too awed by his status and reputation to stand in his way.

'Since when do the scientific men of London glean their knowledge from Captain Essington's whore?' Lord Helton called out.

A thunder of movement swept through the room as the audience shifted in their chairs to face the marquis.

'Get out,' Conrad commanded from the side of the room, practically pushing people aside to get through the crowd. 'You have no right to be here.'

'A man doesn't need permission to point out a travesty taking place in front of him.' Lord Helton pointed his cane at Katie, hate keeping the consumption from diminishing the strength of his voice. 'Will you esteemed men allow Captain Essington to dress his mistress up in the mantle of science in order to foist her upon you?'

'I'm not his mistress, nor will I let you brand

me as such,' Katie objected from the podium and all heads swivelled back to her.

'You aren't his wife either, and you never will be.'

'Strange you should be so bold in your prediction now,' Katie countered, not flinching from his or the audience's scrutiny, 'when a year ago you had to hide behind others to spit on me. I wonder if it's the chance you might fail in your efforts to besmirch me which drives you out from under your shadows.'

'How dare you try to belittle me, woman.' Lord Helton banged his cane against the floor before a hacking cough nearly doubled him over. He pressed his handkerchief to his mouth, trying to quell it.

While he worked to recover himself, Katie stepped out from behind the podium and down the three small stairs leading off the stage. Men shuffled out of her way, making a path from her to Lord Helton, one she strode with her head raised and her chin defiantly in the air. The sight of it brought Conrad to a stop, awestruck by her confidence.

'I'll speak to you as I see fit and I won't be

judged by your or any other men's lies, but by the strength or weakness of my work.' Katie stopped in front of Lord Helton, meeting his hard glare with one of her own.

Pride filled Conrad at her blatant defiance, her stance revealing a force of will and strength he'd thought crushed by her troubles. She wasn't going to be defeated like Aaron, but meet whatever challenges awaited her and survive.

Lord Helton bared his teeth at her like an irritated badger. 'You're no scientist and unfit to pollute such an august institution.'

'You're the one darkening it and your name with all your hate,' Conrad called out as the crowd at last parted to let him through. He marched up to his uncle, ready to drag him from the room.

'Lies, are they?' the old man challenged, clutching the handkerchief to his chest. 'I have it from your own cousin's lips how you and Miss Vickers spent nights together alone at Heims Hall.'

The image of Matilda in Lord Helton's landau rushed back to Conrad. The woman who'd hated Katie had only been too happy to take something private and beautiful and give it to Lord Helton to wield as an ugly weapon against Katie. He wouldn't allow either of them to succeed.

'You there.' Conrad snapped his fingers at the two footmen flanking the door. 'Escort Lord Helton from the room. He doesn't belong here.'

The footmen exchanged uneasy looks and cowered back as though trying not to be noticed.

Lord Helton threw back his head and let loose a phlegm-filled laugh. 'The famous Captain Essington can't even get two footmen to obey him. You're pathetic, just like your father and like him sullying the Helton name with a woman who's bedded half the scientific men in London.'

'Lies,' Katie yelled.

'I can attest to her licentiousness,' Mr Prevett added. 'She and I were lovers in the country.'

Women gasped and their husbands began to hustle them towards the exits, as if the ladies who'd borne the trials of childbirth were too delicate to hear the frank talk of men.

'What did Lord Helton offer you in exchange for your lies?' Conrad stepped up to the man, nearly nose to nose with him.

The coward hustled behind Lord Helton, who was only too happy to shield him.

'I'm publishing his most recent work,' Lord Helton smugly answered.

'Is that the price you paid to come here tonight, Mr Prevett?' Conrad growled. 'Selling your integrity to him?'

'We know what price she paid.' Lord Helton pointed one gnarled finger at Katie, but she stood stern against his accusation.

'And what price will you pay for the sins you've committed?' Conrad charged.

Lord Helton narrowed his eyes at Conrad. 'Don't you dare.'

'What? Reveal the truth? Isn't that what you're after, why you're here? Then allow me to help you.' Conrad threw out his arms in mock theatricality, relishing the horror twisting his uncle's lips. 'Let me tell all of London how, when your brother married my mother, then refused to stand as an MP, choosing instead to seek out a second term as the president of this very society and defy you again, you decided to teach him a lesson. You paid a quack doctor in St Giles to declare him insane, waiting until my mother, pregnant with me, was at Heims Hall with her brother to have him seized and thrown into Bedlam. When she returned to London, you refused to tell her, a woman you thought beneath you, where he was, but left him to rot for months until my mother could find and free him.'

'Lies, all lies,' Lord Helton charged, pink spittle dripping from his quivering lips.

'It's true, every word of it. You ruined his health and killed him as if you'd stuck a blade between his ribs.'

Lord Helton levelled his walking stick at Conrad. 'You think you've bested me, but you haven't. I'll see to it you pay for betraying the Helton name and punish all those who dare defy me.'

Without warning, Helton swung his walking stick at Katie. She cried out as it landed with a hard whack against her arm, knocking her to the ground. He raised it to strike her again, but Conrad caught the ebony and wrenched it from his uncle's hand. He broke it over his knee and tossed the pieces down to clatter against the floor.

Conrad knelt beside Katie, who cradled her arm, white with pain. 'Is it broken?'

'I don't know.'

'Get away from her. Get away.' Lord Helton grabbed Conrad by the coat and tried to pull him up, but Conrad knocked his arm away, making the marquis stagger back before Mr Prevett steadied him.

Lord Helton lunged forward again like a rabid dog, then jerked to a stop, blood trickling from his nose. He clasped his hands to the side of his head, then cried out as his knees buckled and he dropped to the floor at Mr Prevett's feet.

'Help him, someone help him.' Mr Prevett kneeled beside him, most likely more horrified at losing his patron after sacrificing his integrity than at Lord Helton taking ill.

The crowd, shocked silent by the drama unfolding before them, was slow to act until one of the many eminent physicians in attendance hurried to the stricken marquis. He was soon joined by numerous compatriots.

Only Dr Mantell came to Katie's aid. He touched her arm and Katie flinched, grabbing it and holding it close.

'I need a more private place to examine her,' Dr Mantell said, his voice nearly lost in the confusion behind him.

'We'll take her to my house.' Conrad helped Katie to her feet and wrapped his arm around her shoulders to protect her, careful to avoid bumping her wounded arm.

'Step aside, make way,' Henry commanded, clearing a path for Conrad and Katie and leading the way to the door.

Dr Mantell and Mrs Anderson stayed close behind him until they all left the warmth and light of the Naturalist Society for the damp darkness of the London streets. The chaise wasn't far away and they reached it just as Henry pulled open the door. Inside, it wasn't much warmer than outside and Conrad settled Katie next to him on the seat, then pulled up the folded blanket to cover her. Mrs Anderson and Dr Mantell climbed in after Conrad, their faces long with concern.

'To the captain's house,' Henry instructed the driver and, in a jangle of equipage, the chaise set off.

Katie winced when the chaise hit a bump and

Conrad drew her tighter against him to rest his chin on her head. 'Everything will be well.'

'No, it won't,' she muttered, eyes closed tight against a pain both physical and heartfelt, a pain he knew all too well. 'This is worse than last year, worse than what happened to my father.'

Conrad laid a tender kiss on her hair, unable to dispute her because she was right.

Chapter Eleven

'It's a nasty bruise, but nothing's broken,' Dr Mantell confirmed in the candlelit upstairs hallway of Conrad's town house. Downstairs, the tall clock in the sitting room began to chime midnight. 'I suspect it's more the shock of the evening than her injury affecting her now. A little laudanum should help calm her nerves and allow her to sleep.'

'Thank you, Dr Mantell. My driver will see you to your lodgings.'

Entrusting the doctor to Mr Moore, Conrad stepped into his bedroom where Katie and Mrs Anderson sat together in the matching wingback chairs by the fire, a heavy blanket draped over Katie's shoulders. This room was the warmest in the house and the first place he'd thought to bring her.

'I'm glad to hear nothing is broken,' Conrad offered.

'Unlike what's left of her reputation.' Mrs Anderson scowled at him.

Conrad didn't dispute the widow. With his fame, the story would reach the papers and the ears of all in London by morning. As much as the people loved their heroes, they cherished smearing them even more.

The widow rose and marched up to him. 'I know she isn't a grand man's daughter, but she's a good girl and I expect you to do right by her.'

'I will, Mrs Anderson, you have my word.' It was Katie's word which would determine if he could keep his. 'If you don't mind, I'd like a few moments alone with her.'

With a disapproving sniff, Mrs Anderson left.

Conrad took the older woman's chair and faced Katie. 'I'm sorry for what happened.'

'I didn't think tonight would be worse than before.' She stared into the fire and the despair darkening the circles beneath her eyes ate at him.

The rage Lord Helton had attacked her with

had startled Conrad out of the anger he'd carried for the past three days. It also renewed his determination to see through the promise of their engagement. He'd placed her before the society, making her vulnerable to attack, and brought Lord Helton's wrath down on her. With her reputation even more compromised than before, he wasn't about to walk away. 'In the morning, I'll send word to my man of affairs to secure a licence. We'll wed as soon as possible.'

'Why? It won't change anything.' She tightened the blanket around her neck and leaned heavily against the back of the chair.

'Of course it will,' he seethed, frustrated by her continued stubbornness and the entire debacle of tonight, the last two months, the last year and a half. 'You'll have the protection of my name and home. You need never worry.'

'You can't silence them all, not now and not when you're a marquis.' She rubbed her sore arm. 'I won't spend my life surrounded by whispers and sneers, nor taint my children with them the way my mother's poor decisions tainted me.'

'Then you'll let my uncle and men like Mr Prevett win?'

She met his fierce look with one of her own, as if to say they'd already won. Then she turned back to the fire and dropped her head in her hands. 'I don't want to think of it now. Please, leave me alone. I'm tired.'

Realising the futility of further discussion, Conrad gathered up his patience and left. With the shock of tonight so fresh, this was no time to decide something as serious as marriage, although she was mistaken if she thought she could refuse his proposal now.

Katie took a deep breath, but her chest remained tight as the lonely life she'd tried so hard to escape began to close in around her. She might have sent Conrad away, but tomorrow she'd have to face him and a decision, to be alone in marriage, or alone in the world.

'Katie? Are you all right?' Aunt Florence asked, coming to stand over the chair. 'Captain Essington looked in a fury when I passed him in the hall.'

Katie reached up and touched her aunt's arm, moved by the worry drawing down the older woman's face. At least there was one person who truly cared for her. 'I'm sorry to cause you so much trouble, especially when everything is difficult for you already.'

'Nonsense. This is the most excitement I've known in years.' She squeezed Katie's fingers. 'Though it isn't me I'm worried about, it's you.'

'Conrad intends to make me his wife, if that's what concerns you.'

Her aunt pressed one hand to her chest and let out a relieved breath. 'Thank heavens. I knew he'd continue to stand by you.'

And he would. Despite all the aspersions Katie had cast on him, deep down she knew he was worthy of her respect and admiration. She could give him these things and receive the tenderness he'd shown her both tonight and so many times during the past two weeks. It was his love and commitment to her she struggled to accept. He was seeking her hand out of a sense of duty, because he felt compelled to protect her as he always did. Once she was his wife, his obligation would be fulfilled and he'd sail off again, forcing her to endure the relentless attacks of society by herself.

'Then you have nothing to worry about,' Aunt

Florence assured her. 'You'll have a long and happy life with Captain Essington.'

'I'm not so sure.' She could always escape back to Heims Hall in Conrad's absence, occupy her days with the fossils, but she didn't want to be a wife and a widow, or return to such an isolated existence in an empty house surrounded by dead things.

'You can't think to turn down his offer? After tonight you won't even be able to find work as a governess. You know I can't support two,' her aunt exclaimed in a passion of flapping hands and shallow breaths.

'I know.' She stroked her aunt's arm, trying to soothe the flustered woman and herself. Her aunt wasn't being selfish but honest. As a woman on her own, Katie well understood her aunt's worries. She'd vowed not to become a burden to the widow and she wouldn't. 'I'm going to America. The *Thomas George* leaves tomorrow evening. I can easily make the ship.'

'You're too out of sorts to decide anything right now,' her Aunt Florence twittered as she snatched up the bottle of laudanum Dr Mantell had left on the table between the chairs. She measured out a spoonful, so agitated by the idea Katie might reject Conrad that she spilled a good bit of the drug on the floor before she filled the spoon. 'We'll talk about it again after you've slept. Now, take this.'

She pushed the medicine at Katie.

Katie wanted to resist, to lie in the dark with a clear head and plan her future, but the pain in her arm and the fatigue pulling at her limbs demanded she sleep. She took the dose, the sweetness of it as sickening as everything which had happened tonight.

Her aunt helped Katie undress, then lifted the bedclothes so Katie could slide beneath the crisp sheets. She tucked the thick coverlet up beneath Katie's chin before settling herself in the chair beside the bed.

Katie snuggled down under the comfortable weight, the scent of Conrad's sandalwood cologne as thick as the fabric and soothing her more than the laudanum. He'd brought her here instead of taking her home, ready to take charge of her care instead of leaving her solely to her aunt's charity. There wouldn't be such comfort in America or another chance with Conrad if she left, only the solitude and perseverance which had been her constant companions for so long, but staying with him didn't guarantee happiness either. She couldn't compete with Mr Barrow for his fealty, nor did she want to. After a lifetime of trying to capture first her mother and then her father's attention, she was tired of fighting for recognition from society men, of defending herself and her reputation from unwarranted attacks, of begging those closest to her to love and cherish her. It wearied her as much as the drug until her thoughts began to tangle and she dropped into a deep but fitful sleep.

'Captain Essington, Captain Essington.' Mrs Anderson's high voice pulled Conrad from a restless sleep on the narrow guest-room bed. He rose, still dressed in his uniform shirt and breeches, and hurried to pull open the door. 'What's wrong?'

'Katie's so restless, I can't calm her. I fear she's taken ill.'

Conrad rushed down the hall, Mrs Anderson close behind him, her worry for Katie as sharp as his. Inside, a single candle burned on the bedside table, casting its light over Katie who lay tangled in the white sheets, her gold hair spread out on the pillow around her.

Conrad felt her forehead, relieved to find it cool. The pressure of his touch calmed her and she settled against the mattress, though she continued to mumble words he couldn't understand. It was then Conrad noticed the bottle on the table. 'I'm sure it's just the laudanum affecting her dreams.'

'I'm so sorry to wake you with my worries.' Mrs Anderson stood over him, drawing her borrowed wrap tighter around her. 'But she's all the family I have.'

'I'm glad you did. Now rest, I'll sit with her for a while.'

Mrs Anderson returned to the small couch near the window. The rumpled pillows and blanket told Conrad she'd been sleeping there before she'd fetched him. Within a short time, she was breathing as steadily as Katie.

The worry created by Mrs Anderson's appearance eased as Conrad watched Katie's full chest beneath her chemise rise and fall. He longed to climb into bed beside her, wrap his arms around her and hold her close. He didn't, not wanting to disturb her from the much-needed rest. In time there would be many pleasurable nights between them until the anxiety and troubles of this one were forgotten.

He brushed a strand of hair off her cheek, ignoring the ridiculousness of his dogged determination with her. Any other man would have given up on such a stubborn woman, but he couldn't. All would be well between them. In the stillness of the early morning he knew it, just as he'd known in the Arctic that if he led his men away from the sunken ship they'd find salvation. It was intuition, something he couldn't explain, like the strange images he'd seen in the sky above the northern sea which made ships seem forty times larger than they really were on the horizon.

Her willingness to stand before the Naturalist Society and defend herself against Lord Helton boded well for their future together and the challenges she'd face as his wife and a marchioness. However, it wasn't the fortitude she'd exhibited tonight as much as the faith she'd placed in him which fed his belief in everything turn-

ing out all right. Deep down, she still believed
in him as she had during their first spring together. If not, she never would have sought out
Mr Winston and offered Conrad the one chance
to free himself from his guilt and the ravages
of the north.

The winter came early.

Conrad pulled the sheets up higher to Katie's
chin, waiting until he was sure she was sleeping deeply before he slipped from the room and
made his way downstairs. The house was lit
by the faint light of the coming dawn flood-
ing in through the front windows of his study.
It turned everything an ash grey, including the
brown leather journal on top of his desk. Nightmares awaited him there, but so did the possibility of peace.

Conrad lit a reed in the grate and set it to the
candle perched on the edge of his desk, then sat
down before the journal and opened the cover.
His hand shook as he combed through his entries until he was forced to grip his thigh to
keep it steady. He loathed going back over the
details, but kept at it, certain the truth was there.
While he read, he copied out passages on to a

clean piece of parchment, teasing from the blistering entries the evidence he needed to prove Katie was right.

Hours passed and the sunlight in the room soon overwhelmed the candlelight, making the words easier to read.

At last, he set down his pen and stretched his back which smarted from having been hunched for so long. The yellowed and water-stained journal stood in stark contrast to the crisp cream paper on the blotter beside it. So was there a noticeable difference in his penmanship. Where the copy was filled with the flourishes of a warm and somewhat steady hand, the letters in his journal were cramped, blurry, written in the misery of hunger, cold and privation.

He picked up the list and read over every entry he'd made about the weather. It was a vague jumble of observations, but temptingly promising— the Inuit who'd stumbled upon them in the early days of their imprisonment and muttered something about the cold being fiercer than any year he remembered and the whaler captain who'd made a similar remark. Over a matter of hard months, the scattered and unconnected remarks about the weather had meant nothing. Taken together, they offered Conrad a chance to reclaim the peace stolen from him the moment he'd spied Aaron lying dead in the cold.

The sound of Mr Moore clearing his throat drew Conrad's attention to the door. 'Mr Winston to see you, sir.'

Mr Moore led the older man into the room and Conrad rose to greet him.

'Mr Winston, thank you for coming on such short notice.' Conrad had sent a note to the gentleman at sunrise, hoping he might offer more insight into Katie's cryptic comments. Conrad could ask Katie himself, but he was reluctant to disturb her, especially when he was so agitated. They'd left too much unfinished and tense last night, he didn't want to make things worse by pestering her, not when there were others who could answer his questions and set his mind at ease.

'It was no trouble at all.' Mr Winston took the offered chair by the fireplace and brushed some clinging snow off the leather folio he carried. 'Though I'm surprised you wanted to see me.'

Conrad sat down across from him. 'I'd like to know what you discovered about the winter when I was trapped. Miss Vickers told me something about it last night, but was unable to provide more details.'

'Yes, I heard what happened.' He trilled his long fingers on the folio. 'She's doing well?'

'She is.'

'Good. What a dreadful business and so disgusting to think Mr Prevett was willing to assist a heinous man like Lord Helton. I'm always amazed by the lengths some will go to further their ambitions.'

'And your research?' Conrad prodded, turning the conversation back to the reason for Mr Winston's visit.

'Of course.' Mr Winston handed Conrad the folio. 'The year you set out, winter descended much earlier than even seasoned whaling captains expected. It'd been steadily arriving in August instead of September for the last four years, but it swept in with most quickness and severity the winter you and your ship were trapped. It's all outlined in the paper I just gave you, the one I hope to publish next spring, perhaps with your support?'

'Of course,' Conrad mumbled, too focused on the charts to care if he was patronising Mr Winston's work or a pedlar's in Piccadilly. Everything Katie's comments had suggested, and all he'd gleaned from his journal last night, was laid out here in neat numbers and solid proof.

While Conrad read, Mr Winston described his findings, how the ice pack hadn't broken up as much as in previous years. He'd found the information from the logs of any captain or harbour master who'd been willing to answer his enquiries and provide the information. All of them attested to the colder temperatures, the animals migrating sooner and winter coming nearly a month earlier than anyone, even Conrad, could have anticipated. 'It wasn't your decision to sail north which caused the problem. The year before you would have been able to press ahead and not encounter such fierce ice.'

Conrad closed the folio and rose, tapping it against his hand as he paced the room. 'No matter what decision I could have made, *Gorgon* would have become trapped.'

'Yes. You had no way of knowing how brutal winter would be.'

Conrad sagged against the edge of his desk, relief crashing through him as strong as he'd felt when he'd crested the last snow bank to see the whaler anchored in the harbour. The guilt he'd carried like a scar from the Arctic began to fade in the face of Mr Winston's research. It wasn't Conrad's fault *Gorgon* had become trapped, any more than Aaron's decision to surrender to his desperation instead of continuing on was. He'd never forget having to leave Aaron behind, but for the first time in months his hand didn't shake at the memory and the remorse didn't tear at his soul.

Mr Winston shifted forward to the edge of the chair. 'I hope my work is of some benefit to you. Miss Vickers said it would be.'

Conrad straightened. 'Miss Vickers encouraged you to create this for me?'

'She did. She came to me three days ago, asking for me to have it ready by last night, but it took much longer than I expected to compile my notes. It's why I wasn't in attendance. I was hurrying to finish, but you can see it's done now.'

Conrad scratched at the stubble on his chin, stunned into silence for the second time this morning. He'd told Katie of his guilt and she'd pursued an answer, a way to absolve him. She'd stood with him in his fight against his demons when a few days ago he'd accused her of abandoning him to face them alone. Then last night, she'd been willing to add her voice to Conrad's in their condemnation of Lord Helton. She'd stood strong against Lord Helton's accusations instead of fleeing, just as she'd found a way to help him even after he'd vowed to walk away from her for good.

Half an hour later, Henry looked up from Mr Winston's notes, his pipe dangling from his open and surprised mouth. 'Well, I'll be damned.'

'Mr Winston's research proves she was right.'

'I always said you weren't to blame, even in my report. It figures it would finally take a woman to make you believe me.'

The optimism he'd once known at Heims Hall, and at the start of every previous expedition, filled him again.

'I have some more interesting news, if you're up for it?' Henry handed the papers back.

'This morning, I feel as if I could face anything.' Conrad gripped the folio tight, amazed at the strength in his hand and the lack of pain in his joints. It wasn't his fault, he hadn't let down his crew. Though the trials they'd faced would always be with him, they wouldn't command him as they had these last few months, or guide his decisions ever again.

'Good, because you'll need your stamina.' Henry enjoyed a few puffs, drawing out his long pause before recovering his tongue. 'Your uncle died last night. You're the Marquis of Helton now.'

Conrad stared at Henry. Mr Winston's report had changed so much. This news altered his life even more. He'd seen the attack Lord Helton had suffered, but he'd thought little of it after they'd left, too focused on Katie to care what happened to the vicious old man. He peered through the door of the study into the sitting room across the entrance hall and at the portraits of his parents on the far wall. 'It's strange to think the man I've spent so many years hating and fighting, the one who wreaked so much damage on so many I love, is now gone.'

'A few people at the club are saying it's your fault he died, that you helped him along to the afterlife to gain the title.' Henry smiled wryly around the white pipe stem. 'If I didn't know you so well, and how much you loathe this inheritance, I might believe the rumours, too.'

Conrad shook his head at his friend's joke, enjoying his humour despite the gravity of the charge. He didn't give a fig for what people thought, but Lord Helton's death complicated matters with Katie, and his future in the Navy. Even if he wanted to take the helm of the Melville Island expedition, Mr Barrow wasn't likely to send a peer halfway around the world and risk him dying of fever, not when he could make use of his influence here. Initially, Conrad might have rejected his uncle's suggestion to follow him into the House of Lords and employ the power of the Helton name for the benefit of the Discovery Service, but he had been coming round to seeing the potential in it.

'So tell me, what will your first act as a newly minted peer be?' Henry asked.

Conrad tapped the edge of the desk. 'To resign my commission.'

The pipe nearly fell from Henry's mouth before he took hold of the bowl. 'So the old man has finally ended your career.'

'It appears so, but it's not entirely about me and what I want any more. It isn't just the title I've inherited, but also the lands and people who depend on the estate.' *Including Katie.* 'I can't imagine my uncle treated them well or fairly, but I will.'

'As you have all the men who've ever served under your command,' Henry offered with heartfelt commendation. 'When will you tell Mr Barrow?'

'At once, before he hears of it through the whisperings of his wife. I'll advocate for your promotion to captain and command of the Melville Island expedition,' Conrad offered, laying Mr Winston's folio on his desk on top of the journal. 'If you want it.'

Henry lowered the pipe, facing his choice as Conrad had faced his. Then he stood up straight, standing before Conrad as he would aboard ship in front of the men. 'I do. My time in the Arctic is over and now I must carry on, but Mr Barrow isn't likely to promote me, not with so many other, better-connected men lobbying for commands.'

'You're the friend of a marquis now, a powerful and influential one. I doubt Mr Barrow will deny me such a request.'

'Thank you, my lord.' Henry executed a deep bow somehow both mocking and reverential.

'Don't,' Conrad commanded. 'Not even in jest.'

He wouldn't have people bowing and scraping before him, or burn a swathe of respect borne from fear through society like his uncle had done.

'Yes, sir.' Henry straightened, shooting Conrad a cocky but understanding smile.

Conrad nodded his gratitude, grateful for his friend's confidence and support, eager to do all he could to reward it. 'I'll fetch my coat and we'll be off.'

Conrad hurried upstairs, pausing at the door to his room. He listened, but all was quiet inside. He slowly turned the knob and peeked in.

Mrs Anderson slept on the sofa, her borrowed

cap rumpled over her face. The heavy curtains kept out the morning light, but in the glow of the fireplace, Conrad spied Katie in bed, curled on her side beneath the coverlet. The curls covering her shoulders and resting against her cheeks invited Conrad to step closer and brush his fingers through her hair. He could wake her and thank her for what she'd done, then tell her the news of Helton, but he didn't. Sleep made her serene and he was loath to disturb her peace.

He backed out of the room and quietly shut the door. He'd tell her all when he returned from the Admiralty. The power of his resignation from the Discovery Service could better mollify her concerns about his elevation to the peerage and hopefully smooth the way to her accepting him and the future he offered.

Hurrying to the guest room, he slipped on his discarded coat and stepped up to the mirror. He fastened the brass buttons, then ran his hands over the dark-blue wool to smooth it before straightening the white lapels. He stared at his reflection, knowing this would be the last time he'd don his uniform.

It seemed strange to be leaving the life of an

explorer behind, especially after he'd fought so hard against his uncle's influence to achieve so much, but it was the right decision. He'd achieved a great deal since the day Uncle Jack had first taken him aboard ship as a boy. It was time to forge another path through the halls of Parliament and Helton Manor and embrace the future laid out by both his heritage and his heart. A greater love than that of uncharted waters waited for him when he returned to Katie later today as both a civilian and a lord and he was ready to embrace it.

Chapter Twelve

Katie stood at the window overlooking the street, watching as Conrad and Mr Sefton passed below, deep in conversation. Over the noise of the carriages, carts and hawkers, only a few words drifted up to her.

'Mr Barrow won't be pleased.' Henry laughed.

'I think we'll be surprised at how he reacts to the news.'

They disappeared inside the chaise and it rolled away, leaving tracks through the thin snow which had fallen overnight. Conrad hadn't come to her this morning, but was already off to see Mr Barrow, reinforcing again exactly where she stood in his priorities.

Katie rubbed her arm and the sharp bruise which stood out as a hard circle against the skin surrounding it. She detested Mr Barrow almost as much as the Marquis of Helton. The Second Secretary of the Admiralty held more influence over Conrad than Katie could ever hope to obtain. Whatever Conrad was going to discuss with his superior now, she was sure it would do her and her future with him no good. Yet for all the desperation she'd experienced in the darkest parts of last night, when the laudanum had made her toss and turn among the sheets, dreaming of Conrad, only to awake and find herself alone, one small comfort remained—America.

'Don't stand there in your chemise, you'll catch your death,' her aunt chided as she picked up the black dress lying over the footboard and held it up. 'I'll help you get dressed.'

'I hate that dress.' Katie frowned. *Especially the memories clinging to it.*

'Well, you won't need it much longer,' Aunt Florence offered cheerfully as she slipped the dress over Katie's head, then did up the buttons. 'Once you're married to Captain Essington, you'll have a proper dressmaker and nothing to worry about except gowns and dinner menus.'

'I'm not going to marry him,' she stated with

more conviction than she felt. 'I'm going to America.'

Her aunt took Katie by the shoulders and turned her around. 'How can you be so foolish?'

'I can't marry a man I don't love, who doesn't love me.'

'You don't love him?' Aunt Florence balled her hands on her hips. 'That's as big a lie as if the captain were to come in here and tell me he doesn't love you.'

'He doesn't, not any more. He's marrying me out of duty. It has nothing to do with love.'

'Nonsense. I've seen the two of you together. You think I didn't notice how you both crept away at Miss Benett's and the way you looked when you returned for dinner?'

Katie's mouth fell open and her shock emboldened her aunt. Gone was the frail woman who spoke and moved like a mouse; in her place was a forceful creature Katie had never seen before.

'My husband might be gone, just like my youth, but I know what it is to steal whatever moments you can with a man you adore. I also remember the bliss of having a man who loves you. Do you really believe Captain Essington helped you, risked his reputation to bolster yours, simply because he felt honour bound to do it? No, he did it because he cares about you as much as you care about him. And don't say you don't, I heard you comfort him the other night in this very house.'

'But you were asleep,' Katie cried, aghast to hear her secrets being revealed one after another.

'No, I wasn't. I was enjoying listening to the two of you be so open and honest with one another. Now you must be honest again and with yourself.'

'Being honest means admitting there's no future here for me and Conrad,' Katie insisted, more to convince herself than her aunt, refusing to doubt her decision. 'The *Thomas George* is leaving tonight and I intend to be on it.'

'So Captain Essington is expecting a wife and instead he'll get a note,' Aunt Florence spat. 'Just like your mother, you'll have your own way, then blame others when it doesn't work out to your liking.'

'How can you say such a thing?' Her aunt had never spoken so harshly to her, or so meanly of

Katie's mother, not even in the days after she'd disappeared.

'Because I saw how it was between them. You think your mother retreated because my brother paid her no mind. It wasn't like that at all. After he got her with child and she married him, she wasn't content to be merely a country doctor's wife. She missed her old life and all the fancy balls and dresses and insisted he give it back to her. She pushed him to make money, to work all hours of the night and day, demanding so much from him. He tried to make her happy, but nothing he did was enough for her, so he gave up and focused on the fossils, thinking they, not his medical practice, would be the making of him. Then your mother left and your father disappeared deeper into his work because what else did he have?'

'He had me,' Katie gasped, all the heartache of the past welling up inside her and forcing the tears to slide down her cheeks.

'I know.' Aunt Florence wiped Katie's wet cheeks with her calloused fingers. 'He cherished his work instead of you. I used to chide him about it in my letters, but he wouldn't listen to me, but you can. Your parents could've been happy together if they'd reached out to one another and treasured the love which brought them together and created you. Instead, they insisted on having their own way until they could barely stand to speak to one another and you were the one who suffered because of it.'

Katie slid the opal ring from her finger and laid it in her palm, everything she'd thought of her past and her parents changing. They'd both been at fault for the failures between them and now Katie was behaving more like them than before, demanding so many sacrifices and compromises from Conrad, while never once making one for him. Despite his reaching for her time and time again, she was embracing the shallow comfort of past grudges instead of the true joy of Conrad's arms.

Her aunt took up the ring and closed her fingers around it to hide it. 'Don't be like your parents, Katie, don't put your own desires above love, or insist Captain Essington be a man he isn't. Accept him for who he is and love him with all your heart. You'll both be so happy if you do.'

Katie looked around the room, his room, at the paintings of ships on stormy seas and the mementos of his previous journeys covering the tables. This was who Conrad was, the brave man she'd first come to adore in West Sussex, the one who always made her believe she could achieve anything, including the joy and love she'd sought her entire life. Even when she'd cursed him for leaving, she'd prayed every day for him to return and he had. His desire to be reunited with her had given him the strength and fortitude to survive the Arctic, now it was her turn to believe in their future together. It was time to accept him and stop running away.

'I do love him and he loves me.' She'd never stopped loving him, but had been too afraid to believe in it or Conrad. 'I should have admitted it long ago, but I couldn't.'

'It's difficult to open your heart when you've spent so many years being strong in order to protect it.' Aunt Florence patted Katie's cheek. 'Now, go downstairs and wait for him. Let yours be the first face he sees when he returns.'

Katie nodded and made for downstairs, hope for the future welling inside her for the first time in too long. Sacrifices could be made and she and Conrad would create the deep affection she used to wish for between her parents, the kind she longed to give her own children. He'd spoken before of resigning his commission; perhaps he would and she'd give up her work on the bones. Maybe then she could at last rest from her relentless pursuit of science and look instead to another purpose the fossils had always eclipsed.

'Good day, miss.'

Katie halted on the stairs at the sound of a strange man's voice.

In the entrance hall stood a young officer in a simple blue uniform, a long paper tube tucked beneath one arm. 'I've come from the Admiralty with a ship plan and maps for Captain Essington. I don't know where the butler has gone to, but I must leave these and get back at once.'

Cold lead poured through her insides as she approached the officer. 'What need does Captain Essington have for maps and plans?'

'They're for his expedition to Melville Island.'

'He's been assigned another expedition?' The day Mr Sefton had summoned Conrad to the Admiralty came rushing back to her.

'He's due to leave in a week or two, once the ship is ready,' the officer explained, obviously baffled by her lack of knowledge. 'Didn't he tell you?'

'No, he didn't.' Betrayal overwhelmed her as the future she'd imagined a few moments ago began to collapse. Yes, there'd be sacrifices made in order for them to be together, but they'd be expected from her. Conrad would never leave the Discovery Service. It was only her misguided hope which had led her to believe he might. She'd remain at home, always waiting for him to return while he continued his life of exploration until it either garnered him more glory or killed him.

'I'm to leave these here for him. Please see he gets them,' the young officer pleaded.

'I will,' Katie muttered through a dry mouth as she accepted the paper tube with the hated plans.

His order executed, the young officer left.

Katie tilted the roll and the papers shifted to hit the cork stopper. She was tempted to wait for Conrad to come home and confront him with his deceit, but there was nothing he could say to excuse his actions. His secrecy had proven the

Discovery Service was more important to him than her and always would be.

She flung the tube to the floor and started up the stairs, refusing to waste another moment of her life waiting for someone to return. She'd already squandered nearly three months of her childhood sitting in the window at Whitemans Green willing her mother to return, then a year and a half waiting for Conrad. It was time for her to set out. Let him have his parting note and his precious Discovery Service. She'd have her own adventure and a new life in America.

Chapter Thirteen

'How does it feel to be a civilian again?' Henry clapped Conrad on the back as they stepped from the chaise and made their way to Conrad's front door.

'Strange.' It'd been difficult signing the paper ending his career, but he'd served his country well and it was time to let other men do their duty and find their glory. 'And how do you feel about your appointment, Captain Sefton?'

Henry gripped his lapels with pride. 'Never thought a mere butcher's son could rise so high.'

'My lord,' Mr Moore greeted him and Conrad started at the sound of his new title. 'Miss Linton is waiting for you in the sitting room.'

Conrad's smile faded and he exchanged an irritated look with Henry.

'It seems Mr Barrow isn't the only one impressed with my elevation to the peerage.'

Conrad strode into the morning room, anger making his boots fall hard against the carpet.

Matilda rose from the chair as he approached, clutching her beaded reticule in front of her and cowering like a small dog about to be kicked for barking too much.

'What are you doing here?' Conrad said sharply. If she were not a woman, he'd take her by the scruff of her neck and toss her into the gutter where she belonged.

'I came to congratulate you and pay my respects to the new Lord Helton.' Shame lent her pasty cheeks a hint of colour as she dipped into a wobbly curtsy.

'I hope you got from the last Lord Helton whatever it was you wanted in exchange for lying about Katie, because you'll get nothing from me.'

'I didn't mean to hurt her,' Matilda whimpered. 'I didn't think he'd use what I told him in such a way.'

'You knew exactly what you were doing and how he'd use it.' Conrad raised one menacing finger in front of her face. 'I've been kind to you, Matilda, looked out for you when no one else would and all you've done is spite me for it.'

She stomped her foot, the red on her cheeks heightening with anger. 'What have you done for me except throw me crumbs, just like Uncle Jack? He did everything for you, seeing you into the Navy, treating you like the son he never had, all the while overlooking me. Heims Hall should have been mine, but instead he left me a paltry inheritance, hardly enough to catch a good man's interest.'

'If your character wasn't so ugly, you might find a gentleman willing to overlook your lack of fortune. Now get out of my house.'

'You can't turn me away. My friends have all shunned me because of what Lord Helton did and the scandal of you and Miss Vickers.' Her pale eyes filled with tears, turning them red. 'What am I to do?'

'Go to Bath. I hear spinsters with limited means do well there.'

Burying her long nose in a handkerchief, Matilda scurried out of the room, nearly knocking Mr Moore aside to get out of the door before he could fully pull it open.

'Never seen you so harsh on anyone, not even Boatswain James.' Henry leaned against the door jam, as amused as always.

'I'll give her some time to think about what she's done, then I'll settle some money on her and have nothing more to do with the witch.' He'd once pitied his cousin, but time and her vile tongue had eroded his sympathy. Yet no matter how much he disliked his cousin, he wasn't about to see her sink into poverty or starve, any more than he would have set Boatswain James out in the snow for stealing food. 'Now, if you'll excuse me, I must speak with Katie. Unlike Mr Barrow, I think she'll be quite pleased to hear I've resigned my commission.'

'Miss Vickers and Mrs Anderson are no longer here, my lord,' Mr Moore informed him.

Fear gripped Conrad as it had when Henry had peered out of the tent flap and told him he couldn't see Aaron in the snow. 'You mean they've gone for a walk?'

'No, my lord. The ladies departed for home after you left for the Admiralty.' He levelled a paper tube at Conrad. 'This arrived for you from Mr Barrow before Miss Vickers left.'

Conrad took the tube and pulled out the cork stopper at the end. He tilted it up and a few rolled pieces of paper slid out. He unrolled them to reveal the plans for *Medea*, the ship he was supposed to have commanded for the Melville Island expedition. 'Did Miss Vickers see this?'

'I believe she did, my lord.'

Conrad and Henry exchanged an uneasy look. *Medea* was Henry's ship now, but there was no way she could have known it when the courier inadvertently revealed the only secret Conrad had ever kept from her.

'What are you going to do?' Henry asked as Conrad handed him the plans.

'Go after her.'

The sun continued to rise overhead as Conrad's chaise rolled to a stop in front of Mrs Anderson's tumbledown lodgings. It melted the snow in the streets, making tiny rivulets of water run along the gutters and through the piles of dung and trash. He hurried inside the dark building and up the stairs to the first floor, the dank and dirt from outside seeming to follow him. He shouldn't have hidden the expedition from her. Telling her would have kept her in his house, instead of driving her back here.

'Katie, it's Conrad.' He banged on Mrs Anderson's wooden door, making it rattle on its hinges before he stopped to wait for an answer. He wanted to pace and shake off his worry, but he forced himself to remain still. In a few moments she'd know everything, including his unwillingness to leave her again, and all would be well.

The door opened. They weren't Katie's eyes which met him, but Mrs Anderson's.

'Katie isn't here.' Mrs Anderson took him by the arm and pulled him inside, slamming the door closed behind her. 'She's gone to Greenwich to catch a ship for America.'

'What business could Katie have in America?'

Conrad listened, stunned as Mrs Anderson revealed Mr Lesueur's request for Katie to join him on his expedition. It was the first he'd heard of it.

'She was ready to be your wife, then she found

out you were leaving for Melville Island,' Mrs Anderson finished.

'I'm not going. I resigned my commission this morning.' Conrad fingered the button on his jacket. 'I was wrong to keep it from her.'

'Just as she was wrong to keep her plans from you.' Mrs Anderson gripped his arm. 'You must go after her. She loves you, Captain Essington, she told me so, but she thought you didn't love her enough to stay.'

'She's wrong.' He did love her, her strength and courage, even the stubbornness driving her to Greenwich. He wanted her beside him when he accepted his summons to the House of Lords, needed her to ride next to him when he set out to inspect the fields of Helton Manor and ensure the welfare of his new tenants and staff. They wouldn't be the grand adventures of an unexplored shore, but the more quiet responsibilities which could make a man as respected as any captain aboard ship. It was the quiet life he'd dreamed of from the tomb of *Gorgon*, the life he couldn't allow this last failure to be honest with her to steal from him. She loved him and he loved her and he wouldn't let her run away.

'You must stop her before it's too late,' Mrs Anderson begged. 'She's on the *Thomas George*.'

'I'll reach her before she sets sail and bring her back.' He patted her hand reassuringly. 'I promise.'

'Godspeed, Captain Essington.'

Conrad hurried from the room, back down the stairs and out to the chaise. With any luck the winds would not favour her ship, leaving it stranded in port and giving Conrad enough time to find her. He looked up at the fast-moving wisps of clouds, trying not to let their swiftness increase his dismay. He would make it to Greenwich in time. He had to.

'Make your way aboard now, miss,' a grizzled old sailor instructed, doffing his cap at Katie as he walked towards the ship carrying a small barrel.

Katie smiled her thanks, then left the shelter of the side of the cooper's shop and began the slow walk to the gangplank. The stuffed satchel hung heavy in her hand, increasing the ache in her bruised arm. The tall masts of the ships towered ominously over her, casting tangled shadows of rigging and sails across the wharf and the sailors hurrying to load the last of the cargo.

Regret echoed in the soft click of her heels as she approached the *Thomas George*. All around her, other passengers exchanged tearful good-byes with the family who'd come to see them off. Only Katie stood alone, secretly wishing the tide wouldn't come in, but there was a stiff breeze and the river already lapped near the high-water mark on the piers.

Stepping in line behind a thickly built man and his small wife waiting to board, Katie looked back at the crush of carts, horses and people along the wharf, faintly hoping to see Conrad among them. No, he wouldn't come and she wouldn't stay. This was the right decision, it had to be. She might be alone here, but there were friends and colleagues waiting for her in America and a chance for a new start. Let Conrad have his expedition; she would have hers, no matter how much she wished she could stay.

Over the clang of ships' bells and yelling seamen, the Greenwich clock sounded out the three o'clock hour as Conrad's chaise hurried towards the wharf. The tide was up and the river filled with the tall masts of ships unfurling their sails to catch the wind. It'd taken nearly two hours for the chaise to force its way here through the crowded London streets. The clog on London Bridge had nearly driven him from the vehicle to set out on foot before the way had cleared and the driver had at last made good time to the river.

Reaching the docks was only one success. He must find the *Thomas George* before it set sail. With few ships still moored, Conrad feared he was too late, but nothing was lost until the *Thomas George* set out to sea. Even then it would most likely dock in Portsmouth before sailing off across the Atlantic, giving Conrad at least one more chance to reach the ship and Katie.

The chaise came to a stop near the wharf and Conrad jumped out and sprinted down to the dockmaster's office. He entered the rickety shack perched over the water and a rotund man wearing a worn fisherman's coat looked up from where he hunched over a small stove in the corner.

His rheumy eyes filled with suspicion at the

sight of Conrad. 'Navy don't usually send such fine men to press sailors.'

'I'm not here in search of a crew, but the *Thomas George*. Which berth is she in?'

'Ain't in no berth, but set out with the tide like all them others.' He pointed a thick finger at the filthy window.

'How long ago?'

The man shrugged, the hole on the shoulder of his coat widening, then closing with the movement. 'Can't say. Don't pay much attention to ships leaving, only those coming in which has to pay their duties.'

Conrad wanted to throttle the man for being difficult, but he couldn't blame this stranger for his problems, besides, there were other ways around them. 'Is there a small boat I can hire to take me out to the *Thomas George*?'

'None here at the moment. All taking advantage of the good sailing to ferry goods and people. If you wait by the wharf, one might return and you can hire it, but I can't say for certain. It'll be up to you to find one.'

'I will.' Conrad marched back outside, cursing

the steady breeze whipping over the river and rippling the murky surface.

On either side of him, the emptiness of the wharf mocked him. There wasn't a rowboat or dingy to be seen, only sailors shuffling about to shift the cargo unloaded by recently docked ships. He turned to make for the few vessels still tied to their berths, ready to commandeer the nearest sloop if it meant reaching the *Thomas George* before she sailed out of the mouth of the Thames. Katie wasn't going to put herself so far beyond his reach it would mean crossing an ocean to find her.

He'd just reached the nearest ship, ready to ask to come aboard, when a lonely figure coming up the dock made him stop.

A woman carrying a satchel weaved around two sailors hauling coils of rope. Her steps were hesitant but steady and over the clatter of seagulls and the slapping of the water against the piers, Conrad could just make out the fall of her half-boots against the wood. The satchel brushed her legs as she walked, disturbing the swish of the thick blue pelisse covering her slender body.

'Katie?' Conrad rushed down the planks to her, stopping a few feet from where she stood.

The late-afternoon sun reflecting off the water glittered in her eyes and deepened the gold of her hair. He opened his arms to embrace her, then lowered them, waiting as he would for a sounding before he sailed closer. 'You didn't leave.'

The satchel dropped to the ground with a soft thud.

'I couldn't. I know I've given you little reason to stay with me or want me, but I want you. I don't care if people sneer at me, I don't care about the whispers or the rumours, I don't even care if you leave, only that we're together before you go and I'm here waiting for you when you return.' She moved closer, raising her hand to his face, her fingers achingly close to his cheek, but not touching it. 'I want to be with you and know you love me as much as I love you, wherever you are.'

'Where I'll be is here.' He pressed her hand to his face, covering it with his to warm her slender fingers against the chill. 'I'm not going to Melville Island. I resigned my commission this morning.'

Hope whispered through her eyes. 'You aren't leaving?'

'No.' He brushed a round tear from her cheek, then slipped his hand behind her neck. 'I'm sorry I didn't tell you about the expedition.'

'I'm sorry I didn't tell you of America.' She slid one hand around his waist and pressed so tight against him not even the breeze could slip between them.

'No secrets between us.'

'Never.'

Conrad leaned into Katie and a kiss more precious and deep than any he'd ever experienced with her before. She wanted him as much as he wanted her. It was all he could have asked for and everything he wanted.

A few sharp whistles sounded from somewhere above them. Conrad and Katie broke from their kiss to peer up at the numerous sailors hanging from the rigging and pointing at them.

'It seems we've scandalised the sailors.' Katie laughed, the sound as beautiful as her smile.

'Then let's take our scandalous behaviour somewhere more private.' He swept her into his arms and carried her from the wharf, leaving her sad satchel behind. There was no weakness or worry as there'd been in the mine or even last night, only the surety of her body so close to his, her breath stroking his cheek where she nuzzled against him. The heat spread down though his chest to consume him, the desire filling him stoked by the lazy play of her fingers in his hair.

He quickened his pace as the chaise came into view, eager to reach it and answer the invitation in the subtle press of her lips against his neck. He carried her into the vehicle, closing the door behind him and pulling down the shade. Without a word, she reached over and drew closed the other, leaving them to the intimacy of the faint sunlight creeping in through the sides of the darkened windows.

Once alone, Conrad freed her hair from the pins holding it up, pulling them out one by one and dropping them to the floor. Her golden curls spilled over her shoulders like the way the sun from the Downs used to grace her skin. He slid his fingers through the silken tangle to draw her to him.

'I want you, Katie, all of you,' he murmured in her ear, taking the lobe between his teeth to graze the tender skin as she freed herself from her pelisse.

'I'm yours,' she breathed, laying her head on his shoulder as he began to undo the buttons on the back of her dress. At length the fabric opened and he slid it from her arms to reveal the stay and chemise beneath. Sliding a finger between the cotton and the stiff boning, he eased one full breast from its confinement and lowered his head to taste the tender point.

Her hands on his shoulders tightened and she moaned as he made circles on the tip with his tongue, exhaling on the wet flesh to tease it. While his tongue worked, he slid his hand beneath her dress and raised the fabric above her knees, caressing the length of thigh beneath.

She fumbled with the buttons of his coat until the blue wool dropped to the chaise floor to join the pins. Her fingers against the fall of his breeches stilled as he found her wanting centre. His body tightened at her readiness, the desire to be one with her more powerful than any he'd known before. She'd waited for him, come to him instead of running away, at last willing to accept him whether he was a captain or a marquis. He shifted her on to his lap, the firm pressure of his thighs against hers making him want to rush forward, but he waited, continuing to caress and tease until she whimpered in his ear.

'Please, Conrad, please.'

Her plea broke his resolve and, raising her hips, he settled himself between her legs. The tip of his erection just touched her as he waited, as ready to bring them together as he was to join their lives.

Katie straddled Conrad's thighs, eager to surrender to him and take this last step to declare herself his. With knowing hands, he guided her down over him. The sound of the carriage driving over the streets drowned out her cries as he filled her in both body and spirit. It was an intimacy she'd sought her entire life, one she'd never imagined she'd find. Yet here it was with Conrad.

She arched her back as he rocked into her, ready to make any sacrifice to be with him. Nothing mattered except Conrad, not the fossils, the future or anyone's condemnation. Let them judge and whisper, they couldn't touch either of them now, not with his chest hard against hers, their hearts beating in rhythm with their passion.

With his stroke steady and firm inside her, she opened both her being and heart wider to him. Her fingers dug into his arms as she clung to him, racing faster and faster with him until at last her body shattered around his. With a groan, he met her release, his breath hot and powerful in her ear as they clung to one another, united, never to be separated again.

Epilogue

Two years later

'Lady Helton, I have the most wonderful news,' Miss Benett's clear voice rang through the Heims Hall conservatory like the sound of a hammer against a rock on a clear day.

'What is it?' Katie twisted around on her small stool, the charcoal still between her fingers as she looked away from her sketch. The palm trees which had once filled the room were gone, replaced by a forest of easels and canvases and tables covered with sketchbooks and boxes of pencils.

'It's not what I've found, but what Mr Buckland has discovered.'

Young Aaron slid off the chaise where Katie had positioned him by the tall windows and toddled on fat legs to clutch Miss Benett's skirt. The lady geologist bent down to ruffle his sandy hair, the same shade as Conrad's hair, and pinch one chubby cheek. 'My, how big you've grown, almost as big as Anne Marie's boy.'

Miss Benett picked Aaron up and carried him back to Katie, handing her the paper instead of her son. 'You must read this.'

Katie took the article with a slight gasp of surprise. There at the top was the picture of a beast so similar in shape and form to her creature. It smiled with sharp teeth above the thick content printed below.

'Mr Buckland found a creature like yours, here in England. And look there.' Miss Benett reached down to point to a paragraph midway down the page. 'He references your paper and your presentation from the Naturalist Society.'

Katie smiled, the old part of her which had fought so long and hard for recognition proud of the accolade, no matter how late or small.

'This could be the making of you. If you wanted it,' Miss Benett prodded.

'But I don't.' Katie folded the paper and

handed it back to her. 'I employ my talents else-where now.'

Katie picked up her son and nuzzled his neck, making him giggle. All her life she'd been pushed by her father to assist him, eager to learn what he'd taught her in the hopes he might one day cherish her as he had his work. Then, after he'd died, the work with the fossils had been the only thing left, until Conrad had made her see she could have and be so much more.

She looked to the illustrations of her child, Conrad and Heims Hall covering the one con-servatory wall. The most cherished watercolours of Conrad holding Aaron hung on either side of the door, their smiles a lively encouragement for her work. Within the love and security of their marriage, Katie had found her true calling and real happiness at last.

'Yes, you're a brilliant artist,' Miss Benett con-ceded.

'Have you brought my wife another stone to illustrate for your book?' Conrad asked as he strolled into the room.

'Daddy.' Aaron wriggled off Katie's lap and ran to his father. Conrad gathered his son up in his strong arms and tossed him above his head, making the boy squeal before Conrad caught him and settled him on his hip.

'She has enough to draw, what with Captain Sefton shipping so much back from Melville Island.' Conrad laughed as he carried Aaron over to stand behind Katie and admire her unfinished sketch. 'He's lieutenant governor there, a post he writes quite suits him.'

'He should send her specimens, for there's no better artist who can render them. In fact, Mr Buckland should have come to you to do his drawing, instead of whoever he hired for his.' Miss Benett wrinkled her nose at the illustration, then set it down on the table next to Katie's watercolours, exhibiting as much pride in Katie's work as the artist herself. 'Yours of the creature were far superior. Whatever did you do with the animal?'

'It's at Helton Manor, along with so many other relics,' Conrad answered, laying one hand on Katie's shoulders. She revelled in the weight of it and the steadying influence of him, unable to believe she'd once nearly thrown this life with him away. Katie covered his hand with hers, curling her fingers to join with his. Those days were gone now and there was no reason to dwell on them.

'Perhaps we should donate it to the British Museum,' Conrad suggested.

Katie tapped one charcoal-stained finger against her chin. 'Or sell it to benefit your hospital for wounded sailors.'

Conrad wiped the charcoal smudge from her face. 'Or your charity for impoverished young women.'

'Aunt Florence would love to have something so sensational for the charity, so would Mr Edgar.' She rose and slid her arm around Conrad's waist, enjoying the warmth of the sun which lingered on his coat from his time outside.

'How is Mr Edgar? Still prattling on about transmutation?' Miss Benett asked.

'He is, and Aunt Florence is all too happy to listen.' Aunt Florence and Mr Edgar had married shortly after Conrad and Katie, bringing both of their long years of loneliness to an end.

'They aren't the only happy couple,' Miss Benett teased.

'Indeed, they aren't,' Conrad concurred, smiling down at Katie with the same deep love swelling her heart.

'No one could be as happy as we are.' Katie pressed a kiss to Aaron's chubby cheek, then rose up on her toes, her lips meeting Conrad's in a searing kiss which blotted out the world. They were together, a family, in love. It was everything she'd ever wanted and the answer to all her dreams.

* * * * *

Author Afterword

New discoveries and research in the natural sciences had been brewing all through the eighteenth century, but it began to really come together in the early nineteenth century.

Fossil-hunting and the study of ancient creatures along with rock strata and attempts to date different geological time periods were happening in both England and Europe. Identifying previously unknown animals based on fossil records had also been taking place in both France, under Georges Cuvier, and in England under such men as William Buckland.

Certain terms, including *ichthyosaurus* and *proteosaurus*, while very modern-sounding, did come into common use around the time of Katie and Conrad's story. *Saurus* comes from the Greek word for lizard. I had a great deal of fun researching the early fossil-hunters and geologists and incorporating real historical figures like Etheldred Benett and Dr Gideon Mantell into the story. The Naturalist Society is a fictitious one I created for the story, but it is modeled on many different scientific societies in existence at the time.

Another real historical figure I incorporated was Second Secretary of the Admiralty, John Barrow. Mr Barrow's obsession with discovering the Northwest Passage for Britain led to his sending out many expeditions to the Arctic over a number of years, including the famous and ill-fated Franklin Expedition. Naval ships sailing to the Arctic were fitted out to resist ice and other severe conditions and were often provided with tantalising leads to follow from the whalers already working the far north.

Exploration of the Arctic was limited to the very short summer and most expeditions only lasted roughly six or seven months. Ships were able to sail into uncharted bays and inlets once the sea ice broke up in the spring and then had to be sure to sail out again in late summer before the ice froze again. As Conrad discovers in the story, any ship lingering after the end of summer risked the very real nightmare of becoming trapped and having to spend the winter in the ship.

While I did a great deal of research for this story and did my best to remain true to the facts, words and events of the time period, I did take a little historical licence with the departure point of Katie's ship bound for America. Although there were docks and wharves and a naval shipyard in Greenwich, there wasn't as much commercial travel from the Greenwich area. However, for the sake of Katie and Conrad's story, I needed the convenience of a closer wharf than Portsmouth.

It was great to research maps and plans of early Greenwich, as well as the scientific discoveries and excitement of the early nineteenth century.

The creature Conrad brings back for Katie is based on the Nanuqsaurus, a small tyrannosaurus-like dinosaur that has been found in Alaska.

MILLS & BOON®

Why shop at millsandboon.co.uk?

Each year, thousands of romance readers find their perfect read at millsandboon.co.uk. That's because we're passionate about bringing you the very best romantic fiction. Here are some of the advantages of shopping at www.millsandboon.co.uk:

* **Get new books first**—you'll be able to buy your favourite books one month before they hit the shops

* **Get exclusive discounts**—you'll also be able to buy our specially created monthly collections, with up to 50% off the RRP

* **Find your favourite authors**—latest news, interviews and new releases for all your favourite authors and series on our website, plus ideas for what to try next

* **Join in**—once you've bought your favourite books, don't forget to register with us to rate, review and join in the discussions

Visit **www.millsandboon.co.uk**
for all this and more today!